Only dimly aware of what
I was doing . . .

I willed the ring to carry me in the direction from which I'd come. I passed through the globe without effort and continued away from it, moving toward the hole I'd made in the barrier, buffeted by hurricane-force winds rushing through the hole into space. I put a bubble around myself, trapping some of the air inside, and then the winds didn't buffet me anymore.

I had no idea how long it had been since I'd started chasing the vanishing planet, nor even any clear idea of how long it had been since I'd left Earth. Years? Days? Time was becoming elusive and almost meaningless.

The hole in the barrier was enlarging and other holes were appearing. The entire thing was cracking, fragmenting, the pieces drifting into space, pushed by what was left of the Oan atmosphere.

I felt a great weariness. I didn't just want to sleep—I wanted not to be. That was the Oan plan for me, and for everyone else, and I thought, *Okay, bring it on.*

Also available from Pocket Books

JUSTICE LEAGUE of AMERICA™
GREEN LANTERN™

HERO'S QUEST

DENNIS O'NEIL

POCKET STAR BOOKS

New York   London   Toronto Sydney

This book is a work of fiction. Names, characters, places and inci-
dents are products of the authors' imagination or are used ficti-
tiously. Any resemblance to actual events or locales or persons, living or dead, is entirely coincidental.

An *Original* Publication of POCKET BOOKS

A Pocket Star Book published by
POCKET BOOKS, a division of Simon & Schuster, Inc.
1230 Avenue of the Americas, New York, NY 10020

Cover painting by Alex Ross
Cover design by Georg Brewer

ISBN: 0-7434-1712-7

First Pocket Books printing April 2005

10 9 8 7 6 5 4 3 2 1

POCKET STAR BOOKS and colophon are registered
trademarks of Simon & Schuster, Inc.

www.dccomics.com

Manufactured in the United States of America

For information regarding special discounts for bulk purchases,
please contact Simon & Schuster Special Sales at 1-800-456-6798
or business@simonandschuster.com.

To John Ingallinera, Lizzie Fagan, Michael O'Shea,
and Bryan Holihan. I owe them everything.

The truth is Silly Putty.
—Paul Krassner

PART ONE

1

*The first mortars came arching out of the jungle,
screaming like angry banshees. They were lost in the glare
of the early morning sun for a moment and then reappeared
as they crashed into the barracks, spewing flame and debris
as the panicked solders scurried around the compound,
blind with fright. . . .*

Before we go any further, I should admit that I have
no idea whether mortar shells scream at all, much less
sound like angry banshees. In fact, I don't know if banshees scream or get angry. For all I know, they may be
the most even-tempered, taciturn monsters on Earth.
I've never met a banshee I didn't like, because I've
never met a banshee, period. As for the rest of the para-
graph immediately preceding this one—well, I'm not
too sure about any of that, either. The attack *was* at
dawn, so the part about the morning sun has to be
about right, though whether the shells got lost in its

glare is something you'd have to have been there to know. And it seems logical that the soldiers would be scared, though it may not have affected their eyesight and, heck, maybe they were calm as dew; maybe they were *used* to being attacked at dawn. Or maybe they were disappointed when they *weren't* attacked at dawn.

I'll admit it: I wasn't there. I should have been, and I got really yelled at for my absence. Everyone in the Justice League agreed: Kyle Rayner screwed up. But I'll tell you all about that in a while.

One more thing before we get back to the attack. I'm not a writer. I'm an artist. So I looked around for something to imitate and found, lying in a pile of empty soda cans and pizza cartons, the latest Rip Riley novel. That became my model for writing this . . . I don't know exactly what to call it. Memoir? Reminiscence? Anyway, the Rip Riley novel—*Rip Riley's Cairo Crushdown*—became the model for writing at least the first chapter of whatever it is that I'm writing. You may not have ever read a Rip Riley, but you must have seen some. *Cairo Crushdown* is number 156, according to the cover. I'll bet there isn't a paperback rack in the country at this moment that isn't graced by at least one Rip Riley.

I apologize for this digression. I'll try not to do it again, but no promises.

Anyway, back to the attack, which, by the way, was taking place on a tiny Caribbean Island called Santa Prisca:

The thunder of high explosives continued to rock the jungle and the adjoining beach as the mortars erupted.

Then, snarling with hate, the rebel forces burst from the lush greenery and charged down the slope, their AK47s spitting fiery death as they went. The soldiers, still gripped by panic, were easy victims in the merciless onslaught.

Then, the Justice League appeared!

Actually, it wasn't the whole League. Batman never comes along on missions like this. Neither does Plastic Man, which is too bad because he's always good for a laugh and that's cool—when you're saving the world a little comedy doesn't hurt. Martian Manhunter and the Atom were busy elsewhere. Am I forgetting someone? Oh, yeah. Green Lantern. Him. I'll give you his excuse in a while, but I'm warning you right now, it's lame.

So I guess the Justice League was represented by Superman, Wonder Woman, and the Flash. Not a bad group, when you come to think of it. I mean, what *can't* they handle? Certainly not some lame rebellion on a postage stamp–sized lump of Caribbean dirt.

Which brings us back to our story:

Superman hovered above the spot where the mortars were located and caught two of the deadly shells, one in each hand. He smashed the shells together, causing them to explode in his bare hands. When the flame and smoke had been blown away by the morning breeze, the Man of Steel was smiling. He flew down to where the mortars were positioned and fixed a steely gaze on the rebel terrorists who had been firing.

"Go ahead, lovers of evil," he grated. "Do your worst."

"Do not hurt us," a rebel pleaded in his own language.

"Well, okay," was the Man of Steel's reply.

Meanwhile, Wonder Woman was also busy. She was spinning her golden lariat as she looked at a dozen oncoming terrorists. Before they could take aim at her, the lariat flashed out and encircled them, pinning their arms to their sides. One, however, did manage to work his left upper limb free, and took a 9-millimeter Browning semiautomatic pistol from his filthy waistband. This he fired at the Amazon Princess. Casually, she raised her arm and deflected the bullet with her Amazon bracelet.

"Don't try that again, my friend," was the Amazon Princess's sweet but stern admonition. Awestruck, the would-be killer dropped his weapon and promised he wouldn't.

Nor was the Flash idle as Superman and Wonder Woman quelled their share of the lawbreakers. This could be attested to by a squad of rebel troops who saw a red blur, momentarily experienced a wind of almost hurricane force, and then were suddenly bereft of their firearms. They looked up the slope upon which they were standing to see a tall man clad in scarlet standing at the top, his arms laden with their guns.

"You fellows won't be needing these," the Flash called cheerily. One of the rebels turned and began to run down toward the beach. Again there was a red blur and a brief hurricane, and suddenly the Scarlet Speedster was standing in front of the fleeing malcontent.

"Don't leave yet," the Flash hissed merrily. "The party's just getting started."

Within moments the rebel troop was completely disarmed and marching toward the government compound,

where soldiers, their calm restored by the cessation of dan-
ger, waited with ready weapons.

Superman spoke to the captain of the government de-
tachment. "They're all yours."

The uniformed Santa Priscan was gaping. "Are joo re-
ally Superman?" he gawked in his charmingly accented
English.

"We helped too," chimed in the Scarlet Speedster in his
kidding way.

The Amazon Princess, known to the world as Wonder
Woman, smiled in a fashion that combined maternity with
a hint of flirtatiousness.

I guess I should apologize for that last line, but I
won't because when I'm around Wonder Woman I
half want to ask for home-baked pie and half want to
ask her what she's doing Friday night (and Saturday,
and Sunday . . .). So what I wrote reflects the truth as
I experienced it, and as an old uncle of mine would
have said, "Them as don't like it can lump it."

One further confession: That line I gave Superman
about lovers of evil—I got it off a sweatshirt that I am
absolutely certain was manufactured without his
okay. That kind of thing happens all the time to Justice Leaguers—that use of their names and likenesses
without their okay. The unofficial policy seems to be,
don't sweat the small stuff. It *would* be pretty undigni-
fied for Superman to appear in court and say something like, "I'm the mightiest creature in the solar
system, if not the entire universe, and I want five hundred bucks from this shirt merchant because he

ripped me off." Of course, if it were *Batman's* image
ill-used, the story might be different. Nobody messes
with the Batman. Nobody. And I'm not sure exactly
why.

Was that a digression or what?

I'm returning to the events of the day the League
put down the rebellion on Santa Prisca, but not to the
Rip Riley style of writing. You want Rip, go buy one
of *his* books.

So, anyway, what happened next was . . . I'm not
sure. I guess Superman, Wonder Woman, and the
Flash went back to League headquarters, which is a
satellite in stationary orbit high above the Earth they
call the Watchtower. Normally, the Flash and Wonder
Woman would use one of the teleporters the League
has stashed around the planet, but that day, I'm bet-
ting, they just hopped a ride with Superman. Although there's not enough air that high to breathe,
and the pressure outside a human body is a lot less
than the pressure inside, which could cause terminal
problems, it's possible to fly to the satellite so fast
that lack of atmosphere doesn't matter.

I know. I do it all the time. I'd done it that day.

2

I'd left a park near my apartment building at 7:15 in the pee-em and stepped through the airlock onto the League's satellite at 7:17:40, give or take a few nanoseconds.

I stood breathing in the tinny-smelling air, which always made me slightly nauseous, and steeling myself for whatever the next few minutes would bring. Then, wobbling slightly in the artificial gravity, I walked onto the control deck.

They were waiting for me: Superman, Wonder Woman, the Flash and, on the mattress-sized video screen, Batman, presumably coming to us from wherever his cave is. They were not happy, any of them.

"I know, I know," I said before they could start in on me. "We had something to do this morning and I wasn't there."

"I'll just *bet* you have a reason," the Flash said.

"Well, I do," I replied. "But you probably don't want to hear it."

"On the contrary," Superman said softly.

"We're quite interested," Wonder Woman said, also softly.

I stared at the metal floor, wishing I could sink into it. This is not, for me, an unfamiliar feeling.

"I forgot. I mean, I didn't forget so much as over-sleep. I mean, I had this date last night and things were going really well until about midnight, and then I did something dumb—"

"Care to tell us what?" Wonder Woman asked. She was smiling; she wasn't really mad at me.

"I'd rather not," I answered, and I may have been blushing, but if I was I hope she didn't notice. "Anyway, by the time I got done apologizing it was three, and after I got in bed I kept replaying the whole scene in my mind, trying to figure out how I could have been such a doof—"

"I think we've heard enough," Superman said.

"Especially since it's just another variation on his usual theme," the Flash added.

"Hey," I protested. "Last time I had a real excuse."

"Meaning that this is *not* a real excuse?" Wonder Woman asked.

"Well, *no*, not exactly."

"This inquisition is pointless." That was Batman, speaking from the video screen. As always, I didn't so much hear him as feel his words in my bones.

"Yes, it is," Superman said. He planted himself in front of me and I realized that I was about to be reprimanded by a guy who takes sauna baths in the heart of stars, who probably eats asteroids for breakfast and doesn't need an Alka-Seltzer afterward, and who takes day trips to places like Jupiter—and that it didn't feel a lot different from being given hell by my grade school principal.

"You're not dependable," he began, and I thought, Where have I heard *that* before? "You have great potential, but unless you harness it to discipline, it will remain just that—potential. You could eventually be a credit to us all, or you could end up an embarrassment."

"Bet on the embarrassment," the Flash murmured.

"I'm not a psychologist, a teacher, or even a parent," Superman continued. "I have no idea how to motivate you. I wish I did."

This guy could chew through mountains, and I was stumping him. Maybe I should have felt flattered.

"Would you believe me if I said I was sorry?"

"I might," Superman said. "But would *you?*"

"We've heard his 'sorry' before," the Flash said, and I wished he would use his superspeed to run off a short pier.

I stared at my boots for a very long minute, a mannerism I perfected in the seventh grade, and then I raised my eyes and said, "Look, guys, I never asked to be a super hero. In fact, I feel a little silly saying the word—'super hero.' It's the kind of word that belongs on cereal boxes, not resumes. But I was given this ring"—I held up the glowing green band that encircles the middle finger of my right hand—"and you all told me that some duties go with it. Okay. I won't argue. Maybe I'd like to, but I won't. But I'm learning a job I don't want and probably don't have any aptitude for. So cut me *some* slack, okay? I promise I'll try harder."

"How *did* you get the ring, anyway?" the Flash asked.

3

Well, Flash, that's a good question and—surprise!—I have an answer to it, but an answer that even *I* have trouble believing.

It began with Sharon Klingerman, who was the girl—excuse me: *young woman*—who sat two seats away from me in a life-drawing class the local Y offers free of charge to indigent wannabe artists. Sharon was cute, which is like saying the Marianas Trench is deep, and the third finger of her left hand was as nicely tanned as the rest of her, meaning it didn't have any clunky old ring between it and the rays. I had a trick she seemed to like: When she looked at me, I became invisible. I know this because she often looked my way and, I swear, she saw whatever was behind me.

Okay. What does this charming person have to do with my becoming a Green Lantern? Just this: During a class break about six weeks ago, while we students were loitering in the corridor next to various food and drink machines, I overheard Sharon telling a friend that she hung out at a music club called Omfrey's. In fact, she continued, she planned to be at Omfrey's that very night.

The instructor called and we went back to our sketch pads.

After class, I went to the half-basement my landlord insists is an apartment, shivering because a cold rain was pouring onto the city and, as usual, I'd neglected to wear proper clothing. I pushed open my landlord's gate and glanced at something he'd planted in the tiny front yard a few weeks earlier—a dogwood tree, he'd told me. It was sad: a single, scrawny stick jutting up from the mud, getting rained on. Every time the wind blew, it seemed to shiver. Lonely, scrawny little tree. I felt sorry for it. What were its chances of surviving until spring? Call them slim. But I nodded to it anyway and continued my trek homeward.

I paused by my mailbox, a rusty antique nailed to the side of the house, opened it, and saw that I'd gotten no mail, also as usual. Then I spotted a flat, brown package in the mud a few feet away. Obviously, it had been way too big for the box, and so the postman had leaned it against the wall. I guess the wind had decided to move it into the mud. I picked the package up, knowing that it contained the latest batch of art I'd submitted, on speculation, to a magazine and, probably, a curt rejection note. Rain had soaked through the wrapping, undoubtedly ruining the work inside. No big loss. The magazine I'd submitted to was called *The Cactus Farmer Hobbyist*; the work I'd done for that market probably wouldn't be appropriate for, say, *The New Yorker* anyway.

I went inside, dumped the unopened package into a waste can and my wet clothes onto the floor. I put on a ratty old terry-cloth bathrobe and switched on the television, hoping I was in time to catch the *Star Trek* reruns on Channel Eight. The TV sputtered, displayed a series of jagged lines, and darkened. Dead, Jim. Again. And not likely to be resurrected soon. Repairmen have this really annoying habit of charging for their services, darn their pesky hides.

So now what? I could have read—I'd gotten a book from the library titled *The Tao of Physics* that looked interesting. Or I could have stewed about Sharon Klingerman. Of course, stewing would have accomplished nothing, but I wasn't to be deterred by such a minor consideration, not me, no sir. However, let's be charitable and say I didn't stew, *I considered*. Okay, consideration: What if I went to Omfrey's and I was just as invisible to Sharon there as I'd always been in class? Downer. Weekend-ruiner. *But* . . . what if the invisibility trick didn't work at rock clubs and she saw me and said, *"Say, without your sketch pad you're* hunky."

In fifty years, we'd be doting on our beautiful grandchildren. But not unless I took a chance.

So, at nine that night, I hopped on my bike and went. Pretty embarrassing, a guy who'd lived to the mature age of twenty having a bicycle instead of . . . oh, a Porsche. A BMW. At least a used Hyundai. But anything fancier than a bike was out of my price range, and thankfully bikes don't use gasoline, which

I certainly couldn't afford. I pedaled as fast as I could, both because I was anxious to find out if Sharon could see me and because in my neighborhood even the rats don't go out after dark. At one point, somebody threw an empty bottle at me (and missed, I'm happy to report) and a block later three punks—excuse me: *young men*—were systematically trashing somebody's car with bricks and boards. Life in the city. . . .

I fastened my ride to a *No Parking* sign with a lock that cost as much as the bike and was guaranteed to withstand anything short of a nuclear blast, and entered Omfrey's. Gasping, I rubbed my suddenly watering eyes: There were enough carcinogens in the air to keep an army of oncologists busy for the rest of the century.

At the far end of the long, narrow, ill-lit room was a stage, and on that a kid—no older than me—with lots of tattoos and piercings, a guitar, and two amps the size of basketball courts. I guess what he was doing was singing. Whatever it was, it numbed both my eardrums and my brain. But it was okay, really. It just took some getting used to. I allowed myself to listen and enjoy for a few minutes.

Then I finally spotted Sharon at a side table, sitting across from some slab with a buzz cut and shoulders the width of ironing boards. She was smiling and leaning forward, and so was the slab, but what did that mean? Maybe he was her brother. Maybe he was a guy from school she always secretly despised but had decided to be nice to because she was a wonderful person. Maybe, in fact, he was her boyfriend, but they were in the process of breaking up and she was smiling because she was so relieved to be rid of the jerk. And she was leaning forward because perhaps she had a pulled muscle in her back. Anyway, I decided to stay around for an hour in case any of my dumb *maybes* turned out to be true or something happened to cause the slab's early exit.

I scored a Pepsi from the bar. Nothing stronger. I tried something stronger once and was sick for the next three days. I'll never be a drinker—don't have the stomach for it, literally. Never be a smoker, either, of anything. After fifteen minutes in that alleged air, my mucous membranes were swollen like overinflated truck tires, and I could feel my lungs curling into the fetal position and whimpering, "Mama."

I hauled my drink out a rear exit, thinking I'd breathe for a little while before returning to my Sharon watch. I found myself alone in an alley, staring at a dirty, windowless brick wall, probably the rear of a warehouse. The only light was from a bare bulb under a metal shade that hung above the door to Omfrey's.

I drained the soda. I shivered. Kind of cold for September. Maybe an early winter this year.

Then the weirdness began.

For less than a second, for less than *half* a second, the dirty brick wall suddenly glowed white and wavered, as though it were dissolving and becoming transparent, and through it I glimpsed the street on the other side. Which was not possible, and I *knew* it was not possible. So, while I rubbed my eyes with my fists, I started formulating explanations: . . . *something*

*in the drink . . . something I inhaled with the smoke . . . lack
of sleep . . .*

"It was a time stasis," someone said. I turned and
saw . . .

Okay, this is the part that's most hard to believe.
Not that a small man about a yard tall was somehow
standing five feet from me, nor that the small man
was blue—maybe he got an overdose of Omfrey's
air—but that the small man was wearing what looked
like a red nightshirt. Why would a small blue man
wear a red nightshirt?

Ah, I had it! A costume party. He had come as Yoda
and gotten the details way wrong.

"You shall have to do," he said, and I felt I had
wandered into a cheesy sci-fi movie because his lips
didn't move and, boys and girls, how often have we
seen *that* cliché on screens large and small? Okay, he
was a ventriloquist or he was wearing a mask.

He extended a fist and then opened it, revealing a
green ring that glowed faintly. "Take it," he said/didn't
say.

Why not?

It looked a bit big for me (and *way* big for the guy
in the red nightshirt), so I tried it on my middle finger
instead of my ring finger. It slid past my knuckles
without touching skin—yep, pretty big, all right—but
then it . . . I didn't know what it did at the time, and I
still don't. Shrunk, you could say and not be telling a
lie, but it did more than decrease in size. It sort of
molded itself around my finger, almost became a
green-glowing part of me.

Nifty trick.

"Okay," I said. "So what happens now? What am I supposed to do?"

"Wear the ring," Red Nightshirt replied.

"For how long?"

"Until you die or something worse happens to you."

Something worse?

"It's a gag, right?" I asked, looking around. "Where's the camera. Gotta be a camera *some*where." I gestured to the wall. "One of those bricks a phony? A one-way kind of deal with the lens behind—"

And, again, the wall glowed white and wavered, became transparent, only I didn't see the street through it, I saw . . . some kind of movie set, or cyclorama, or Christmas window. Or something. Fat snowflakes wafting down—and remember, this was only September—and horses pulling carriages, and men wearing frock coats and derbies, and women in long dresses with bustles: a scene from at least a hundred years ago.

I whirled. A projector, inside Omfrey's and aimed out at the warehouse wall? Had to be! Some kind of variation on a light show?

"Cute," I said to Red Nightshirt. "I gotta admit, you were freaking me out for a while there—"

He vanished.

I walked around the place where he'd been, knelt, and ran my fingers over the floor of the alley, searching for a trapdoor or at least a seam in the asphalt or a place that could hold a mirror and puff out smoke. . . .

Of course, there had been no smoke. No mirrors, either, or seams, doors, or gimmicks of any kind.

Okay, I said to myself, *how about a hologram? That has to be it—a hologram, and some extremely advanced, voice-throwing sound system.*

I relaxed, unaware until that moment how much I had tensed. I hate being made a fool of. But now that I was sure I knew how the stunts had been accomplished . . . I turned to go back inside.

But what about the green thing that encircled the longest finger on my right hand. I rapped it against the wall. Solid. Tangible. No damn hologram—

Then *it* vanished too.

Vanished, but did not go away. I could still feel it, still hit it against solid objects and get a noise. I just couldn't see it.

I briefly considered that some prankster, whoever was doing the holograms, had gotten hold of the military's stealth technology and . . .

And I was weary of thinking up explanations. Enough was enough.

I went back into the sea of noise and poison that was Omfrey's. The guy with the tattoos and piercings was gone; the music was still heavy metal, but it was coming from a recording. I saw Sharon and the slab in the middle of the dance floor, clutching each other, swaying slightly, faces mashed together. Okay, he wasn't her brother. If he was a guy from school she always secretly despised I wanted her to find me absolutely repulsive. And if he was her boyfriend and they were in the process of breaking up, she obviously planned to end the relationship by smothering him to death with her lips, which didn't seem likely somehow.

This was not going to be one of the great, happy-happy nights. (It *was* going to change me and everything about me, possibly forever, but I didn't know that at the time.)

I stood for maybe a minute in the midst of the smoke and noise and sweaty bodies, not knowing what to do next, or where to go. Finally, I decided: *Out!* Even my cruddy hole of an apartment would be better than Omfrey's, provided I could reach it alive. There I could kick back, think things over, figure out who was messing with my head and why . . . and, if I had any energy left, make a voodoo doll of the slab and start sticking pins in it.

As I left Omfrey's I saw somebody in the process of stealing my bike. He had somehow removed the flat metal rectangle sign, the part that says NO PARKING, and was trying to lift the bike, expensive lock and all, up and over the metal post. No cops in sight, and even if there had been I'd probably still have been on my own.

I looked at the guy. He could have been the slab's clone. Big. Six-six, if he was a centimeter, and wide, and heavy—two-twenty, easy. Possibly armed, with a knife if not something noisier.

So I should saunter up to him, palms showing, smile, and say, *"Hey, big fella, I kinda need those wheels and I can't afford new ones. . . ."*

Last time I tried something like that, the Gandhi approach, I'd gotten punched.

Run into Omfrey's and yell for help? With the decibel level in the club, I'd have to have a voice as loud as a foghorn, and then the clubbers would probably just go on dancing or face-mashing or whatever.

What else? Attack him from behind and hope that surprise would be a good substitute for brawn? No. Unless I was prepared to find a weapon of some kind and hit him hard enough to maybe kill him—and I wasn't, not even close—I couldn't hope to hurt him as badly as he'd hurt me. To merely annoy him could prove fatal.

So, I leaned against a wall and settled for the final and only realistic option: remain helpless while my property was being stolen. Feel like garbage, seethe with rage, but be helpless.

For a moment, I allowed myself to imagine the thief being hit by a boxing glove—stupid, sure, but the kind of thing an undernourished urban victim like me sometimes did to relieve frustration.

Resigned, I raised my right hand in an ironic, self-deprecating wave, and a big green boxing glove shot from the ring and reached across the street and punched the would-be thief, who promptly ran away. Then the glove vanished.

Well, *that* was nice. I walked over to the bike and unlocked it, realizing what had just happened. . . .

A. Big. Green. Boxing. Glove. Punched. The. Thief.

This time, I didn't bother to look for projectors, trapdoors, any of that stuff. I just got on my bike and rode home.

4

Once inside my apartment, I flopped down on the futon and calmly considered my situation. Two possibilities: 1) I was totally insane, in which case I should hop on down to the nearest psychiatric facility and check myself in, or 2) Everything that I thought had happened had, in fact, happened. In some ways, that was the worse possibility. If I were merely crazy, well, there were psychiatrists and social workers and Dr. Phil to help. But if I *weren't*? Then what?

I remembered Green Lantern and wondered why I hadn't thought of him earlier. He was one of the first of what eventually came to be called "super heroes," along with Superman, Wonder Woman, and the Flash. They had appeared about ten years ago, heralding their arrival by a series of spectacular stunts, all of which saved lives or property or both. They avoided reporters, seldom remained to accept applause after one of their capers, and, of course, got a lot of media attention. MORE POPULAR THAN THE BEATLES, one headline insisted. Considering who the Beatles once claimed to be more popular than, it was quite a statement.

A few years later, the superdoers announced that they had formed an organization, the Justice League, and added a few new members: the Atom, whose trick was to shrink, which didn't impress me too much—I've got T-shirts that can do that; and Plastic Man, who could do the opposite of the Atom and *stretch*—a little better than shrinking, or at least a little more amusing, but still not exactly mind-boggling. There were also some others who either stayed entirely out of the public eye or whom I've forgotten.

I was never a big super-hero fan, any more than I'm a big football fan—just not into muscles and might, I guess—but if I *were*, Green Lantern would not have been my favorite. What he was, what exactly he did, was always vague. We knew it had something to do with a ring he wore, and that he flew, and that he managed some moves that nearly equaled those of his teammate, Superman. But his profile was even lower than the others'; if the Justice League were the Beatles, then Green Lantern would be Ringo. (If there's a pun in there someplace, do us both a favor and ignore it.)

So if I *was* crazy, why fantasize that I'd become a guy I didn't particularly care for? I gave that a lot of mulling—mulled and mulled and mulled. . . .

I blinked at the light coming through the single window of my subterranean palace. I must have slept.

The alarm clock read: 10:23. I'd been out over nine hours.

Had I been dreaming? I wanted to pray, *Oh, please let it have been a dream. . . .*

I touched my right middle finger with my left forefinger and felt the ring. Still there. No dream, unless I was *still* asleep . . . So I did the traditional thing: I pinched myself. It hurt. But maybe I was *dreaming* that it had hurt.

I looked at my finger and felt a rush of anger. "I want to *see*, dammit . . . !"

The ring appeared. *Ask and ye shall receive.*

I hadn't really examined it before. Now, I did. It had a wide green band and a rectangular top shaped like . . . something. I knew I knew that form, but I couldn't name it.

I remembered the boxing glove and, being relatively unmuddled and calm, reached the obvious conclusion.

"Okay," I said aloud, "let's see the glove."

Nothing.

"All right then—vanish."

It did.

I had a thought. *Magic? Real magic?*

I wasted the next hour looking up "magic" in the yellow pages and calling every number listed. No help. One guy tried to sell me a used set of *linking* rings: "I'm sure you've seen the effect on television, fella. You have these eight big rings, see? You bang them together and they . . . *link.*" A woman with a foreign accent who announced herself as Gypsy Gerda said she'd sell me a mystic candle that would solve any problems I had with rings and was also potent against evil siblings and indigestion. I passed on both offers.

But Gypsy Gerda reminded me of what I often try to forget: that in the matter of siblings, I was a washout. No brothers, no sisters, aunts, uncles, or cousins, at least not currently alive, and, of course, no parents. Not even any family mementos, except for a faded photograph of my mother and father, probably taken with a box camera that set somebody back a whole couple of bucks; they're both dressed in white and they're standing in front of an old-fashioned car—the kind with big fenders and running boards. I can make out my father's smiling face, barely, but my mother's face is a blur; maybe she moved as the photo was being snapped. The closest thing I had to a family was a lawyer who sent me a tiny check every month, interest from an annuity my father had established for me shortly before he died. Some months, it was my only income. Enough to pay the rent, but I had to eat, too, and that was a problem sometimes.

I hauled out my sketch pad, set it on my lap, and began working with a number two pencil. I did quick drawings of Red Nightshirt, the ring, the boxing glove. I wasn't just killing time; I often think better when I'm drawing. I looked at what I'd done. The sketches were okay, but something was missing. I added a drawing of Omfrey's. Then, gritting my teeth, I drew one of Sharon dancing with the slab.

I tore the sheet off the pad and dropped it. Stepped on it too.

Then I began sketching again, with nothing in particular in mind. I did a picture of Red Nightshirt, but for some reason I crammed it into the bottom fourth of the page. Then, I found myself drawing a word balloon the remaining three-fourths above Red Nightshirt's head, like the ones in comics that show what's being said and who's saying it. Odd. I was interested in comics, of course—ever meet a twenty-year-old illustrator who wasn't?—but I hadn't done any since sixth grade.

I was writing in the balloon, giving Red Nightshirt some dialogue. Just, you know, making letters, not thinking. Some kind of automatic writing, perhaps?

When I was done, I read what Mr. Nightshirt "said":

Whatever you visualize, the ring will create.

You can use it to fly.

It must be recharged soon.

Okay, that wasn't what I would have expected my subconscious to cough up, and I had no reason, at that point, to believe that my subconscious was any smarter than my conscious, which, as you may have gotten by now, does not win rocket-science prizes. But what the hell? I could easily test the truth of what I'd written.

I visualized the boxing glove and—

Yup, there it was. Big as life. No—*bigger* than life. Sucker was the size of a refrigerator and greener than grass.

I'm a bit ashamed of what I tried next. Yeah, a life-sized Sharon Klingerman—green, but still devastatingly cute. I thought: *Smile*. She smiled. I thought: *Bat your eyelashes*. She batted. I thought: *Walk over here*. She walked. I thought—

This is getting a little sick, man!

So I willed Sharon to vanish, which she obligingly did.

Then, for the rest of the afternoon, I experimented. Using the ring, I created models of everything from the Eiffel Tower to a Hula Hoop. I felt like every kid in the history of Christmas who ever found a humongous, giant-sized Erector set under the tree.

The ring had limitations. I conjured up a pizza that had neither taste nor substance. When I bit into it, I was chewing air, which even I know is not particularly nourishing. Everything was green, of course, and things that had engines in them, like the nifty, full-sized Ferrari roadster I materialized—which occupied my entire room—didn't actually run, but they *looked* great. Some of my creations were as solid as the boxing glove that kayoed the wannabe bicycle thief, and some, like the pizza, weren't.

Obviously, I had a lot to learn about my new toy.

I looked at my drawing of Red Nightshirt again, reread "his" words: *Whatever you visualize, the ring will create. You can use it to fly. It must be recharged soon.*

Okay, let's take those last two items one at a time. I can use the ring to fly? *That's* interesting. I assume that Red Nightshirt didn't mean that the ring would provide me with a boarding pass for the next plane out of the nearest airport. No, it had to mean that I, Kyle Rayner, minus aircraft, balloon, or other mechanical contrivance, could take to the skies.

Oh, boy!

But where to test it? Nowhere too public, just in case I made an utter jackass of myself. So no parks or playgrounds, and certainly no city streets. An empty field would be perfect, but I wasn't up to biking out to the nearest farmland. So where?

I looked at my single window. No light was pushing through the grime, so I assumed that it was dark out there in the world. Time really *does* fly when you're having fun. The question was, could I?

I crept up the stairs, past my landlord's door and farther, onto the roof. Mr. Gloinger doesn't like me up there—something about the tar sticking to my shoes and making the roof leaky. But by now, Mr. Gloinger was sucked into whatever was on television at the moment. He wouldn't hear me if I was reasonably quiet. I hoped.

Okay, the program at hand was, Kyle flies. And how do we accomplish this? I raised both hands and arms above my head and jumped. Went up a foot. Came down.

Next idea: I took a running start and jumped. And came down.

What had Red Nightshirt said? *Whatever you visualize, the ring will create.* Add that to the idea of flying and what do we have?

Wings?

Yeah, wings.

I had the ring equip me with a pair of wings, in-spired by dozens of Christmas tree decorations, and imagined them lifting me—

I looked down. At the tar-paper roof. The size of a postage stamp.

I was about four hundred feet above it.

Then, I was falling, watching the postage stamp grow and knowing that if I hit it I would be instantly killed or go through it to Mr. Gloinger's apartment and die an instant later. Either way, the fall would end me.

Lift, lift, I thought, and maybe a second before I would have smashed into the roof, I began to waft upward. With a little—very careful!—experimenta-tion, I discovered I could control direction and, to a lesser extent, speed.

So this is how the city really looks from on high, without the noise and metal of an aircraft as distractions. Glittery. Car headlights making streaks of the streets. Red and green and purple neon signs. Rooftop gardens.

I was dizzy, literally. Excitement combined with lack of food—air pizza doesn't do a thing for a man's blood sugar. I returned to Mr. Gloinger's roof and touched down light as a whisper. I started toward the stairway and stopped. I had another question: *Are wings my only means of flight?*

What else? I remembered a fairy tale I'd read as a kid about a guy with a flying carpet. Well, why not? I visualized a carpet, which the ring immediately cre-ated, and sat on it and willed it up, up, and away. . . .

Gliding over the city, looking down, I enjoyed the

sights as no one had ever enjoyed them before. My city. Cute little city. Like something on a model train layout. I almost felt as though I could reach down and rearrange it: put the train depot over at the western border, nearer the interstate, move the mall to the center of town, exile the high school I'd attended to a landfill. . . .

I was becoming a bit crazy and I didn't care. But hundreds of feet above the ground was not a good place to be out of my mind, and that's where I was.

I returned to Gloinger's roof, and this time I did descend the stairs, then flopped down on the futon.

Just resting my eyes for a few minutes, trying to make sense of what I'd been experiencing . . .

5

I was awakened by dusty sunlight from the window, and was feeling ferociously hungry. I hadn't eaten since leaving for Omfrey's, more than thirty-six hours ago. My check wasn't due to arrive until the following day, but I managed to scrounge a few bucks' worth of change from various pockets, enough for coffee and a puny but adequate stack of pancakes from the Big Belly Burger down the block.

I didn't fly; I walked. I wasn't ready to deal with all the implications of flying, much less get asked questions I couldn't possibly answer. I returned to my apartment and willed the ring to become visible, which it did. I willed it invisible, picked up my sketch pad, and walked down to the path that borders the river.

For an hour, I sketched what I saw: a strikingly pretty girl on Rollerblades, an even prettier young mother pushing a baby carriage, a guy rowing a kayak on the water, an old couple walking hand in hand.

Then I drew Red Nightshirt.

"Got something to say?" I asked the picture.

I put a word balloon above his head and let my pencil do the talking. *You need to rechange the ring. Use the green lantern.*

"Okay, fine. Now where, exactly, is this 'green lantern'?"

My pencil moved. *The ice cathedral of the Order of St. Dumas.*

"Never heard of it—the Order of St. Dumas *or* the ice cathedral."

It is in the Swiss Alps.

"That narrows it down a bit, but—"

My pencil added a fourth balloon. Old Red Nightshirt was getting to be a blabbermouth. *Draw me drawing a map.*

Can do. I flipped to a fresh page and sketched Red Nightshirt facing away from the viewer with a piece of charcoal in his hand.

New balloon: *Now the map.*

I placed the tip of my pencil at the tip of Nightshirt's charcoal and away we went. When the map was done, the pencil seemed to want to add some lettering, which was okay with me.

I turned to a new page and, while I was speaking, did another sketch of Nightshirt. I was getting very good at drawing him because practice does, indeed, make perfect.

"Is this Order of St. Dumas friendly or not?"

Balloon: *Not.*

"When should I go?"

Now.

"Hold on. I need some more info before I go flitting off to Switzerland and grab something from people who don't like me."

A question, one I should have asked way earlier, suddenly occurred to me, and when I asked it, there was a hot edge in my voice: "Am I the new Green Lantern?"

Yes.

I hesitated, because I wasn't sure I wanted my next question answered. "What happened to the old one?"

I am not certain.

Could a cartoon be lying to me? Had it been telling . . . or writing, or whatever the hell it did . . . had it been *propagating* untruths all along?

My pencil was moving, creating the page's sixth balloon: *The ring will be useless in six of your hours unless it is recharged.*

"So, the program is, I go off into the wild blue yonder, fly over to the Alps, snatch a green lantern, and bring it back here to recharge the ring, whatever that means. That about right?"

Yes.

"No. Not until I get my head straight about a few things. For instance, is any of this really happening? Where's the guy who used to be Green Lantern? Why was I chosen to replace him? What is the Order of St. Dumas and why isn't it my buddy?"

"Pardon me, young fella," someone said close to my ear. I looked up. The male half of the old couple I'd seen earlier was bending from the waist, an expression of polite concern on his face. "Are you aware that you've been talking to yourself? If you need help getting somewhere—a hospital, say—I'd be happy to lend you cab fare. . . ."

"Won't be necessary, sir," I told him. "But thanks."

"You're sure—"

"I am. Have a nice day."

The man sauntered away to join his female companion. He would not have a "nice day," at least not until tomorrow, because the sky had darkened. As I left the park, the streetlights flickered on. Somehow, I'd blown another couple of hours, which drastically reduced the amount of time I had left to recharge the ring, if my cartoon was to be believed.

I walked home. I vowed to myself that I would not fly until I had an idea of how to proceed, and as I made the vow I got an idea.

A compromise. After all, wasn't this country founded on the idea of benevolent compromise? Why should I think I'm better than Thomas Jefferson? What I would do is, I'd assume the identity of Green Lantern and visit the ice cathedral—not necessarily to swipe anything, just to scope out the scene. That way, if I did blunder somehow, Green Lantern would get blamed. Since I was pretty sure Green Lantern, whoever he was, wasn't around any longer, I had myself a no-lose situation.

Pretty nifty solution, I thought. I hadn't completely abandoned the possibility that I was still in the midst of the damnedest hallucination in history, but if I were, I might as well ride it out, especially since I wasn't waking up anyway.

Okay. First, I needed to *look* like Green Lantern. I rummaged through a couple of boxes of clothing Mr. Gloinger had stashed behind the furnace. It would have been nice to be able to report that I found a Green Lantern costume left over from Halloween. Didn't happen. But I found a bunch of stuff that was the right color, and although I couldn't sew, I could *visualize* the ring cutting and stitching, which was all I had to do. Pretty soon, I was standing in front of the mirror next to the futon, checking myself out. "Resplendent" was a word I might have spoken aloud if anyone had been in the room with me. I was *resplendent* in my new Green Lantern costume, complete with mask. Yes I was.

I glanced at my watch. Four hours left to do the old ring recharge. But I had one more chore before I left. From behind the futon, I pulled the laptop computer I'd bought secondhand back when I thought I'd be a college student, plugged it in, fired up the modem, and went to various databases looking for the Order of St. Dumas. On the fifth try, at a website devoted to European legends, I got a hit.

Order of St. Dumas: Said to be a clandestine group founded in the 14th Century which amassed vast wealth. According to the legend, the Order's members were sworn to secrecy; anyone even admitting the existence of the group was penalized by immediate execution. Historians have found no evidence that the Order ever existed. The stories about it may have been inspired by the Knights Templar. See also: Illuminati. Knights Templar.

Okay. A nonexistent bunch of rich guys with a secrecy fetish that somehow had whatever I needed to recharge the ring. No problem *here*, right?

I unplugged the computer and, map in hand, went to the roof, willed the carpet into existence, and flew east. Flew pretty slowly, I might add. I'd never get to the Alps in four hours at this speed, not that it would make any difference since I did not plan to steal the lantern in any case. But no point in closing options.

"Faster," I told the carpet.

The carpet ignored me. I realized that the problem was, I could not bring myself to imagine a really *fast* carpet, and my imagination, filtered through the ring, was actually the carpet's power source.

I visualized myself inside an intercontinental ballistic missile arcing over the top of the world at supersonic velocity—*wheeeee*—and when I was dropping toward northern Europe, I imagined the missile morphing back into the carpet.

I checked the map by the light of a ring-spawned torch and guided the carpet to where the ice cathedral was nestled between two snowcapped peaks. It was eerie and beautiful: two spires rising from an oblong structure with a cantilevered roof, the whole of it glowing in the moon and the light reflected from the snow. I sat on my carpet and stared and asked myself some questions: How could the world not know about something as spectacular as this? That cathedral *had* to qualify as one of the Wonders of the World. Why wasn't it mentioned in every guidebook published? Why was it not swarming with tourists? How did whoever owned the cathedral conceal it in an era of satellite photos

and spy planes and global positioning apparatus?
With bribes? Great *big* bribes? Payoffs to anyone who
learned of it? *That,* I told myself, *has to be the answer.*
Then I remembered that I was here for a reason.

The luminous dial on my watch told me that it was
seven back home, which made it . . . what?—about one
in the morning here. Two hours to recharge the ring.

Probably everyone inside the cathedral was asleep.
Unless there were guards. Would an ice cathedral
even *have* guards? Here, miles from the nearest city,
where junkies ripping off the poor box was not likely
to be a concern?

There was one window lighted in the higher of the
building's two spires. I guided the carpet down to it
and looked inside. Two tall men, dressed in gray
robes, stood at rigid attention on either side of a door
that must have been forty feet high. They had rifles,
or maybe shotguns, slung over their shoulders. Okay,
there *were* guards, or damn good facsimiles.

I edged the carpet around the curve of the wall,
away from the window, and put my palm against it:
cold, but not wet. Not real ice, then. Some kind of
glass? I aimed my ring and visualized a beam melting
the wall. A second later, there was a round hole, large
enough for me to climb through.

Which I did. I was in darkness, but in the glow that
shone through the hole I'd made, I could see that I
had entered a high, narrow corridor that curved off to
either side, obviously girding the spire. I reckoned
that whatever was behind the high doors was on the
other side of the inner wall. Maybe it was nothing

more than a storeroom for altar wine, but anything that well guarded and encased just might be a vault of some kind—a likely place to start my search, anyway.

The ring made a hole in the inner wall. I stepped into a huge chamber lit by a chandelier spangled with shimmering tubes hanging from the ceiling. I closed my eyes for a second to adjust to the dim light, opened them, and gawked.

Treasure. An unimaginable amount of treasure. Gold and silver and gems in heaps on the floor, spilling out of huge chests. Coins, bars, candlesticks, swords, broaches, bracelets, necklaces. And more: gowns decked with pearls and rubies, marble statues, oil paintings—could that really be a Rembrandt? A Picasso over there? A Titian next to a Tintoretto?

The wealth of ages, spread before me.

"Pretty swell, hey?" The voice, high-pitched and squeaky as a rusty hinge, had come from behind me. I whirled and saw the two guards, their weapons aimed at me. Between them stood a short, fat man in a crimson robe—he of the squeaky voice.

"You do speak English? The international tongue these days. Not like the old days when everyone who was anyone spoke Latin. You're surprised to be caught? Oh, we saw you from far off. Our technology is excellent. We've been expecting you, you know. For hundreds of years we've been expecting you."

"I don't understand. . . ."

"Yes you do. What planet are you from?"

"Planet? This one, Earth—"

"Do not lie. Brother Rollo does not tolerate lies."

"You're Brother Rollo?"

The question seemed to surprise him. "Certainly."

"And your job is?"

"I am the supreme pontiff and heir to the mantle of the most blessed St. Dumas." He tipped his shoulders forward an inch—a bow, or as much a bow as his huge belly allowed him.

"Nice to meet you," I said, lamely.

He and the larger of the two gun-toters moved past me to a pile of jewelry on top of a large table. Rollo pawed through the goodies, and I wondered what he was looking for—truffles, maybe?

"Here it is," he said, pulling from the gems what appeared to be a lantern. You guessed it—a *green* lantern. "Is this what you seek?"

"As a matter of fact, it is—I think. May I ask how you got it?"

"There is no harm to come from telling you. Three hundred and seventy-eight years ago, someone from your planet suffered a mishap and died. He had this object with him."

"By any chance, was he also wearing a ring?"

"Yes. It is here somewhere."

"Why do you think he was from another planet?"

"He was *flying*, as were you."

Well, what he was saying actually made some kind of sense.

"All right," I said, smiling as widely as I could. "What do I have to do to make you give me the . . . thing." After a moment, I clarified, "The thing you're holding."

As though we might be discussing some *other* thing.

"Oh, it is part of our treasure. You may not have it. And you must die now."

I'll never know why Rollo hesitated, but I wouldn't be here if he hadn't. I had a couple of seconds to suss out the situation and visualize a shield, which the ring obligingly materialized. Rollo snapped his fingers and the guards shot at me. One of the lighted tubes above us shattered: a ricochet, I guess. The guards fired again, to no avail; the shield was doing its job. Enough: time to go on the offensive. I visualized a giant hand and mentally caused it to slap the guns from the guards' fingers.

Then I had an inspiration. I had the hand grab my three playmates and hang them from a ring-formed hook on the wall, where they wriggled like newly boated trout.

"Now listen to me," I said in what I hoped was a truly stern voice. "I *am* St. Dumas. I've come back to check up on you, and I gotta tell you, I do *not* like what I see. I'm giving you a week to get rid of this treasure. Give it to poor people. Give it to the World Wildlife Fund and the Fellowship of Reconciliation and Greenpeace and the Red Cross and . . . anybody else who needs it. If I have to tell you again, your sorry asses will be in a serious sling. *Kapeesh?*"

Rollo nodded. Obviously, he was the spokesnodder for the group.

Rollo had dropped the lantern—the *green* lantern—when I'd put him on the wall. I picked it up and went back through the two holes I'd made. I was again in the corridor. So there I stood in a place almost nobody knew existed—what's more, a place that had existed for over four hundred years, if Rollo were to be believed. Suddenly, I thought that it would be doofy not to look around, kind of like going to Paris and passing on the Eiffel Tower.

I could spare a few minutes for sightseeing.

I crept through the corridor until it opened out on a huge, vaulted hall full of shadows, the only light coming from a few glow tubes that seemed to have less power than the ones in the treasure room. There were maybe a dozen doorways around the walls, which, I guessed, led to other parts of the cathedral.

They did. Toting the green lantern, I gave myself an unguided tour of the premises—or part of the premises: The place was huge, as big as Grand Central Station in New York, and I'm sure I saw only a fraction of it. What I did see was mostly more of the same: shadowy corridors, shadowy halls, everything colored white. Twice, I encountered guards, guns on shoulders, standing at attention in front of doors. They were as stoic as those guys who stand in front of Buckingham Palace: didn't move an eyelash, and didn't react to my passing. They didn't bother me so I didn't bother them.

After a while, I realized that I was disappointed. I'd been expecting . . . oh, I don't know . . . more treasures, I guess. Or something else equally gaudy. Or at least some nifty architecture. Instead, I got the architectural equivalent of chicken soup: bland and monotonous. Maybe it's what I should have expected from a group that kept itself virtually invisible for over four centuries.

I started to return to where I'd begun my boring little expedition and then stopped: I'd gone around a lot of corners, up and down a lot of stairs and, in typical Rayner fashion, I hadn't been paying much attention. So—surprise, surprise!—I was lost.

"Okay, ring," I said aloud, "show me the way to go home."

The ring did nothing.

I closed my eyes and visualized the first corridor I'd entered, trying to remember something, anything, that might give me a clue as to how I should return there. All my imagination conjured up was the big hole I'd made and . . . voila! That was it. My answer—a hole. I aimed my ring at the nearest wall and burned a gap in it. I immediately felt a blast of cold and saw the hard, blue stars of a blue-black sky. I formed the carpet and wafted into the glowing night. I was in no hurry. I had a lot to digest and figured I might as well digest it while flying home. For openers, I considered how amazing it was that an apocryphal Order was not, in fact, apocryphal. Then I reran my speculations about how it kept hidden. Maybe Brother Rollo and company managed to get the air above the building declared a no-fly zone. Which made me laugh. *I* was flying above it—

Then I remembered why I'd come. As I was glancing at my watch, the carpet began to dissolve, and I realized that ring-charging time was *now*. But my cartoon hadn't told me how to do the recharge.

The carpet melted into nothing and I began falling.

I jammed the ring against the lantern and . . .

Tingled. Like my whole body was a funnybone and I'd just hit it against a car door. While I was tingling, I was also shrieking: *"The carpet!"*

It materialized, and not a second too soon. I was close enough to the ground to see the little bumps in the snow.

We elevated, my pal the flying carpet and I, and skimmed over the mountaintops.

I heard a another shriek and wondered if it wasn't a much-delayed echo of the noise I'd made. But it was coming from somewhere above me. I looked up and saw, silhouetted against the moon, an aircraft—a small jet plane with red dots winking on its wings. A *snap-whir* erupted near my head and I realized that what I'd heard was a bullet passing: The jet was shooting at me.

Apparently, Rollo hadn't bought my St. Dumas story.

But how could he have gotten someone on my trail so quickly? A jet on some kind of launcher, a pilot on twenty-four-hour standby . . . ? Didn't matter *how,* really. Point was, a guy in a heavily armed supersonic aircraft was trying to do grave bodily harm to a guy on a flying carpet.

I surrounded myself with a shield and decided to have some fun. I had the ring form a giant dragon—green, of course—and clamp the jet in its jaws. The dragon descended to a valley between the peaks and spat out the jet. Then it stuck out its tongue and vanished.

Enough jollies. I morphed the carpet into the missile and sped across the top of the world.

6

What I didn't know, and what I would not learn until much later, was that at that moment, 22,300 miles above the Earth, I had an audience: Plastic Man and the Atom were taking their turns at monitoring duty on the control deck of the Watchtower, the Justice League's satellite headquarters.

The Atom was not very atomy. He stood a full six feet tall and wore jeans and a T-shirt. He would have answered to "Ray Palmer," the name he was born with, and he was busy plying his trade, that of scientist, peering at a bank of dials and indicators. He frowned, did a quick calculation on a small computer he'd brought from home, frowned again, and sighed.

"You whipping it or it whipping you?" Plastic Man asked. Unlike the Atom, Plas was unmistakably a costumed hero. He wore dark glasses and a red garment that resembled an old-fashioned swimming suit, but that wasn't what made him distinctive. He was bent over a copy of the Boy Scout manual, opened to the section on knots, and he had twisted his arms into a classic square knot and was in the process of bending his legs into a half-hitch. Occasionally, he had to adjust one of the monitors that lined the walls of the room; this he did by stretching his ear four yards to the appropriate control and tweaking it.

"You hear what I said, Ray?"

Ray looked up from his computer. "Yeah. It's whipping me. By which I mean, I can't figure out why our chronometers lost a tenth of a nanosecond night before last."

"A whole *tenth* of a *nano*second? Guess we're in *ter-ri-ble* trouble, huh?"

"No, but it shouldn't have happened."

"Any clues?"

"Not really. If I didn't know better, I'd say something briefly altered the space-time curvature hereabouts."

"*Do* you know better?"

"I *think* I do."

"Hey, what's happening *here*?" Plastic Man had stretched his neck across the chamber and was peering at a screen. "Something going down in the Alps."

Ray moved closer, squinted, and slid his switch upward. The image on the screen magnified: A giant green dragon was swallowing a jet plane.

"This is being shot from one of the WayneCorp satellites we borrow," Plastic Man explained.

"I know."

Ray manipulated the controls again and the image grew still larger: The dragon was spitting out a jet.

The satellite camera panned upward and focused on a masked guy riding a flying carpet.

"Can't be," Ray muttered.

"Can't be who? Or is it 'whom'?"

"Green Lantern."

"He's before my time—"

On the screen, the carpet morphed into a tapered green cylinder and shot out of the picture. Ray frantically twisted dials, switching from satellite to satellite, as images danced and flitted. . . .

"You channel-surfing?" Plastic Man asked.

"Something like that. Looking for him—*there* he is!"

The cylinder was plunging into a bank of clouds. Ray looked away from the screen. "We've lost him. But at least we have some idea where he went."

"So was he the Green Lantern or wasn't he?"

"I'm prepared to say he was *a* Green Lantern. Whether he was *the* Green Lantern . . ." Ray shrugged. "Your guess is as good as mine."

Plastic Man had unknotted himself and stood beside Ray, who was busy at the controls. "Can I help you? With whatever you're doing?"

"It's done. I downloaded the recordings of what we saw and beamed them to Superman, Wonder Woman, Batman—"

"Why *him*? He doesn't even like to hang out with us."

"Sometimes he sees things. Sometimes he understands things. Sometimes—"

"He ignores us," Plastic Man concluded.

"That too."

1

The eastern sky was just beginning to lighten as I touched down on Mr. Gloinger's roof.

"Gotta stop using this as a landing strip," I muttered. "Sooner or later, somebody's gonna see me."

Of course, somebody already had, from 22,300 miles overhead, but I didn't know that yet.

"Gotta stop talking to myself too," I continued as I crept down the stairs, battery in hand. "Or somebody will think I'm crazy, such as I am."

I closed my door behind me, locked it, and tested the lock, then dropped my improvised costume on the floor and went into the bathroom. There, in the mirror over the sink, was me: Kyle Rayner, pale, too thin, thick brown hair badly needing a trim.

I began to tremble. Within the past eight hours I'd traveled thousands of miles, been to a foreign country, broken into a fortified palace, beaten armed guards, downed a jet plane. By myself. Within eight hours.

Not possible. I had to be crazy. No, I *wanted* to be crazy, desperately. Because if this was true, any of it, I had more power than I wanted and I'd have to do something with it. Wouldn't I? And I had no idea what.

I lifted the battery, tapped the ring against it. Both seemed solid.

"Okay," I told the universe. "Here's the bargain. I'm gonna lie down. Sleep if I'm lucky. When I get up, if the ring's still on my finger and the battery's still here, I'm gonna toss a coin. Heads, I go down to the loony bin and beg to be admitted. Tails, I try to do something heroic, see if I can. Oh, and either way I'm gonna stop talking to myself."

I flopped down on the futon, and for a long while I shivered. Shock, I realized, both mental and physical—my body had ascended and descended thousands of feet within seconds with nothing between it and the air and it had had guns pointed at it and bullets whizzing within inches of its head. Human bodies weren't supposed to do such stuff.

But had I imagined everything?

Darkness all around me except for a faint, dusty rectangle of light to my right. My window. My basement crib. So I *had* slept. For how long? My watch told me that the time was now 6:45. I'd blown another day. How long since I'd seen noon? Three days?

I remembered the promise I'd made to myself. If I still had the ring and lantern, or battery, or whatever it was, I'd either visit my friendly neighborhood psychiatric ward or . . . what? Become a hero?

I hesitated, wishing that I could stop time right then and not have to look at the middle finger of my right hand, much less make any decisions based on what I saw. Slowly, I lifted the hand. No ring. But it would be invisible.

"Show me," I said.

And there it was.

Okay, a bargain's a bargain, even if it's a bargain with yourself.

I fumbled in the coin pocket of my jeans and found a quarter.

I tossed it. Squinted down at my palm. Tails.

What had I decided? Heads I was to be a hero, tails an inmate? Or the other way around? I couldn't remember.

Then I did. Tails equal hero.

That was it. No fanfare, no hosts of admirers toasting the newest addition to the world's supply of good guys. Just a skinny twenty-year-old alone in one of the world's truly cruddy apartments, choosing a bizarre path into the rest of his life.

I put on my street clothes, willed the ring invisible, and left the apartment. The night was terrific. Crisp, cool, halos around the street lamps, the breeze off the river edged with a faint chill. Late September at its best.

So how does one become a super hero? Should I go down to the state employment office in the morning and tell the clerk, *"Hi, I'm the new Green Lantern, at your service. So, where's today's mad scientist? Any berserk robots need taking down?"*

Would I have to file a form? Could I get any benefits—social security, health insurance, Christmas bonuses?

I walked across town to a better neighborhood and used the quarter that had decided my fate to buy a newspaper from a machine. Standing in pink light from a neon sign in the window of a candy store, I scanned the headlines: Stock markets doing the hokeypokey . . . garbage strike likely . . . local politician caught with his hand where it shouldn't be. . . .

Depressing stuff. Nothing requiring the services of a super hero, though.

A fire engine roared past, its siren wailing.

I opened the paper to page two.

Three cop cars wailed past.

Nothing on page two, either.

Another cop car sped by and—

Hey! Firemen and cops, obviously in a big hurry . . . maybe they could use a hero. But how could I follow them without a car?

Duh. The ring.

I looked around and saw no good place to take off from; it was, after all, a busy city street in the middle of the evening. Finally, I spotted a moving van parked in the shadow of an office building. It would have to do.

I ducked behind the van and, staying in the shadows, floated to the top of the building. I glanced down. Nobody looking my way. Good. I shot into the sky.

From about four hundred feet up, I could see the flashers atop the cop cars, moving toward the city's northeastern border where an interstate ran between hills not quite high enough to be called mountains. When I got closer, I saw spotlights on three fire engines aimed at the top of a steel tower, one of a series along the top of the hills with power lines strung between them. The lights were shining on a small airplane that had obviously collided with the top of the tower and was hanging perpendicular to the ground, its lower door torn open, one wing caught in a steel grid. Several of the lines had snapped and were loose and writhing, crackling with hundreds of volts of electricity. If any of them touched the plane, anyone inside would probably be electrocuted.

But *was* anyone inside?

I floated near, stopping just outside the spotlight's glare, and peered at the plane. I didn't like what I saw. A man and a child, a little girl, were in the cockpit, secured only by their seat belts. The man wasn't moving, but the girl was, wriggling around, crazy with panic, trying to free herself. If she succeeded, she'd fall out the door to her death. If she stayed where she was, either she'd be electrocuted or the plane itself would fall.

Rescuers might figure out a way to save her in time. Or they might not.

I realized that I was in street clothes, not my improvised costume; and then, suddenly furious with myself for worrying about something as trivial as *that*, I willed the ring to form a huge pair of ice tongs. I used the tongs to pluck the plane free and was lowering it to the ground when, somehow, the girl got free and dropped from the plane. With no conscious thought, I formed a catcher's mitt as large as a suburban lawn and got it under the girl just before she would have hit the ground.

I set the plane down on a grassy slope.

And then, from a corner of my vision, I saw the spotlight swinging its beam toward me. Was I ready to reveal myself to the world? And if I was, *which* self? Kyle Rayner or the new Green Lantern?

I couldn't deal with it, not at that moment.

8

There's an old saying: "When the pupil is ready, the teacher will come." I was ready, maybe for the first time in my life. The truth is, until then, I'd never been a big fan of teachers. I wasn't a rebel, exactly, but I couldn't often get myself involved in what the people who stood in the front of classrooms wanted to teach me. I read a lot, and I was interested in a lot of things, especially if the things concerned drawing pictures, but studying and taking tests and vying for grades . . . Sorry. Not my trip.

But now I needed a teacher. Somebody who could tell me how my damn ring operated and then suggest what I should do with it.

So, flying back from the site of the plane crash, I had mixed . . . no, *scrambled* feelings. A part of me was happier than I'd been in years. I'd saved a life, maybe two. I'd never done anything *half* that good before, and it felt great. But I hadn't answered any of my big questions. If anything, I'd only made them bigger.

I was dropping down to land behind Mr. Gloinger's house, preparing to will the carpet out of existence, when I realized there *was* no carpet. I'd learned to fly—with the ring's help, of course—without any pseudo–floor covering. How had I managed *that*? Another question.

I hit the alley and went through Mr. Gloinger's back gate to my apartment door, then inside. I snapped on the light. Superman was standing in the middle of the room.

Superman was standing in the middle of the room?

My room?

I didn't doubt that he was the real article, not for a second. This was not some joker in a suit. It wasn't physical—oh, he was tall and muscular and handsome, but so are a lot of actors, athletes, and models. No, his *presence* was what awed me. He exuded a calmness, as well as a sense of tremendous power, that couldn't be faked. Standing there in the familiar blue costume, with the red boots and cape, he was the most impressive man I'd ever seen; the air around him seemed to *glow*.

"You're surprised," he said.

"Yes."

"Please try to relax. This may take a while."

Sure—relax, just chill out, with the strongest, smartest, most famous man in the world taking up space in my crummy apartment.

"Get you anything?" I managed to ask. "I've got water and . . . water . . ."

"I'm fine," he said. "Why don't you sit down."

Well, when Superman tells you to sit, you sit. Not having any chairs, I flopped down on the futon, crossed my legs, and propped my back against the wall.

"You're probably wondering why I'm here."

"The ring?"

He nodded. "The ring. We need to know some things about it, and about you."

"We?"

"I'm here as a representative of the Justice League."

"Other superguys. You've got like, a club."

He smiled. "Something like that."

For some reason I wanted to delay getting to the crux of the meeting. I asked, "How'd you find me?"

"Some colleagues of mine saw your little performance in the Alps a couple of nights ago. They were able to keep you in sight as far as this city before you vanished into the clouds. That caused us to monitor the area, and an hour ago I saw you save that plane. Nice work, by the way."

"Thanks." Greatest man in the world compliments you, what do you say? "Thanks" is what you say.

"Before we go any further, I have to ask if you're from this planet."

First Brother Rollo, now Superman. Why does everyone think I'm an alien? Just because I fly and create huge objects out of nothing?

"Yes," I said. I extended my hand and started to rise. "I'm Kyle Rayner."

"Don't get up." Superman reached down and

grasped my hand. We shook. His grip was firm, but not crushing, and his skin was warm and pliable, not steely.

"Then may I ask how you came by the ring?"

I told him the story of the alley behind Omfrey's, Red Nightshirt, the cartoons, the ice cathedral, all the rest of it.

"These cartoons," he said. "May I see them?"

I pulled my sketch pad from behind the futon and gave it to him. He handed it back immediately.

"The drawings are inside," I said, lifting the heavy cardboard cover to demonstrate—to Superman, not to a somewhat dim first-grader—exactly how to look at my work.

"I know. I've seen them."

"The X-ray vision—"

"A misnomer. It has nothing whatsoever to do with X rays."

"Glad to hear it. I've wondered about the radioactivity—"

"It would be a problem," he said gravely. "May I continue?"

"Please do."

"I've scanned your pictures down to the molecular level. There's nothing unusual about them."

"Well, they're just something I dashed off—nowhere *near* my best work."

"I meant, they do not seem to be receiving transmissions of any kind. I've also taken the liberty of scanning your ring. I can penetrate the outer shell, but inside there is only an undecipherable jumble of energies. All I can say for certain is, it's identical to Hal Jordan's ring."

"Hal Jordan?"

"Your predecessor. The other Green Lantern."

"I've been wondering about him."

"I don't doubt it."

"Could you fill me in? Tell me something about him? For openers, where did he go? Is he still alive? Can I—"

Superman held up a palm and I stopped chattering. "Whoa. It's a long, complicated story, and I don't know all of it myself."

"I'd be grateful for anything. . . ."

"All right."

Then, Superman began to talk:

"As far as we know, it began," he said, "on a small planet called Oa on the rim of our galaxy long ago. It may have been as long ago as a million years; no one is certain. One of the local life-forms evolved much more quickly than is usual. These beings must have developed the level of intelligence humans now possess while the universe was still young, then went on to surpass it. They developed a technology based on principles humankind has yet to discover, and roved the stars and the planets that circled them. Eventually, they became unhappy with the chaos they encountered and determined to eliminate it, or at least control it. They recruited peacekeepers from many worlds and equipped them with devices that operated on the interface between matter and energy. These devices, which were often in the form of rings to be worn wherever the individual's anatomy allowed, could be used as weapons, and often were, but they had other uses too. They could be used to fly within the atmosphere of a planet—"

"Been there, done that," I muttered.

"I beg your pardon?" Superman asked.

"Sorry. Go on."

"—or even," he continued, "to travel between planets. The beings of Oa, or *Oans*, divided the universe into sectors, and assigned one of their recruits to each one—"

I interrupted Superman again, this time deliberately: "How big were these sectors?"

"I don't know."

"And . . . whatshisname—Hal Jordan? He was assigned to the sector that contains Earth?"

"Yes. Perhaps you'd like to save your questions until I'm finished?"

"Oh, sure. Sorry."

"—with a set of rules and duties," he continued. "These included a prohibition against using the rings for personal gain, and a command never to take life. The system worked well for tens of thousands of years. Only recently has it failed."

Superman stopped speaking.

"Well, okay," I said. "I'll have to think about all that for a while."

"There is an obvious question," Superman said.

"You mean, what happened to Hal Jordan?"

"That's not the question I had in mind, but I'll answer it, as best I can."

"Okay, what *did* happen to Hal Jordan?"

"His entire home city was destroyed. Perhaps you heard."

"You mean *Coast City*? Sure, everyone's heard about that. But I don't know exactly what happened—the news reports were kind of fuzzy. Can you fill me in?"

"It's a long, complex, and painful story. The short version is that an entity, a cyborg named Mongul, infected Coast City with a virus. He intended to use it as a base and eventually alter the Earth to his liking."

"But not to yours."

"No."

"So something went wrong."

"We failed. *I* failed."

"Even the Justice League screws up, huh?"

"I'm afraid so."

"You know, you could sell the story to the networks and make serious bucks—"

I became aware of how level his gaze was. Level and unblinking.

"Of course, you wouldn't be interested," I said.

"We would not."

"Okay, so the destruction of Coast City had nothing to do with Green Lantern."

"Not directly."

"Then he got *involved* . . . how?"

"Hal tried to use the ring to re-create it—Coast City and all its inhabitants. Although the ring was extremely powerful, that task was beyond it. Hal's failure apparently deranged him. He blamed the Oans and attacked Oa itself. He was overcome and exiled—and then, for some reason, the Oans exiled themselves."

"Where to?"

"Where did they go for exile? I don't know. Perhaps another universe, perhaps even another dimension."

I clutched my forehead with both hands and squeezed my eyes shut. "All this is *way* beyond me. Other universes, other dimensions . . . hard for me to believe such stuff even exists."

"It does. Believe me."

"You've seen it, huh?"

Of course he had.

I opened my eyes. "Okay, what's the question I *should* have asked you?"

"Not me, Kyle—yourself. The question is: 'Am I a member of the Oan peacekeeping force'?"

"Not that I can tell," I said.

"You have the ring."

"But nothing else. I even had to swipe the battery. How'd it wind up in the Swiss Alps, by the way?"

Superman shrugged. "Your guess is as good as mine. I'd have to say that sometime back an Oan or a peacekeeper made a mistake and lost it."

"So Oans and these . . . peacekeepers . . . ?"

"It might be easier if you do as Hal Jordan did and call them 'Green Lanterns.' He once told me that the term was actually a close translation of the Oan term for them."

"Right. Green Lanterns, then. So a Green Lantern lost a power battery, and one of St. Dumas's ancestors found it."

"A hypothesis, but one that covers the known facts."

"Good enough for me. But we still don't know whether I'm a Green Lantern, and if I'm not, why I have the ring."

"No, we do not. And that presents us with a problem."

"Which is?"

"The ring makes you extremely powerful—second only to myself, perhaps." He said this with neither humility nor cockiness; he was simply stating a fact. "You can either be a force for good, or for evil." Again, simply stating a fact. "We don't know which yet, and I feel that you don't either."

"Hey, I'm not exactly an overachiever, but I'm a pretty good guy—"

"I don't doubt your essential virtue, Kyle. But as Lord Acton said, 'Power tends to corrupt and absolute power corrupts absolutely.' With the ring, you have something very close to absolute power."

"*You* don't seem corrupted."

"I'm not. But I have an advantage: I'm from another world. My DNA is similar to yours, but there are significant differences. My genes make it difficult for me to act selfishly, and most of what we call 'evil' has its roots in selfishness."

"You're hardwired to be a good guy?"

"Something like that."

"And I'm not."

"You just have to work harder at it."

"Looking at my track record, I can see where you'd have doubts about the 'work harder' part."

"I'm not judging you."

"No, *I'm* judging me. Anyway, where does all this leave us?"

"I'd like you to meet the other Justice League members and discuss our mutual problem with them."

"That problem being my great power and general untrustworthiness."

"As I said, I'm not judging you."

"I just had a thought: Why don't you just *take* the ring from me?"

"That would be breaking one of my own rules." He didn't say what the rule was. After a moment, he continued, "When you're as powerful as I am, it's important to maintain your ethical standard."

He didn't elaborate and I didn't ask, which meant I lost a chance to hear what has to be the world's most unique take on ethics. Dumb.

"Say I agree to your proposal." Now I was bargaining—with Superman, no less. Can you say "chutzpah"? "How would this meeting happen?"

"We could go to the Justice League satellite."

"'Satellite' as in circling overhead? *That's* where you guys hang?"

"'Hang' is a pretty good description of what the *satellite* does. *We* don't hang. We make use of artificial gravity generated by centrifugal force. We also have a base on the moon."

I couldn't decide if he was kidding or being totally serious.

"Okay, when do we get together?"

"Tomorrow evening at this time?"

"I really *should* consult my social secretary, but . . . okay. Tomorrow, same time."

Early the next morning, while I was asleep, something happened that has no direct bearing on the tale I'm telling, but I thought it was interesting, and maybe even revealing. There was a fire near my building. A grandma and a couple of kids were trapped on an upper floor. Superman rescued them. End of story. Superman must have done jobs like that a thousand times, but what was just a bit curious was that it happened in *my* neighborhood. Did Superman just happen to be in the area? Or was he keeping an X-ray eye on me? I'll probably never know.

I put in eight hours on the sheets, got up, brushed my teeth, and suddenly felt light-headed. Low blood sugar, I decided. My meals had been even more infrequent and irregular than usual recently, due to both lack of funds and little adventures like flying to the Swiss Alps.

My monthly check was in the mailbox, however. It was 3:15, too late to get to the bank. Reluctantly, I went to a storefront check casher-cum-mail drop and paid the 8 percent they demanded for their services. Then, money in hand, I had pizza—a whole pie. Call me "Sport."

Back at my apartment, I looked at my homemade "costume." Pretty shabby. But it was all I had, apart from my usual ratty jeans and T-shirt ensemble, so I put it on and hoped the light in the Justice League headquarters was extremely dim.

It was now dark outside. I sat on Mr. Gloinger's roof and waited for Superman.

He arrived precisely at nine. Some kids in a tenement window across the street spotted him landing and began pointing and yelling.

"Looks like you may have blown my cover," I said.

"We'd better go," he said, and before I could reply, he scooped me into his arms and we were soaring above the city.

"I can fly myself," I shouted, trying to be heard above the howl of the wind.

He landed on a hilltop outside the city limits, not far from where the plane had gotten tangled in the power lines, and put me on my feet.

"I know you can fly," he said. "But I wanted to get away from the onlookers before we had our discussion."

"Discussion?"

"Practical matters, such as getting to a satellite where there is virtually no atmosphere."

"Hard to breathe, huh?"

"And extremely cold. I suggest you let me take you there this first time."

"Okay."

"Hal had a technique of putting a bubble around himself when he got above the atmosphere to keep him warm. Can you do that?"

"I don't know." I visualized a big ball surrounding Superman and myself and . . . there it was.

"You'll need to hold your breath for about ten seconds," Superman said.

Again, he grabbed me and took off. I looked down: The Earth, seen through the green-tinted ball, seemed to be shrinking. Then I looked up and saw a curving, silvery surface, gleaming in sunlight that wasn't visible in the city we'd just left: the satellite's outer skin.

Superman placed his hand on a small rectangular box. A panel slid aside and, after I'd willed the bubble to vanish, we passed into the satellite.

We went into an inner chamber and there they were: the Justice League.

Wonder Woman. (I've already described the effect she had—*has*—on me.)

The Flash, lounging against a concave wall.

The Atom, only an inch tall and perched on the Flash's shoulder.

Plastic Man, his body twisted into a corkscrew shape with a foot-wide smile—his mouth was actually at least twelve inches long.

And on a video screen atop an elaborate control panel, Batman. *Batman?!*

"This is the new Green Lantern," Superman said. "Kyle Rayner."

They all nodded.

When I was a high school freshman, our English teacher—Mrs. Fraland, if anyone cares—departed from the prescribed curriculum for just one class and told us about mythology: Zeus. Hera. Apollo. Diana. Hermes. Hephaestus. All the Greek gods. I mention this because at that moment, I felt like a human—an illiterate, thumb-sucking, armpit-scratching shepherd, maybe—suddenly hauled to the top of Mount Olympus and confronting the biggies. What does one say?

"Nice to be here," I said.

Superman turned to me. "Before we begin, do you have any questions, Kyle?"

I could probably have asked questions well into the next day, but I didn't want to bore them. On the other hand, it would have been impolite not to ask *something*.

I spoke to Plastic Man. "Are you aware that it's impossible to do what you're doing?"

"Oh, sure," he replied. "But hey, I won't tell if you won't."

Okay, the question was doofy and deserved the answer Plastic Man had given it. Or worse.

I was not off to a glowing start.

"Perhaps we should get down to business," someone said from what sounded like a great distance away. The voice, I realized, came from the Atom and his miniature vocal cords.

"Let me summarize," Superman said, and he did. When he was finished, after about five minutes, he asked, "Any comments?"

"A question," Plastic Man said. "Exactly what are we trying to decide?"

While Superman had been talking, the Atom slid off the Flash's shoulder and grew into a "normal" sized man, whatever that is; now about six feet tall, he stepped forward.

"Whether we invite our friend here into the League," the Atom said, nodding in my direction and answering Plastic Man.

"You sound as though you have an opinion," Wonder Woman said.

"I'm against it."

"Why?"

The Atom assumed the manner of a classroom lecturer. "One: He claims not to know the identity of this hypothetical person in a nightshirt. To believe that is to give him a large benefit of the doubt, but let's do that, for the time being. Which brings us to two: We don't know that he isn't being manipulated by some malevolent force—"

"Such as?" Wonder Woman asked.

"Any one of hundreds," the Atom answered impatiently. "I shouldn't have to tell *you* that the universe is full of malevolence."

"I'd rather call it ignorance," Wonder Woman said, almost in a whisper.

"Call it anything you like," the Atom continued. "We dare not let a possible enemy into our inner circle."

"If he's there, you can watch him," yet another voice said, and for several seconds I didn't know who it belonged to; the Justice Leaguers were standing in front of me and none of their lips had moved. Ventriloquism? Then I looked past them at the video monitor and saw that Batman's lips were moving. I'd forgotten about Batman, which, I had a hunch, is what he wanted.

"Make the newcomer a provisional member," he was saying. "Don't tell or show him anything he doesn't need to know or see. Wait for him to betray himself."

"And if he doesn't, he's a good guy?" the Flash asked.

"Exactly."

"Too risky," the Atom countered.

"Riskier than turning him loose on the world with no constraints?"

"Batman is right, as usual," Superman added.

"As always," Wonder Woman murmured.

"Welcome aboard," the Flash said, slapping me on the shoulder.

"I still don't like it," the Atom muttered. "Can't we wait until we get to know him?"

"That will come," Wonder Woman said.

"Okay, then," said the Atom, not giving in, "shouldn't we at least *train* him?"

"To do what?" Batman asked, his voice edgy. "We all operate differently. Do *you* know how to use the ring?"

The Atom shrugged and looked down at the floor.

"Do we need to vote?" Superman asked the group.

"I'm with Batman," Wonder Woman said.

"Batman's *the* man!" the Flash yelled.

"I agree," Superman said.

"I'm outnumbered," the Atom said, shrugging. "We'll try it."

"I suggest that the newcomer leave the satellite immediately," Batman said from the monitor. "There are things he doesn't need to see."

"Fine with me," I said, moving toward the airlock.

"Hold on," said the Atom. He handed me a small button, about a quarter inch in circumference. "This is a signaling device. In an emergency, it'll beep."

"Then what?" I asked.

"Report here immediately."

"Got it."

"Can you return to Earth without my help?" Superman asked me.

"No prob," I assured him, then waved to the group. "Later, guys."

In the outer chamber, the airlock slid open; one of the Leaguers must have activated it from the control board. I willed the protective bubble around myself—and couldn't get through the lock. I willed a *smaller* bubble and stepped into space. Then I glanced toward a blue-green expanse that filled the sky below me.

The sky *below* me?

Actually, the sky was all around me. I was *in* the sky. The Earth just happened to be six feet closer to my feet than my head, so to me it was *below*.

I hung in the vacuum figuring all this out.

Why hadn't I noticed that on the trip here?

I aimed my head at the planet and began the long drop home. I was in no particular hurry. . . .

When suddenly I was cold, gasping, choking, breathing poison. . . .

9

I'd forgotten that the smaller bubble trapped less air than the one I started with; I'd also forgotten to hold my breath, and my leisurely flight downward had exhausted what air there was. I was surrounded by carbon dioxide. My vision blurring, I looked around at the darkness. How high above the ground (or water) was I?

I had to take a big chance. I willed the bubble to vanish and tried to fill my lungs. It was like breathing in ice, but I stopped gasping.

Now what? I was in free fall. Judging by the thinness of the air, I was still pretty far up, but I decided to err way on the side of caution. Besides, being in free fall in darkness was no fun anyway: nothing to look at.

I willed the ring to create a big green parachute and drifted, squinting at the landmass below me. I could discern a few pinpoints of light but nothing to really indicate location.

Then something hit my feet. It was the Earth. I'd landed.

But where?

By the glow of the moon and stars, I could see that I was on a country road. On either side were open fields with fences around them. In the distance, there were black shapes, probably farm buildings.

My watch told me that it was midnight—assuming that I was in the time zone the watch was set for.

Now what? Fly around aimlessly, hoping to spot some hunk of geography familiar to me? Not a good idea. I might set off radar or run into a flock of geese or at least get even more hopelessly lost. Or something. *Walking* around aimlessly seemed a lot safer.

So I walked. The air was chilly, but not unpleasant. Nice night for a guy to have himself a good, serious think.

So I thought: If I were seeing the glass half *full*, I'd say that I'd just been accepted into the most exclusive club on Earth, the Justice League. If I were seeing the glass half *empty*, which is what I usually did, I'd say that I was accepted only until the other members caught me screwing up, and I'd probably oblige them, sooner or later.

A pickup truck, doing at least 60, bumped over the crest of a small rise in the road. I waved my arms. It sped past me, its red taillights vanishing around the next bend. Driver not interested in stopping for a costumed weirdo on a deserted road in the middle of the night, huh? Hard to blame him.

Where was I? Oh, yeah. Thinking about the Justice

League membership. Well, what was there to think about, really? I couldn't plan because I had no idea what I was doing, or *supposed* to do, and besides, I wasn't sure I wanted to be a member of their high-and-mighty League. Once I'd stopped being awestruck, I hadn't really liked them much. Except for Wonder Woman. Her I liked.

I heard a noise from somewhere ahead, a crash, and, a moment later, a reddish glare shone through a stand of trees.

At first, I ran. Then I stopped running and flew. I got to the source of the glare, about a mile from where I'd been walking, in a couple of seconds. It was the truck that had passed me, its front end mashed against a tree, its rear blazing. I saw barrels, burning and scattered around the wreckage, and I guessed that they contained something nasty and flammable. The fire had spread to the truck's cab. Unlikely that anyone could be alive in there, but I couldn't be sure. I formed a giant fire extinguisher with the ring, aimed its nozzle at the blaze, and . . .

Nothing!

I panicked. *Why isn't the damn thing working?*

It just wasn't. I formed a pair of pliers with the ring, lifted the truck into the air, and . . . dead end. It still blazed. Then I got a better idea, the first good one I'd had all night. I formed a bubble around the truck. The bubble around *me* had run out of air, so this one would too.

In less than a minute, it did. The fire must have exhausted the oxygen fast.

I didn't want to look in the cab, and fortunately I didn't have to. A police cruiser, its lights blinking, skidded to a stop on the road and two uniformed men got out.

"You see what happened?" the taller of them called to me.

"No," I said. He strode across the grass as his partner moved slowly to the blackened and smoking wreckage.

"I got here just after," I told him.

"Why you dressed like that?"

I improvised. "Costume party over at the Gloinger place. Lost my ride."

"Gloinger? Now where exactly might that be?"

I was saved from further lame improvisation by the second cop. He was shining a flashlight into the cab and shouting, "It's Freddy Slother." Then, coming toward us and in a quiet voice: "What's left of him, anyway. I reckanize that big ol' ruby ring 'o his. Damn fool always did drive too fast."

Suddenly, I was aware of a smell in the air and hot bile in my throat.

"Something funny here," the first cop muttered, staring at the truck. "Oughta still be burning." He turned to me. "You manage to put it out someways?"

"Not me," I lied, unable to think of think of anything else to do.

"You don't go anywhere till I say so." He trudged toward his cruiser. "I'll go call it in."

I had no idea how to handle this situation. Should I admit to being Green Lantern? Would I also have to

give them my real name? Would the Justice League
want me to tell the truth about how I got to this for-
saken place?

Questions, questions, questions.

No answers, though.

Well, when in doubt, get the hell out.

"This is going to sound dumb," I said to the second
cop, "but could you tell me where I am? In what state,
I mean?"

"You been drinking, son?"

I opened my mouth wide and breathed at him.
"Nothing on my breath, right? Except maybe a little
pizza. So humor me."

He told me where I was.

"Near what city?"

He mentioned a city.

"Okay, you're a pretty nice guy," I said, "so I'm
gonna warn you. You won't want to believe what
you're about to see, but it'll really happen."

I flew straight up.

With the information the cop had given me, I located a familiar river gleaming in the moonlight and
followed it across a state line and on home. I landed
in a deserted park and walked the rest of the way to
my apartment. By the time the sun was rising, I was
in my shower, scrubbing.

Scrubbing hard.

But somehow, the smell that had risen from the
wrecked truck wouldn't wash off.

The phone rang. I looked at my watch. 6:14. Any
call that came at that hour was probably important.

"Hello," I said into the receiver.

"Recognize my voice?" the caller asked.

"The . . . little guy I met last night."

"Okay, no need to say my name. Not that this line is tapped. We made sure of that."

I'll just bet they did.

"Couple of things," the Atom continued. "First, practical stuff. You'll find all your bills paid and a thousand dollars walking-around money deposited in your checking account."

"Pretty good membership perk," I said.

"No perk. You'll pay it back later. One of our stricter rules—nobody gets a free ride just because they're . . . members."

"Okay, but don't expect it anytime soon."

"Second item . . . an apology. I was pretty rough on you. Bad manners, and I'm sorry."

He wasn't saying that he trusted me, but what he *was* saying was enough.

"Apology accepted."

"See you soon."

I dropped the receiver onto its cradle and flopped down on the futon, more exhausted than I would have believed possible. But I couldn't sleep. I remembered the burning truck, the smell, the taste of bile. . . .

Questions, questions, questions.

What if I hadn't tried to run before I flew? Why hadn't my ring-formed fire extinguisher worked? If I'd been a couple of seconds quicker, could I have saved Freddy Slother?

Was it my fault that he died? This Freddy? This

stranger? Had the ring made me responsible for his life?

"Dammit, I don't *want* that responsibility," I said. "I didn't ask for it and I won't *take* it!"

I pulled the ring from my finger and flung it against the wall.

Then I lay back and stared up into the darkness.

I must have slept because the next thing I was aware of was that nameless color on the inside of eyelids when light is striking them. I opened my eyes. Daylight was streaming through my window.

I got up and went about my life, such as it was. Walk, sketch, check the mailbox, eat something, check the mailbox again in case I'd missed something earlier, stare at the wall, check the mailbox yet again . . . I did that for three days. In that time, the Justice League signaler sounded at least twice. I'd hear it and suddenly remember the smell of Freddy Slother's truck and realize that heroes dealt with a lot of that kind of ugliness, as did cops and firemen and paramedics and lots of other people, and I didn't want to be any single one of them. So I ignored the signaler and later got chewed out for it, remember?

This would be a better story if something had happened to change my mind—something dramatic like Saul being knocked to the ground on the road to Damascus, or at least something wonky, like Isaac Newton getting bonked by the apple. In fact, I'm tempted to make up such an incident, and maybe someday I will. But not now. Now, we stick to the facts.

I changed my mind. I don't know exactly when or how. I just remember going down the steps to my apartment, shivering in the autumn cold, and shedding my jacket and deciding to find the ring.

I felt a little stupid, remembering the melodrama—the throwing of the ring had been particularly corny.

I walked over to the wall. The ring hadn't gone anywhere; it lay against the baseboard in a film of dust. I put it on, felt a slight tingle for the smallest moment.

I tried an experiment. With the ring, I formed a computer. Then I tried to compute on it. Nothing. I began to get a glimmer of an idea. Could I build a computer out of components? I got my sketch pad, did a quick drawing of Red Nightshirt, and as I drew asked aloud, "Do I have to understand a thing for the ring to form it?"

Red Shirt answered with a question mark above his head.

"What does that mean?"

My pencil moved, forming a balloon and the words, *Some things, yes.*

"What kind of things?"

Red Nightshirt replied, *Things you lack a concept for or a working knowledge of.*

Ending a sentence with a preposition—shame on you, Red Nightshirt!

"Like, I have a concept for speed, but I don't really know how a computer works," I said. "Or a fire extinguisher."

The pencil remained still. I took Red Shirt's "silence" to mean *Yes.*

Well, that was bad news. Because, frankly, I didn't have concepts for much. Why pay attention in class when you can draw cartoons in the margins of the textbooks and stare at the backs of girls' heads?

But maybe it wasn't too late. *Of course* it wasn't too late.

I had a library card, somewhere, and the telephone of Jennifer Tulone, an extremely smart and extremely attractive girl I'd never had nerve enough to ask out who seemed to know computers the way most people know breathing.

I dialed the number and when she answered, I said, "Hi, Jenny. This is Kyle Rayner."

"Who?"

"Kyle. We were in science class together."

"Kyle with the red hair?"

"That was *Lyle*. My hair's black."

"Oh." Long pause. "How are you . . . Kyle?"

"Well, you know, hanging in. Listen, Jenny, I have a computer question to ask—"

"Com*pu*ter question?" Her voice had brightened about a thousand percent. "Ask away."

I did, and filled three sketch pad pages with her answers. Forty-five minutes later, I said, "Thanks, Jenny. You've been a big help. Maybe I could buy you coffee sometime—"

"I'm not sure that would be a good idea," she said, her enthusiasm now down the thousand percent. "But if you have any other computer questions, give me a call."

"Count on it. Thanks again."

I hung up and looked at my pad. What Jenny had given me was the URL addresses of the best computer sites for getting questions answered. I booted up my laptop and got right to it. First question: How do fire extinguishers work?

That was how my education began—my *real* education—and how I got in trouble with the Justice League.

I went a little crazy. I'd think of a question, then get it answered, but getting the answer would raise other questions, and when I had answers to them I had still other questions. . . .

At one point, I arose to get a drink of water and fell on my face. The reason, I realized as I sneezed from inhaling the dust on the floor, was that I had neither eaten nor slept for a day. Not good.

I walked from the building into a windy, chilly late morning and got my pizza fix. Then, returning to my apartment, I happened to pass the public library and thought, *Well, I'll just drop in for minute or two, get warm. . . .*

The librarian escorted me to the door eight hours later and told me he would not check out books past closing time, thank you very much.

More pizza. And back to the apartment for more computer.

10

I awoke with my head on the keyboard and
\\\
\\\\\\\\\\\\\ on the screen.

"Sleep well?" a voice I'd heard before asked.

Superman was standing in front of me.

"Uh, hello. Hi. Good morning."

"Afternoon."

I stood, knuckling my eyes. "Afternoon then. What brings you here?"

"You do."

I wanted to say, "Well, I guessed *that*." But I didn't. Not wise to smart off to the mightiest man in the solar system. Instead, I said, "How so?"

"You remember the signaling device we gave you?"

I patted my pockets. "I've got it here somewhere."

Superman extended a palm, on which lay the small red button.

"Oh," I said, taking it from him. "Where'd you find it?"

"On the floor."

"Sorry about that."

"We are too. We thought we might need you."

"Something wrong?"

"There could have been. Solar flares disrupted the instruments on the satellite and made the meteor shower look like a bigger threat than it was."

"Well, of course, almost all meteorites burn up in the Earth's atmosphere. Some years, there are hundreds."

Superman raised an eyebrow. "You know that?"

I'd learned it in the library. "Uh, yeah."

"The point is," he continued, "there might have been important work for you to do. You should have answered the signal."

How do you make excuses to Superman? You don't, I decided.

"Won't happen again," I mumbled.

"Do I have your word?"

"Sure."

He turned to go.

"Uh, Superman," I said, "could you maybe not leave yet? It's broad daylight and if my neighbors see you—"

"They won't," he said and, somehow, they didn't. Obviously, he had a trick I'd have to learn.

I looked around the apartment for something to eat. Nada. No surprise there. Then I became aware of an odor I'd been smelling since I'd awakened, and realized that it was coming from me. I hadn't showered in days, and I couldn't remember when I'd changed my jeans and T-shirt.

I washed, put on my *other* jeans, and selected a particularly fine garment from my vast wardrobe to cover my bod from the waist up—a red shirt with a really dazzling St. Louis Cardinals logo and only the tiniest of holes under the armpit.

Next, I dumped as many bits of clothing as I could find into a shopping bag and went to visit the laundromat. I hadn't brought anything to read, and of course, the computer modem wouldn't work without a phone line—my laptop was so old it was practically steam-driven—but I did find a copy of the *Corvette Quarterly* that someone had left, and while my clothes were tumbling around the inside of a dryer, I filled myself in on the glories of the 405-horsepower Z06. To tell the truth, it wasn't the most fascinating reading of the week.

There were two things I should have been aware of, and if I'd realized the first I would have known about the second. The first was this: In the pocket of the jeans that were spinning in the dryer was the Justice League signal button and, yes, it was signaling.

The second was this: At that moment, the Justice League was preparing to descend on Santa Prisca. Remember Santa Prisca? I mentioned it at the beginning of this memoir, some 18,679 words ago. (My laptop may be primitive, but it *does* have a word count application.)

So, though I didn't know it, for the second time in a

week Kyle Rayner, super-hero-wannabe and all-around boy doofus, was keeping the Justice League waiting. No, not merely keeping the JL waiting—actually *standing it up*, like it was a date and I'd found someone I liked better.

But while I was absorbed in the splendors of the mighty Z06, I was ignorant of my ignorance. After I'd spent three dollars and fifty cents in quarters on various machines, I crammed my stuff into the shopping bag and left the laundromat.

Outside, on the sidewalk, I met a girl I knew from high school. I'll mention her name, which is Jillian Hivers, and I'll disclose that I thought of her as an average female: average looks, average intelligence, overall average attractiveness. On a scale of ten, I'd give her a six-point-seven-five.

There is nothing wrong with a six-point-seven-five. Absolutely nothing.

We chatted, we had coffee, we went to the movies, and then I shoved my foot into my mouth and crammed it all the way down into my small intestine. Remember what I told the Justice League? *"I had this date last night and things were going really well until about midnight, and then I did something dumb—"* Nothing that would get me arrested, or even beaten up by a protective parent, but major-league stupid nonetheless.

I left Jillian fuming on the front steps of her parents' house and fled back to my apartment, still toting my laundry sack.

As I was carefully folding and placing—well, actually, throwing—my just-washed jeans in the closet, the signal button fell to the floor. As soon as I touched it, its color changed from red to green and I heard Superman's voice in what I would have sworn was Dolby stereo: "Report to the satellite at once."

Uh-oh. I was pretty sure I was going to get yelled at.

I waited until dawn. I could say delaying my trip to the satellite was an act of independence—maybe even defiance. But that wouldn't be true. I just didn't want to face the Justice League, and I procrastinated as long as I reasonably could. But, finally, I started to put on my costume. Then I stopped. Did I really need to be shabby? I understood clothing, kind of, and I had the ring. I shut my eyes, not that it was necessary, and visualized a new costume. When I opened my eyes, I was wearing it. I put my windbreaker on over it, willed the mask to vanish, and walked out into the darkening streets.

A wind with more than a hint of winter in it was caroming around the city, and most people were walking with their heads down, looking only at the sidewalk in front of them. Nobody would notice what I had on below the hem of my jacket, and even if they did, well, for all anyone knew, black tights and green boots were a fashion statement.

I reached the park, found a secluded spot among some trees, and went into the sky, carefully—I wasn't about to risk running out of air again. Then I had an idea. I willed the ring to home in on the Justice League satellite; the satellite and homing-in were concepts I could handle easily.

I went higher.

"Faster," I said aloud.

I arrived at the satellite at 7:17:40, and found Wonder Woman, Superman, the Flash and, on a video monitor, Batman. I've already described the beginning of that meeting, up to the point where the Flash asked how I got the ring. Now, I guess I'd better report how it ended.

After I'd finished telling my story, the Flash said, "Interesting. But it raises more questions than it answers."

Superman nodded and Wonder Woman asked, "What would *you* do if you were us?"

"Do about me?" When it comes to asking the dumb ones, you can't beat ol' Kyle.

"Yes, about you."

"Look, I'll admit I've screwed up—"

"Big time," the Flash interjected.

"—but I'm new at this stuff and, let's face it, I never asked for any of this."

"Do you want it?" Wonder Woman asked.

"I don't know," I muttered. But I knew I wasn't telling the truth even as I said it. Before the ring, my life was confined by my apartment, the pizzeria, the park, and hankering for a girl I knew, in my soul, couldn't possibly ever return my interest.

Now . . . well, I was standing in a satellite 22,300 miles above the Earth with three of the most fascinating individuals who ever lived—four, if you count Batman. I'd been around the world and high over it. And I was learning. I may have hated school but, I was discovering, I liked to know things.

"Well?" That was from an impatient Flash.

Well . . . I was still Kyle the Doofus—C-minus student, slacker, dateless wonder. What business did I have with the likes of the people standing in front of me? Not to mention the one whose face filled the monitor.

"Can I have some time to think about it?"

"How much time?" Wonder Woman asked.

"One day. Twenty-four hours."

"That seems reasonable," Wonder Woman said to the others.

"Twenty-four hours it is," Superman confirmed.

I nodded to them, left the chamber, passed through the airlock, and into space. No stupid mistakes now: I remembered to form a large bubble around myself and instruct the ring to take me back to the park, fast. The area was almost fully dark—very little danger of somebody spotting my arrival. I dropped into the stand of trees I'd started from, got rid of the bubble, and walked across the dying grass to the path.

I trudged into the wind toward the avenue, head down. Beneath a street lamp, I saw something gleaming against the asphalt. I picked it up: a quarter. Was this a good omen or what? A whole United States of America quarter! A block farther, on the avenue, I blew my newfound wealth. Fed it into a newspaper vending machine and took out a paper, folded it, and tucked it under my arm. I resisted a powerful temptation to visit the library and continued to my apartment.

I switched on the light and surveyed my domain. It

was still cramped, dirty, shabby, messy, and barely fit for human habitation. But it was mine. Somehow, it suited me.

I had a decision to make, and of the many things I did badly, decision-making was probably the worst. I had no idea how really quality decisions were made, what the process was, the procedures.

Time to consult with my two-dimensional Red Nightshirt. I dropped the newspaper on the floor, sat cross-legged beside it, and picked up sketch pad and pencil. I flipped open a fresh page, did my sketch of Red, and asked, "Am I good enough to be a hero?"

Red spoke, as always, in comic strip balloons.

Red: *No one is.*

Me: Then I'm not good enough?

Red: *I didn't say that. I said no one is.*

Me: Same thing.

Red: *?*

Me: Can I get a straight answer, please?

Red: *No such thing.*

Me: Is this your world-famous Yoda impression?

Red: *?*

Me: Look, just answer this: Should I accept the Justice League's invitation? Given that I screw up everything I get near? Like Freddy and the fire . . .

My hand started moving, lettering in a balloon over Red's head before I could finish speaking.

Red: *Read the paper.*

The paper? The one I'd bought a half hour ago?

I picked it up and scanned the front page. Stock market woes. Hassles in the Middle East. Gotham

City rebuilds after another earthquake. Second page: more of the same. Third page: ditto. I found it on page eight of the second section. The headline was: PLANE RESCUE STILL A MYSTERY. The story, only four paragraphs long, was about how nobody had yet figured out why the passengers of a small plane that had gotten tangled in power lines weren't killed. Eyewitnesses were telling a tale about a big baseball glove, but experts thought they must have been suffering from stress, or reacting to the excitement, or hallucinating, or doing anything else that didn't involve seeing a giant baseball glove.

What the eyewitnesses were *not* saying was that it was a big *green* glove, sprung from a ring. Of course, they couldn't have known about the ring.

I turned back to the sketch pad.

"So I rescued the little girl and the pilot. That makes me a hero?"

Red: *You did what a hero does. That is the criterion.*

Me: So there's nothing inside a person that equals "hero"? No gene or hormone or something?

Red: *Do not be silly.*

I couldn't think of another question—which did not at all mean that there weren't other questions to be asked—so I closed the pad.

I sensed that I was actually getting close to an answer, but Red's latest pronouncement needed mulling, and my broom closet of a messy pad didn't seem like a good place to mull. What would be? A church? None would be open at—I glanced at my watch—11:15.

I heard a buzzing. What? Too late in the year for an insect to have wandered in from Mr. Gloinger's garden, and I had no appliances that might buzz. Where was the sound coming from? From me. From my left jeans pocket. The Justice League signaler? Yes, indeedy. I took out the button, which was both buzzing and glowing. What did Superman say I was supposed to do when I got buzzed? Oh, yeah, report to the satellite, chop-chop.

The phone rang. It hadn't rung at 11:15 since . . . well, never. I lifted the receiver and recognized the Atom's voice: "Don't bother going to the satellite. You're needed at Lankerville. The railroad yard."

Lankerville, a small town about twenty miles past the northernmost city limit, has been described as a blot on the landscape. Anyone who's ever been there knows the description is charitable.

"Why am I needed?" I asked the Atom.

"Doctor Polaris escaped near there. Your job is to recapture him."

"Why me? I mean, isn't Polaris some kind of heavyweight? I'm the new kid—shouldn't someone more experienced chase him?"

"Everyone else is busy. Major Disaster is causing earthquakes in Costa Rica. You're the only one of us who's near and available."

Major Disaster? Oh, yeah. Another so-called supervillain. They seemed to like fancy titles: Major Disaster, Captain Boomerang, Doctor Polaris. . . .

"What do I do when I catch him?"

"Hal Jordan found that it was possible to encase

him in a cocoon formed by the ring. That seemed to nullify Polaris's magnetic power."

"Okay, say I've got him encased. Then what?"

"Wait for instructions."

Suddenly, there was nobody on the line. I went into the backyard, glad the rain had stopped, and angled up into the dark sky.

II

During the short trip north, I allowed myself a few minutes to wonder about guys like Polaris and the rest. I'm not exactly a history buff, but I do read, and I didn't sleep through *all* my high school classes—apparently there were no super-powered bad guys before there were super-powered *good* guys.

Nobody ever described a flying cowboy gunslinger or a Roman legionnaire who walked through walls or a musketeer who laughed when hit by a minié ball— not outside fiction, legend, myth, and plain old tall tales, anyway. Such people, good and bad, appeared suddenly, in a cluster, near the beginning of the twenty-first century. Nobody seemed to know why.

Hell, I was now one of them and *I* sure didn't know why.

A few minutes later, I saw a bunch of flashing red lights on a road leading to a large railroad facility, a freight yard that was Lankerville's scenic glory. The lights were from four cop cars skewed across the road at odd angles. I landed in the middle of them and watched a bunch of uniformed lawmen gape. The one nearest me approached. If two hundred and forty pounds of raw hamburger could talk and wear sergeant's stripes, it would be this guy.

"Whaddya want?" he demanded.

"I'm from the Justice League," I murmured.

"Got any ID?"

"No. But I *did* just drop from the sky. Does that count?"

Apparently, it did. "You after the geek?"

"If by 'geek' you mean Doctor Polaris, yes, yes I am."

"He's in there, somewheres." The officer jerked a thumb in the direction of the railroad yard.

"And you're not chasing him . . . why?"

"Creep somehow shorted out our engines."

"And you're not going in on foot because . . . ?"

" 'Cause we ain't crazy."

"Well, since I don't have an engine to short out and I don't even have to walk . . . I guess it's up to me."

I rose off the pavement a foot and said, "Wish me luck."

When Sergeant Hamburger remained silent, and scowling, and his brother officers didn't say anything either, I saluted and went up.

What I saw, as I glided over the yard, was mostly shadows. The only light came from lampposts spaced about fifty yards apart, and not all of those were working. There were about a thousand places Polaris could be hiding, if he was even still in the vicinity: in and around boxcars, in and around sheds, behind piles of crates, in gullies, in culverts. . . .

I wished the Atom hadn't terminated our phone conversation so abruptly; I could have used a briefing from him. All I knew about Polaris I'd got from glancing at a tabloid during one of my rare visits to the local supermarket. He was a former physician—at least he'd *earned* his "doctor"—who'd experimented with magnetism as a healing modality. Somehow, a powerful magnetic field had permeated his body, causing him to go nuts and become a baddie; I don't know why, and I don't know that Sigmund Freud could have figured it out either. I had no idea what motivated Polaris, where he was from, what he liked and disliked—no idea whatsoever how to find him in a gloomy railroad yard.

And I didn't have to. He found me.

Something flickered in my peripheral vision, and I turned my head in time to see a boxcar—a big mother of a steel freight hauler—rising from the darkness at about two hundred miles an hour and heading straight for me.

I put a wall of ring energy in front of it and watched the boxcar slam into the green barrier, bounce—actually *bounce!*—and tumble back down. It smashed onto a silvery tank car, and a moment later a geyser of flame spewed from the twisted steel. A moment after that I heard what sounded like a giant, economy-sized thunderclap; I guess whatever was in the tanker exploded. Flaming debris arched up and down, some striking a stack of wooden crates, which began to smolder and burn.

I reconstructed that sequence of events later, piecing fragmented memories into a coherent narrative. At the time, I was busy dealing with a barrage of steel rails newly ripped from the ground and flung at me by Doctor Polaris. I ring-formed a giant tennis racket and swatted the rails into the next county. I scanned the ground, now lit by the burning tanker, and spotted Doctor Polaris.

He was, I judged, about six feet tall, and wore a skintight outfit of blue and purple. His legs were spread wide, his left hand on his hip, his right hand gesturing toward a small locomotive that, I suppose, was intended to be his next weapon. I dropped a ring-formed dome over him and shrunk it until it wasn't much larger than his body.

The Atom was right. The green energy ended his magnetic shenanigans.

Now what?

Darned if I knew. Finally, I simply decided that my work was done and flew away, leaving Polaris in the railroad yard, presuming that the authorities would know what to do with him.

Bad move.

12

A few seconds after I'd entered my apartment, the phone rang. The Atom, of course: How the *hell* had he known when to call? When I said my hello, he began to chew me out: "You screwed up badly tonight. You destroyed two railroad cars and their contents. You destroyed a shipment of farm machinery. You destroyed a fast food restaurant—"

I interrupted: "Hey, there was no restaurant. No farm machinery, either . . . Oh, yeah, the crates. Okay, farm machinery, but no restaurant."

"—in Ossaville, forty miles from where you were," the Atom continued, ignoring my protest.

"The rails I swatted?"

"Yes."

"Okay, the restaurant, too. I didn't kill anybody, did I?"

"The place was closed."

"Okay, good . . ."

"Your worst mistake," the Atom said, "was leaving Polaris in a cocoon. If Superman hadn't arrived a minute after you left, the man would have smothered to death."

Because if an energy bubble kept air *in*, it also kept air *out*. Dumb dumb dumb.

"Look, I admit I wasn't exactly brilliant tonight, but I was defending myself."

"No excuse. You must always act thoughtfully, considering all possible consequences, regardless of circumstances, especially when you wield something as powerful and potentially destructive as the ring."

I wondered if he'd read that last bit off a prepared statement of some kind. Sounded like it, but probably not.

"So now what?" I asked. "You rescind my invitation to join your club? You confiscate the ring?"

He didn't answer me directly. Instead, he said, "We all make mistakes."

Not exactly forgiveness, but not harsh condemnation, either. Okay, I was willing to take what I could get.

While I was thinking about taking what I could get, the Atom broke the connection and I was listening to a dial tone.

I cradled the phone and remembered what I'd been trying to do before I'd been summoned to deal with Doctor Polaris: make a decision about whether or not to join the Justice League. Pacing didn't help, and neither did staring into an empty refrigerator, nor staring at a cold television screen.

In the end, I simply crept to the roof and flew away,

straight up until I began to have trouble breathing because the air was so thin. Then, I stopped, hovered, and looked all around, and for the first time I had a sense that I had not *risen* from the Earth, but *fallen* from it—fallen into infinite space toward stars I saw, really saw, for the first time. They were at once the most beautiful and the most ordinary of things: ordinary because somehow these unimaginably fierce, blazing nuclear furnaces, these supremely inhuman entities, felt like part of me.

Believe me, I know how idiotic that must seem.

But it's as close as I can come, in words, to what I was experiencing while I was hanging there, staring. I had gone beyond language to a place I'd never been before.

My apartment *had* been too small. Confining myself in those walls, I'd never seen how immense the universe is, or maybe I'd never *allowed* myself to see it. I'd been my own jailer.

But I wasn't now. Without realizing it, I'd made my decision. I was existing in a boundless, scary, exciting universe, and I wanted to leave my little corner of it, to explore and experience it as fully as possible. Being Green Lantern and a member of the Justice League was my ticket out, if they'd still have me after the Doctor Polaris fiasco.

I looked down—or up!—at the Earth and figured out where the equator was. Once I knew that, it was easy to plot a course to the Justice League satellite. But did I even need to? I'd been to the satellite twice, and the ring had been there with me.

I formed a bubble around myself and gave the ring a mental command—

—and I was speeding toward the doughnut-shaped Justice League headquarters, suspended in space, its rim gleaming with the rays of a sun that was still mostly on the other side of the world.

Once again, I touched the metal plate on the hull and the airlock slid open. I entered and moved into the inner chamber. For an instant, I saw Superman, Wonder Woman, the Flash, Plastic Man, and a full-sized Atom obviously waiting for me, and I wondered *why* they were waiting for me—why had they all assembled? I glanced at the monitor to see if Batman was present—

—and then I was alone in the emptiness. The satellite was gone, the Justice League was gone, and I was gasping and something in my temples and eyes was pounding and my mouth was filling with the taste of copper. . . .

Later I realized that, at the instant the satellite vanished, I had about ten seconds to live, the length of time a human body can survive in a near-vacuum before the lack of outside pressure causes something vital to burst. But, as I hung there, gasping like a beached codfish, I wasn't giving myself science lessons. It may have been reflex that saved me, or I may have had help; I've never really been sure. Whatever the reason, I formed a bubble around myself, which didn't do much for my gasping because there was no air to trap, and shot toward the Earth.

I didn't have to go far, just deep enough into the at-

mosphere to allow me to gulp a lungful of thin, but sufficient oxygen. To do this, I had to eliminate the bubble,
which meant that I was instantly, bone-chillingly cold,
and that gravity was pulling me toward the ground.
For some reason, I willed the ring to form my old friend
the flying carpet, and I rode it to my apartment.

I don't remember getting into the building or onto
my futon, but since that's where I was when I awoke
the next morning, I must have. I soon became conscious
of a pounding, not inside my head, but on the door.

I got up, and almost fell again: The room seemed to
tilt, and a grid of glowing color got between my eyes
and what I was seeing. It melted away and I saw that
I was still wearing the Green Lantern costume; I
willed it to vanish and, clad in socks and briefs,
opened the door a crack. My landlord, Mr. Gloinger,
was on the landing outside, peering at me from behind his rimless glasses; another man, wearing a
brown suit, stood behind him.

"Kyle?" Mr. Gloinger asked.

"That's me, Mr. Gloinger. What can I do for you?"

"Fella here to see you. Says he's a doctor. A *real*
doctor, not one 'o them other kind."

"I'm a medical doctor," the man said.

"Okay," I said. "Just a second."

I pulled on jeans and a T-shirt and opened the door
all the way.

"You don't need me," Mr. Gloinger said, turning
toward the steps.

The medical doctor came in. He had one of those

black bags doctors are supposed to carry, though I don't know if many actually do.

"Doctor William Blessington," he said, extending his hand. There was something familiar about the name, but I didn't know what.

"Kyle Rayner," I replied as we shook.

The room was tilting again. "Mind if I sit down?" I asked, and dropped onto the futon without waiting for an answer. "What brings you to my humble but lavish abode, Doctor Blessington?"

"I've been paid to examine you," Dr. Blessington said, opening his bag and removing a small flashlight. "Extremely well paid, I might add."

"How'd that happen?"

"A messenger came to my home early this morning and gave me five thousand dollars in cash. He said you might need medical attention, and that I was being requested to provide it. So here I am. Open your mouth please. Wide."

I remembered where I'd heard the name. "Hey, are you the Doctor Blessington who invented the whatsis and got the big prize?"

"I am."

"I'm impressed."

"I don't blame you," he said, grinning. "If I met me, I'd be impressed too. Now open."

For the next hour, the good doctor did all the usual things doctors do when they're scoping you out: the ears, eyes, nose, throat, tongue, heart, pulse, reflexes. For another hour, he questioned me about my family, diets, habits. Then when I'd dressed he led me to the curb, where a shiny gray Lexus was parked. We got in and he drove me to a hospital—a small, private, very ritzy hospital; his Lexus looked shabby next to the other cars in the lot. We went inside and began the examination procedure again, this time using an array of machinery hooked up to what I'm pretty sure were computers.

Finally, he led me to a small office paneled in dark wood and smelling of something pungent. I think a real Picasso was hanging on the wall behind a desk made of the same wood as the paneling.

"Sit," he said, and I sank into a red leather chair.

"Bad news?" I asked.

"Not particularly," he said. "You need rest and a change of lifestyle. Judging from what you told me, you've needed the lifestyle change for years. Man doth not live by pizza alone. But there's something else, something recent. . . . Tell me again, have you done any drugs lately?"

"Not lately and not ever. Not my vice."

"I didn't think so. Okay, question numero two: Have you been scuba diving recently? Or any kind of deep-sea diving?"

"Never in my life."

"You're sure?"

"I'd tend to remember something like that."

"Okay. Well, you're suffering from shock, and you have the kind of internal injuries that usually accompany sudden changes in pressure. How did those occur?"

I shook my head.

Dr. Blessington stared at the ceiling. "I wonder . . ." After a minute, his eyes found mine. "Anyway, I'm keeping you here overnight, just to be on the safe side."

"Wait a second, Doctor. This place must cost ten thousand a night—"

He smiled. "Close."

"—and I don't have insurance."

"Not to worry. Your mysterious benefactor left another package for me. Twenty thousand this time. That'll cover you."

"You do business like this often?"

"New experience. I can't help wondering what it's about."

"Me too."

"You really don't know?"

"Doc, if you have a lie detector, bring it on."

"I believe you. The nurse will be in to show you to your room. Have a good night. And Kyle, about those lifestyle changes—I wasn't kidding."

The nurse was compact, energetic, gray-haired, brisk, and kindly, and the room was bigger than my apartment and had its own bathroom. The bed was firm and comfortable.

I had a restful night and a tasty breakfast—how long since I'd eaten breakfast?—and, a few minutes after noon, I signed a release and ambled outside.

It was a beautiful day. The air was brisk and the sunshine had that amber tint it sometimes has on fall afternoons. I could have taken a bus home, but instead I decided to enjoy the day.

A block from Mr. Gloinger's building, I passed the pizzeria, and turned to go inside. But I remembered Dr. Blessington's admonition—*"Man doth not live by pizza alone"*—and instead went across the street to a Greek coffee shop. I sat in a window booth and ate a chef salad, washing it down with a glass of orange juice. Healthiest lunch I'd had in years.

I nodded to Mr. Gloinger, who was sweeping the front walk near a sad little dogwood tree, and descended to my apartment. There was a note taped to my door:

Meet me in rm. 248,
Gotham Arms, Gotham City,
Midnight.

Mr. Monitor

Who the hell was "Mr. Monitor," and what business did he have telling me to go to Goth—

Oh. Of course. Him.

At six, just after dark, I went to my favorite stand of trees in the park, willed the ring to replace my jeans and jacket with the Green Lantern costume, and shot into the night sky. Gotham City was about four hundred miles to the east as the crow flies, if the crow was just a bit directionally impaired. I had plenty of time to get there by midnight and do a few other things, too.

Well, actually, one other thing. I located the equator, put a bubble around myself, and flew to where I guessed the satellite had been. Nothing. After a while, the air inside the bubble was exhausted, and I had to drop into the atmosphere to restock. This I continued to do for the next three hours as I searched space for some trace of either the satellite or its occupants. I was amazed at the amount of stuff I saw. I'd had no idea there was that much man-made junk circling the Earth, and I looked at a lot of it. None of it was what I wanted to see, however.

But something unexpected did occur: After a while, I discovered I was enjoying myself. So I abandoned the search and just flew—soared and dipped and loop-de-looped, flapped my arms as though I were a bird and stiffened them, pretending to be a jet plane. Went up like a rocket, dropped ten thousand feet before stopping and hovering. It was like skydiving times ten; the most fun I'd ever had.

Finally I plunged to within a few hundred feet of the Atlantic seacoast and followed that to Gotham City. I could hear the waves thrashing below and glimpse an occasional whitecap in the darkness.

Kyle Rayner, boy seagull.

13

I saw the glow of Gotham's lights against the black sky from a long way off. I realized that I had no idea where I should go once I reached the metropolitan area. Gotham is a big place—population 7.5 million— and it sprawls along the coast and partway into the ocean with landfills and populated islands.

Well, okay, time for a little logic. I was supposed to meet "Mr. Monitor" at the Gotham Arms, which didn't sound like a flophouse or sleazoid motel. Probably downtown somewhere, the kind of place a lot of locals can direct a man to. But I didn't want to drop from the sky into the middle of a busy, bright avenue and ask the nearest pedestrian where to go. I wasn't a star hungry for attention, I was a guy trying to sneak into town.

So I chose a railroad yard at the edge of the city, landed between two empty boxcars, a good fifty yards from the nearest lightpole, and began hiking toward where the glow in the sky was brightest.

I was walking through an industrial area full of warehouses and small factories, deserted at this hour except for the occasional stray cat and lunchbox-toting maintenance worker, and that enabled me to save time; when I came to a deserted block, I used the ring to put a skateboard under my feet and go from one corner to the next in about five seconds. Then I thought, *Hey! Suppose somebody* does *see a guy with a green skateboard going like hell, what's the worst they would say? Something like, "There's a guy on a green skateboard going like hell."* I was wearing the costume, but the ring could and did disguise it as the kind of outfit a guy on a skateboard might wear if he were going like hell.

I arrived in downtown Gotham in less than an hour. I ducked into an alley and made the skateboard go away, though I retained the skateboarder's threads, and strolled onto the avenue.

Gotham City, Saturday night. Noise, light, people. Couples, arm-in-arm, looking into shop windows. Neon ads four stories high. Street performers—jugglers, magicians, mimes—on every corner. Taxis jamming the street. Crowds rushing into and out of theaters. Energy and excitement. It was hard to believe that only a few years earlier, an earthquake had leveled the entire area.

Finding the Gotham Arms was no problem. It was a glass-and-steel monolith that occupied an entire block. I was surprised; I'd been expecting something small, unobtrusive, and vaguely European—the hotel equivalent of the hospital I'd been in the previous night.

I went past a doorman who looked at me as though I were something green and fuzzy he'd found on a front tooth, and across an acre or so of crimson carpet to the front desk.

"I'm here to see Mister Monitor," I told the clerk, a statuesque, fifty-something woman with silver hair and a killer smile. "Room 248."

"Mr. Rayner?"

"That's me."

She handed me a key card. "Go on up, sir. Mister Monitor will join you shortly."

I took the elevator to the second floor, which was actually the third floor because they didn't count the mezzanine, and found room 248. The key card got me in.

Nice room. Small, but nice. Two twin beds. Thick carpet. Sofa, chairs, table, TV, mini-refrigerator. Surprisingly quiet, considering it was only a couple of floors above a busy, noisy avenue. I looked at my watch: 11:15. Forty-five minutes until "Mr. Monitor" arrived, unless some joker delayed him.

I bounced on the bed. Checked out the bathroom: tub with a built-in Jacuzzi and enough soap, shampoo, and conditioner to keep a sorority clean for a month. Slid open the mirrored doors to the closet: ironing board, extra blankets, a terry-cloth bathrobe on a hanger. Turned on the TV and channel-surfed for a few minutes. Opened the refrigerator with a tiny key already in the lock and emptied a bottle of orange juice as I looked out the window at the bustle below.

"Enjoying yourself?"

I simultaneously started and whirled. He was standing between me and the door, a large, dark figure in a black cape and half-mask who seemed to absorb the light around him. I was pretty sure I knew who I was looking at, but I felt compelled to ask anyway.

"Mister Monitor?" I asked. *"Batman?"*

"Yes." The voice was deep and cold.

I'd just recently met Superman and he awed me, for sure, but he didn't *scare* me. For some reason, Batman did.

I waited for him to say something. And waited. And waited. I felt the silence as a tangible thing.

And then I blurted, "Okay, *Batman* then. How long have you been here?" Thereby replacing the tangible silence with tangible dumbness.

"An hour."

I looked at my watch: 11:51. *"I* haven't been here an hour!"

"I know."

"But I looked all around the room—"

"Yes, you did."

"And you were here the whole time?"

"Yes."

"How?"

He was silent.

"You gotta teach me that trick."

"No." More silence.

"Well, I guess I can't *make* you—"

"No, you can't." The icy voice was level and empty. Did he know I'd been joking?

"I've got a pretty good idea why I'm here. The satellite, right?"

"Yes."

"But before we get to that, can I ask you a few questions? Of course, you don't have to answer them."

"That's right."

"Okay," I began. "Why did I have to come to Gotham?"

"Because it's where I am."

"You don't travel?"

"Seldom."

"Not even to find out what happened to your teammates?"

"It was not necessary. You came here."

"Gotcha. Okay, this next one's personal, and you can tell me to go catch a train, but . . . what exactly do you *do* in the Justice League?"

"Supply it with integrity, investigative skills, and deductive intelligence."

It was actually more of an answer than I'd expected.

"You're not superhuman? Come from another planet or have special genes or anything like that?"

"I am human." There was just the faintest hint of heat in the voice now.

"Last question. Why am I here?"

"Before we leave this room, I hope to know if you're responsible for the disappearance of the satellite."

It took me a moment to reply. "Why do you think I *might* be?"

Batman reached behind himself and tapped a light

switch. The room was suddenly dark except for a neon glow coming in through the window.

"Circumstantial evidence," he said. "First, you're a newcomer. Apart from the barest facts of your biography, nothing is known about you. You claim to be ignorant of how you came to possess your ring, which strains credulity. Finally, there is this."

He glided to the television set and produced a disc from beneath his cloak. "I record all interactions with the League. I taped this just an hour before their disappearance."

He put the disc into a slot on the DVD player and touched a button. There was the requisite hiss and sputter, and then a shot of the satellite's main deck. The Atom, Plastic Man, Superman, and Wonder Woman were in their usual places.

The Atom was speaking: *"You with us, Batman? Okay. We all got a call from Kyle Rayner—I still have trouble calling him 'Green Lantern'—asking us to meet him here. Anybody have any thoughts?"*

Apparently, nobody did.

"I have to admit," the Atom continued, *"that I don't trust the guy. Don't like him either."*

"Any particular reason?" Wonder Woman asked.

"Gut feeling."

"Not too scientific there, Chief," Plastic Man said.

"No, it's not," the Atom admitted.

"I suggest we suspend judgment until we hear what Green Lantern has to say," Superman said.

Batman switched off the recording. "Comments or questions?"

"Yeah. My homey the Atom said I asked for a meeting. Just how am I supposed to do that? I don't know your real names, phone numbers, e-mail addresses, if any—"

"The summons came via the signal button."

"You can do that? Use the button to call a meeting?" I paused and slapped my forehead. "Of course you can. That's what it's for. But I didn't know how to work it."

"No, you didn't. We deliberately withheld that information from you."

I was torn between insult and relief. "Okay, case closed."

"Not at all. You could be smarter than you seem."

He really knew how to make a kid feel loved! But I found his harsh, uncompromising manner comforting. He was solid, unimpeachable, a man who *knew* and could be counted on to do the right thing.

"Well, I'm not," I said. "I'm dumber than the average rock—ask anyone. Anything else on that disc I should see?"

"This is an hour later," he said, switching on the player. I saw myself coming through the hatch onto the main deck and—

—*and I was alone in the emptiness. The satellite was gone, the Justice Leaguers were gone, and I was gasping*—

—and I remembered that something in my temples and eyes was pounding and my mouth was filling with the taste of copper. . . .

The image blinked, dissolved, split, and for an instant I felt I was somehow looking *through* it at another, identical image. It reminded me of something I'd seen recently. . . .

"Do you see the anomaly?" Batman asked.

I didn't know what "anomaly" meant, and Batman wasn't going to be fooled by my faking it. "Not sure what you mean," I confessed.

"The camera doing the recording was part of the satellite," he explained. "It should have vanished with everything else. Yet it showed you in space *after* the satellite was gone."

"Meaning what?"

"I have no idea," he said. I didn't like the sound of that.

"I have data from every observatory, both optical and radio, and every seismograph on Earth and every satellite equipped with sensing gear above it. There was no explosion, no sudden release of energy, no abnormalities in light, no disturbances in radio frequencies, nothing amiss in the entire electromagnetic spectrum. Something as large and elaborate as the satellite just *goes* without any clue as to how or where? It is beyond reason."

"No clue at all?"

"The Atom mentioned that he'd detected what may have been an alteration in the fabric of spacetime. He couldn't be certain because no such disturbance has ever been detected before."

"This was when?"

"Wednesday, the twelfth."

Something familiar about that date . . .

"Yes," Batman said, as though he were reading my mind. "The night you received the ring."

I sat down on the bed, wondering what to say next. Batman neither moved nor spoke. Finally, I said, "Pretty big coincidence, huh?"

"It may be just that—a coincidence."

"I thought you supersleuths didn't believe in coincidences."

"I believe in them. I've seen too many not to. I just don't *trust* them."

"Looks bad for me, right?"

"Not necessarily. I'm far more inclined to believe your innocence than I was fifteen minutes ago."

"Why?"

"I've been listening to you speak. You aren't lying."

"How do you know?"

"Practice, training."

"Can you be sure?"

"No."

"But you're willing to take a chance."

He may have nodded; in the darkness, I couldn't be sure.

"Suppose I *was* a bad guy. I'm wearing the ring. I could zap you."

"Could you?"

"Sure. I . . ."

I held up my hand and willed the ring to become visible. My finger remained ringless.

Batman dropped it onto the bed next to me.

"How the hell did you do *that*?"

"Hal Jordan once told me the secret of getting the

ring off his finger. He thought I should know how in case of an emergency."

"But how did you do it without my seeing you?"

"Easily."

I slipped the ring back on and said, "You're doing this to impress me?"

"No."

Good answer. Why should *he* care about impressing *me*?

"Where do we go from here?"

"There aren't a lot of avenues to explore," he said, for the first time sounding less than absolutely confident. Then, astonishingly: "Do *you* have any ideas?"

"Me?"

"I thought not," he said, and the cold emptiness was back in his voice. "Then you'll have to tell me everything you can remember since you got the ring."

"That'll take a while."

"Yes, it will. By the way, how *is* your memory?"

"I dunno. Average, I guess."

"Not good enough." For a time, there was silence except for the faint sounds of traffic from outside, and then: "Can the ring help you remember?"

My turn to take a while to think. Then: "I have no idea. I can try, I guess."

How to visualize this? Finally, I simply created a mental image of myself saying, "*I remember everything.*"

"Ready?" Batman asked.

"As I'll ever be."

"Let's begin."

Back in high school, in sophomore year, I found a book that someone left on a bus seat. It was by a guy named Rex Stout, about a detective named Nero Wolfe who had a sidekick named Archie Goodwin. This Goodwin was a world-class rememberer. He would tell ol' Nero everything, down to the smallest detail, and when he was done Nero would be a genius and solve the murder or whatever they were working on. Well, I mention this because for the next four hours I played Archie to Batman's Nero. The ring must have been doing its stuff because I droned on and on, telling Batman things I had no idea I'd remembered.

The street below us was quiet when I finally shut up.

"The pad," Batman said.

"You mean my apartment?"

"The sketch pad," he said. "When you draw those pictures of the being you call 'Red Nightshirt,' you're either accessing some part of your subconscious or there is something in the pad itself that's replying to you. Where did you get it?"

"Art supply store on Kimberson Street. I've had it for maybe four months."

"You noticed nothing strange before you began drawing Red Nightshirt?"

"Nothing at all. Hey, it's a *sketch* pad."

"Perhaps."

"I mean, if there's some kind of gadget in it I'd have noticed—"

"Bring me a drawing pad and a number four lead pencil," Batman said.

"Where am I supposed to get those at this hour in a strange city?"

"I wasn't speaking to you."

We waited. He and I had very different waiting styles. I fidgeted, paced, looked out the window, fidgeted some more. Batman stood. Period. He must have been breathing, but I couldn't swear to it.

After fifteen minutes, I thought of something to ask him. "The Justice League paid my bills and put some money in my bank account, right?"

Silence. Which, I was learning, meant yes.

"But my hospital bills and Doctor Blessington's fee . . . those were paid after the Justice League vanished. Somebody spent serious money on me. Was that you?"

Silence.

"Well, thanks. I don't know when I can repay you—"

"Mandatory repayment is the League's rule, not mine."

"And you don't always play by their rules?"

Silence.

There was a gentle knock on the door.

"Stay put," Batman ordered, and glided across the room. He opened the door, wordlessly accepted something from someone in the corridor, and closed the door. He came toward me, removing wrapping paper from a sketch pad. Two pencils were taped to the pad's cover.

He then dropped the stuff in my lap and said, "Draw."

I didn't have to ask him *what* to draw. I switched on a table lamp and got busy. A couple of minutes later, a somewhat lopsided Red Nightshirt stared up at us from the pad.

"There," I told Batman. "Of course, it isn't my best work, I was in a hurry—"

"Ask something," Batman said.

"What?"

"Something it can answer."

"Like a test, huh? Okay." To Nightshirt: "Where are we?"

The pencil moved, drew a balloon, and lettered: *Gotham City. Gotham Arms. Room 248.*

"Wasn't exactly a brain buster," I muttered.

"Who am I?" Batman asked.

The pencil didn't move.

"You ask it," Batman told me.

"Who am I with?" I asked Red.

Batman.

"Ask it my real name," Batman said.

"You sure?"

"It's a chance I'm willing to take."

"Okay. What is Batman's real name?"

?

"It doesn't know," Batman said.

"That makes two of us," I said.

"Which would seem to indicate that you're having a conversation with yourself."

"You think I'm faking this?"

"No. But you may be having some kind of psychotic episode."

"I think I've just been insulted. Have I?"

"We have to consider every possibility," Batman said.

"Okay, let's ask." To Red: "Are you part of me?"

No.

"Am I talking to myself?"

No.

"We're getting nowhere," I said.

"Ask it where the Justice League satellite is."

"Okay," I said to Red. "Where is the Justice League satellite?"

Where it always was.

"It's invisible?"

No.

Disgusted, I threw the pad on the floor and looked up at Batman.

"You feeling as frustrated as I am?" I asked him.

"Probably not. Ask if it is possible to restore the satellite to its former status."

I picked up the pad and asked the question.

Yes.

"How?"

You must go to Oa.

"You know where *Oa* is?" I asked Batman.

"Nowhere on the Earth."

"I guess you've got the whole planet memorized."

I should have known.

To Red: "How do I get there?"

Through a wormhole beyond Pluto.

Pluto, I knew from recent reading, was the planet farthest from the sun in our solar system. As for a wormhole . . . I'd skimmed a magazine article about wormholes. They were some kind of holes in space, which made no sense to me. I mean, how can nothing have a hole in it?

"How do I find this wormhole?"

The ring can take you there.

I asked Batman, "The Justice League wouldn't happen to have a spaceship stashed somewhere, would it?"

"No. But the ring can transport you outside the Earth's atmosphere."

"One little problem. Breathing."

"Hal Jordan flew in space."

"I'll bet the Halster got an A in all his courses, too. But I didn't. And the damn ring didn't come with an instruction manual."

"I wonder why," Batman said.

"I'm beat," I said. "Can we continue this some other time?"

"We do seem to have reached an impasse," Batman said.

"If I get any ideas, how do I get in touch with you?"

"You still have the Justice League signal button?"

"Yeah."

"Press it. I'll respond." He paused. "I hate to say this, but you might be the only person able to save the League."

I closed the pad and dropped the pencil on an end table. "Are you sure? I mean, there must be others, government agencies or—"

"You aren't listening." The utter lack of emotion in Batman's words made them deeply scary. "I'll say it one more time: You might be the only person able to save the League. Surely I don't have to tell you how important that is?"

"I guess you don't."

"You said you would get in touch with me if you got any ideas."

"Yes, I did."

When Batman spoke again, his voice was no longer merely scary. It was commanding and furious: *"Get an idea."*

I stared out the window for about a minute, and when I turned back to look around the room, I was alone.

14

Outside, the street was empty except for a gutter-prowling cat and a cop car that slowed as it passed me and then sped up again. The sky in the east was just beginning to glow. I materialized a skateboard and began going like hell. But after a few blocks I got bored, dematerialized it, and shot into the air. Leaving Gotham was a lot easier than entering it. Once again, I followed the Atlantic coastline until I spotted a few landmarks. It was still pretty dark when I landed on Mr. Gloinger's rooftop.

My crummy little apartment was somehow different, and for a long while I couldn't understand why. The walls were still the same drab green; the shabby furnishings hadn't changed, nor had the clutter, or the dirt. Then I realized that the difference was in me, in how I was looking at it, my attitude. It was no longer home. It was just a place I was passing through.

I had problems to solve, but I knew I was too tired to solve them.

I slept until mid-afternoon, got up, did the stuff people do when they get up, went to the diner, and managed to persuade the waitress that it wasn't too late for her to serve me breakfast. I tipped her generously for her trouble. I now knew it was Batman's money I was spending, and he said he wasn't expecting repayment, so what the hey?

I needed information about Pluto—the planet, not the cartoon dog—but the library was closed. Which left the computer. I went back to the room Mr. Gloinger was renting me, which is how I was thinking of the apartment now, booted up the laptop, and began to search the Web.

An hour later, I'd acquired a lot of information about Pluto, which can be summarized as follows: Pluto is small (1,485 miles in diameter); cold (average temperature minus 355 degrees Fahrenheit); and very, very far away—at least 3.5 billion miles from Earth. (That's *billion*, with a "b." As in a number followed by nine—count 'em—*nine* zeros.) Not exactly anybody's vacation spot of choice.

How long would it take me to get there, and at what speed? I couldn't begin to do the math. Offhand, I'd say a jaunt to Pluto was impossible for anyone. But Hal Jordan had gone there. Or had he? Maybe the Halster flew in space but had stuck close to home.

I needed answers, as was usual these days.

I got my sketch pad, quickly drew Red Nightshirt,

put a balloon over his head, and stated, "You said the ring can take me to the wormhole near Pluto."

Red did not reply. He wasn't one for chitchat, any more than Batman was.

"Do I have to ask the ring to go in a specific direction at a specific speed?"

No.

"So what do I do? Assuming I'm operating the ring, of course."

Visualize Pluto and conceptualize going as fast as possible.

Visualize Pluto? The photos I'd seen were nothing more than smudges of light against the blackness of space.

"I don't know what Pluto looks like. How do I visualize it?"

Use your imagination.

"How fast will I be traveling?"

Fast enough.

"What happens when I get there?"

Will the ring to take you to the transit.

"That's the 'wormhole' thing?"

Yes.

I guess there was no reason I couldn't have left for Pluto then. But I wanted more time—to procrastinate, I guess. So I decided to find out about wormholes. The laptop was a foot from my elbow.

I went to work.

The stuff I found on the net was full of terms like "super-fluid helium analogue," "momentum distributions," "Kuchar hypertime formalism," and—my favorite—"geometrodynamics of cylindrical gravity waves." For about the eightieth time I found myself wishing I'd occasionally stayed awake in high school, though I doubt my general science class would have helped me understand those lovable cylindrical gravity waves even if I *hadn't* slept through the class. Finally, at a site called askJeeves.com, I found this definition of a wormhole: "A hypothetical structure of space-time envisioned as a long, thin tunnel connecting parts that are separated in space and time." Well, at least I could understand that, sort of.

I picked up my pad and pencil, sketched Red Nightshirt, put a balloon over his head, and asked, "How big is this wormhole . . . or 'transit,' as you call it?"

A millionth of a centimeter.

"How am I supposed to fit into *that*?"

The pencil stayed still.

Obviously, I needed a lot more information—a couple of PhDs' worth ought to be about right—and some good, solid advice. But who could advise me? The only person I could think of was Superman, and his absence was part of the reason I was contemplating a little jaunt to Pluto in the first place.

Well, I thought, *maybe I should take some more time, give the whole matter a lot of serious consideration.*

But I knew that I was just finding reasons not to make a scary decision, and that if I waited until I was tripping over my long, white beard, I still wouldn't be ready to make it.

Should I toss a coin?

I found a quarter in my jeans pocket and flipped it into the air: "Heads I go, tails I don't." The coin landed tail side up on my palm.

"Okay," I said to the empty room. "Better make it two out of three, just to be sure."

I flipped. Tails again.

"Three out of five," I said, and flipped and slapped the coin across the room before it landed. I *knew* what I wanted to do—what I *had* to do. I was just afraid to do it.

But a curious man might ask *why*. Why did I have to do something that might get me killed. I sat cross-legged on the futon and stared at the ring.

Why?

Because the Justice League was worth saving, if they weren't already dead. Because Batman had said that I might be the only person able to save them. And because my life has been, until now, a fat zero. I have done nothing except waste time and opportunities, and I am not likely to do any better in the future. I might as well try to do something worth doing. The alternative is to sit in this dreary basement, draw my stupid cartoons, and yearn for women who are way too smart and beautiful to consider a relationship with a loser.

I willed the ring to vanish and—it didn't. Now what? I shook my hand and said, "*Disappear*, dammit."

Then I remembered the battery. How long since I'd used it to charge the ring? *Too* long, obviously. I got the battery and pressed the ring against it. Again, I willed the ring to vanish, and this time it obeyed.

Nice to know that the ring was in working order if I was going to ride it to Pluto.

And I'd have to remember to take the battery along.

I had two questions to answer before I took off: When should I leave, and how do I breathe in space? Leaving was no problem—no reason why one time would be better than another. But the breathing . . . Hal Jordan had done it. Maybe. But how?

I'm not a very analytical guy. I never figure out logic problems, and I did miserably in freshman algebra class. Someone once told me that I am predominantly "right-brained," which means that I grasp images and whole concepts and do not think in neat, straight lines. But now I had to somehow overcome my right-brainedness (did I just make up a word?) and solve the problem of getting to Pluto. Okay. For openers, how fast would I have to go and how much air could I take with me? I went to the computer. The answers I needed were probably lurking in cyberspace somewhere, but I couldn't find them. Now what?

I remembered Jennifer Tulone, the cute computer whiz. I called her, and she answered on the first ring.

"Jennifer? Hi. Kyle Rayner again. Kyle with the brown hair."

"Hi, Kyle." She actually sounded friendly.

"Got a little problem you might be able to help me with."

"I'll try."

I told her what I needed to know, and for the next

forty minutes we exchanged monosyllables as she worked her computer. What she didn't learn was how much air a person breathes in, say, an hour. What she *did* learn was that Pluto was roughly 3.5 billion miles away from the Earth, which I already knew, though knowing it didn't make it any easier to grasp.

"So if you were traveling at the speed of light, you could make it in about four and a half hours," Jennifer told me. "But you couldn't do that."

"Why not? In theory, of course."

"Because according to quantum theory, at the speed of light mass is infinite," she said. "I'm not sure what that means, but it doesn't sound like a human being could survive it."

"No, it doesn't."

"So let's run the numbers at, say, ninety-five percent of the speed of light."

For several minutes, I listened to the phone hum. Then: "Okay, at ninety-five percent of light speed, you'd need about four and a quarter hours."

"Got it. Thanks, Jennifer."

"Kyle, if you don't mind my asking, what's this about?"

I thought fast. "I'm writing a story. Science fiction."

"Really? I didn't know you were into SF."

"Oh, sure. Huge fan."

"I just finished reading *Stars My Destination* for like the fifteenth time. What do you think of Bester?"

I could tell from her tone of voice what *she* thought of Bester, whoever that was, so I said, "None better."

Ah. A revelation. The way to a girl's heart was

through the books she read. "Maybe we could have coffee sometime and talk about, ah, Bester."

"Sure. Gotta run. Take care, Kyle."

She hung up, and I wasted a few minutes remembering how attractive Jennifer Tulone was before returning to my problem. It wasn't solved yet, but I was getting there.

One more question to answer: Could I put a big enough bubble around myself to encompass the air I'd breathe in four hours and fifteen minutes? I didn't know.

I got another idea. Why not take a bunch of air tanks, the kind divers use, with me? I looked up a sporting goods store in the yellow pages, made another call, and finally had a plan.

I went to the store and bought all the scuba tanks they had. Eight of them. Then I went to another store and bought six more. I paid both places serious bucks to deliver them to my apartment.

It was nearly eleven when I got all that done. I was as ready as I'd ever be. Nothing left to do but go.

Go—and probably never come back. Because I wasn't fooling myself: The chances of going to the far end of the solar system, encountering a black hole, and then returning were almost nil. I couldn't begin to imagine the ways the journey could kill me. It would be the biggest jump into the deepest hole anyone had ever taken.

And no one would ever know that I'd taken it.

That bothered me.

Should I call someone? Who? My cousin in California? Some ex-classmate? I wasn't close to any of those people, and I didn't want them to hear what would certainly be my last words. I would only be confirming their already low opinion of me; they'd scoff, or patronize, or call me crazy.

Then who?

Strangers?

Strangers it would have to be. Maybe someone in a crowd of strangers would listen, be sympathetic, admiring even. I didn't know if that would pan out, but at least I could cherish the hope that it might.

I used the ring to form a band around my tanks and to dress me in the costume. I looked at my watch: 11:20. Where could I find a crowd at this hour? The mall? The last show at the mall's fourteen-screen theater would be ending about now. Okay, the mall it was.

I raised my tanks a foot off the ground and, toting them behind me, stepped into the street. Not caring if anyone saw me, I flew to the mall. As I'd thought, several dozen people were emerging from it, fanning into the parking lot. I hovered above them, willed the ring to surround me in bright green light, and when I saw them looking up, I shouted, "Listen, everyone, my name is Green Lantern and I'm going to Pluto."

Their upturned faces were smudges in the light from the parking lot lamps. Several of them swiveled their heads around, probably looking for hidden cameras, pretty much as I'd looked for hidden cameras outside Omfrey's.

I said, "Just thought you should know."

Then I went higher and used the ring to surround myself in a big, airtight bubble. I had no idea how big the bubble was. When I was forming it, I'd merely thought, *Big!*

I raised my eyes. Lots of stars and lots of nothing between them. It wasn't too late. I could still decide not to go.

I rose above the Earth's atmosphere.

Still not too late.

I visualized words written in green light:

Pluto.

Ninety-five percent of light speed.

Go!

I went.

PART TWO

1

I don't know what I was expecting. Probably something like a movie special effect—those stars that suddenly become streaks of light when Han Solo really puts the pedal to the metal in *Star Wars*, or the flash of light when the *Enterprise* goes into warp drive in *Star Trek*. Instead what I got was this:

That's right: nothing.

Which doesn't mean that nothing was happening, not at all. Actually, there was a lot going on, but my senses and my brain weren't equipped to see, hear, taste, or smell it. I didn't even have a feeling of motion. I just hung there, with a green bubble outside and a fuzzy mind inside. I was aware that I was going somewhere, on some kind of grand mission, but it really didn't seem important. And I wondered, vaguely, how soon I'd have to start gulping oxygen from a tank. Otherwise, time just passed.

Passed slowly. Something I hadn't remembered from my reading, and that Jennifer Tulone had neglected to tell me, is that, according to Albert Einstein, as a thing goes faster, time goes slower. Einstein was right, which is why I never needed the oxygen tanks. The air trapped inside my bubble was enough to get me to Pluto because, traveling at 95 percent of light speed, my time—the time inside the bubble—dragged. How long was I en route? On Earth: almost five hours. Inside the bubble: I don't know. An hour and a half, maybe. I was too—pardon the pun—*spacey* to check my watch (assuming that it was even working properly).

I'm now understanding why the preferred language of physicists is mathematics. It's very difficult to express this stuff in words.

So I'll describe Pluto instead, which won't take long because there isn't much to describe.

I became aware that the initial leg of my journey had ended slowly. First, I realized that I was no longer floating in the center of the bubble; my feet were touching the part farthest from my head, which meant I was being pulled "down." Gravity will do that.

The presence of gravity meant I was on a planet. Then I moved to the interior surface of the bubble and squinted, trying to see what was outside.

It was almost totally dark, the only light coming from the stars. I could make out silhouettes of shapes that may have been mountains or boulders, or may have been something else entirely, and toward my left there was a flat streak of white—frost? snow?—and that was about it. I looked at the sky. One star shone a bit brighter than the rest, just a bit, and I gasped when I realized that it was the sun. Our sun. *My* sun. So distant, so faint. My throat tightened and my eyes filled with tears and loneliness and terror swelled within me. I heard my voice asking, "What am I doing here? How will I ever get back? Please, please, don't let me die here. . . ."

I'd never before, for even one second, been religious, but I guess I was praying.

I knew that in a few moments I might be so overcome with awe and dread that I wouldn't be able to move.

What did I have to do next?

Locate the . . . *transit*? Was that what Red Nightshirt had called it?

But I didn't know how. I hadn't asked Red Nightshirt what it looks like. And I had no way to visualize it.

Stupid stupid stupid. I'd been too dumb to ask the obvious question, and now I was going to die billions of miles from home, a frozen lump in an alien landscape.

And would the Justice League die too, because of me?

I looked at the ring. "Take me to the transit," I said, for want of anything better to do.

Then Pluto was dwindling beneath my feet, shrinking until it was swallowed by the blackness around it. I was moving away from the planet, away from the solar system, probably *out* of the solar system entirely. Toward "the transit," which was a hole in space a millionth of a centimeter wide. I wasn't likely to survive trying to squeeze into something so small, but my fear had vanished. Why worry? I'd gotten *this* far. . . .

Farther than any human, with the possible exception of Hal Jordan, had ever gone before.

About to go farther still.

2

I expected to enter some kind of opening, experience passing through a long tube, and then pop out the other side. But it wasn't like that. I experienced no sense of transition, of motion from one place to another. I just felt an indescribable *shift* and the green of the bubble was suddenly a different shade, which means, I guess, that the light outside it had changed.

Had I dwindled into something smaller than a millionth of a centimeter? Had the transit enlarged to accommodate me? Or had size somehow become irrelevant? Bet on the latter.

Still keeping my loop around the tanks and battery, I slowly, cautiously, shrank the bubble, leaving only enough to protect me from the cold and to retain some air. For a second, I thought I was home again. There was the now-familiar feeling of floating in a vacuum between stars and a planet, but when I looked closely I saw that they were *different* stars and a *way* different planet. Instead of the blue-green-white of Earth, the world I saw glowed with hundreds of colors that were continually changing—dissolving, re-forming, melting. A gigantic kaleidoscope.

So this was Oa.

I knew next to nothing about planetology, but I didn't think what I was seeing was possible, not if Oa was made of anything more substantial than gas.

I hung and considered my options. I could command the ring to relocate the transit; maybe it would. Then I could return to Pluto and from there to Earth. Or I could investigate Oa. To go back now would be *worse* than vacationing in Paris and not seeing the Eiffel Tower—it would be like going to Giza and not visiting the pyramids, I decided.

I was definitely cooler than *that*!

I moved toward Oa, which seemed smaller than Earth, an estimate based on how far above it I thought I might be and what Earth looked like at the same distance—not exactly rigorously scientific methodology.

Still towing the battery and unused oxygen tanks with a ring-formed rope, I approached the swirl of color and—stopped. I was against a barrier made of something I couldn't identify. Carefully, I skimmed the surface, searching for an opening.

Suddenly, I found it—or it found me.

I was being sucked into and through the swirl and, caught by gravity, falling through an orange haze, with the tanks and battery also in free fall. I commanded the ring: *Fly*. Instead, I kept falling. I looked down. I was approaching a flat plain at terminal velocity, and in a few seconds I'd be a grease spot on it. Better that than being a frozen Plutonian lump, I supposed. But better yet to stop falling—you don't visit the pyramids only to have them drop on you.

I tried again: *Fly, dammit!*

Nothing.

I stopped falling. It wasn't like hitting a wall, or being yanked from behind while running, actions that tend to do nasty things to you, such as dislocating portions of the anatomy. It was simply . . . not falling anymore.

I was standing—wobbling, actually—on the ground, if "ground" is what the surface of Oa could be called.

I looked around. Oa, or at least this portion of it, was a pleasant place, but an eerie one too. I saw no "natural" colors—no greens, browns, whites, blacks. Everything was a light pastel blue or tan or orange or aqua. There was no single source of light, no sun in the sky or Oan equivalent of a lamppost. Rather, a gentle glow came from everywhere. I breathed deeply; the air was warm and sweet.

Oa was a lot nicer than Pluto.

Nothing rose from the horizon: no mountains, hills, buildings. There had to be more than this. I decided to fly, completely around the planet if necessary, and find what there was to find. There had to be something. Red Nightshirt must have sent me here for a reason.

I willed the ring to take me up. It didn't. The ring was no more useful than a trinket I might have gotten from a gumball machine. Maybe it needed a dose of the battery. I'd recharged it only a few hours ago. I had no idea *where* I was—on Oa, but where was that?—much less *when* I was. I remembered learning that passage through a wormhole could be travel through *time* as well as space. And who knows how traveling at 95 percent of light speed had affected whatever mechanism governed the battery?

No point in thinking about that.

I knelt and examined the battery, which was lying, apparently undamaged, among the scuba tanks, and pressed the ring against it. After about a minute, I told the ring: "Up."

I stayed down.

Okay. Next, I cupped my hands around my mouth and shouted, "Hello! Anybody here?"

There was no echo. No answer, either.

I started walking, thinking that Oa had to be inhabited—somebody had done that neat trick of breaking my fall. Unless some*thing* had done it. Maybe Oa wasn't inhabited by any sentient beings, just the odd automatic fall-breaker and ring energy killer. I was marooned in this pastel, sweet-scented demiparadise without food or water. Or a ring that worked. All I had were scuba tanks, and breathing wasn't my problem. By contrast, Pluto suddenly wasn't looking so bad. At least my demise there would have been quick.

In a moment of unexpected frustration, I shook the ring and hit it on the sole of my boot. "Work, damn you!" I shouted, stupidly.

"All right," the ring said, and—this is really hard to explain, much less expect anyone to believe—somebody emerged from the ring. Oozed out and grew simultaneously. But he didn't grow large. He was no bigger than when I'd first seen him in an alley behind the music club several weeks earlier.

3

"Hello," Red Nightshirt said.

I sat down.

"Welcome to Oa."

"You've been in there all along?" I asked.

"Yes."

"Wasn't it cramped?" I wasn't joking; it was a sincere question. My head was seriously messed.

"Not at all," Red Nightshirt answered, equally sincere. "I merely rearranged the spatial-temporal energy flux within the ring's reality parameters, and accommodated my own energy flux to it."

"Oh," I said, understanding nothing he'd said. "I'm not sure I understood that."

"I would not expect you to," he said.

"I've got a lot of questions," I said.

"That does not surprise me. Unfortunately, I will have to answer them before you can proceed with your mission."

"What *is* my mission?"

"That is one of the questions."

"Which you won't answer?"

"Later."

"Why is answering my questions 'unfortunate'?"

"Another question. That one I might not ever answer."

"Why not?"

"Another question."

I was exasperated. "You enjoy frustrating me?"

"And another."

"Okay, Mister. . . . what *is* your name?" Before he could answer, I said, "I know, I know—another question."

"But *that* is a good one."

"Does that mean you'll answer it?"

"We haven't needed names for eons. The last one of us who had a name stopped using it five hundred thousand of your years ago."

"And he's long dead."

"Not at all. In fact, he was me."

"You're a half-million years old?"

"Older."

He'd answered me twice. I was making progress, sort of.

"I was called Ganthet."

"Can I call you Gandy?"

"We've only just met."

Was he bantering? Joking?

"So, Gandy, what happens next?" I was pushing my luck.

"Most of your questions get answered," he said.

"Hooray."

"I haven't decided whether or not I'll tell you why answering your questions is unfortunate," he continued.

"Your privilege."

"I know."

I'd been so intent on my little give-and-take with Red Nightshirt—excuse me: *Ganthet*—that I hadn't noticed a gradual change in my immediate environment. The air had darkened to a navy blue and was in the process of solidifying. As I watched, it became walls and a domed roof. I was now inside a huge chamber of some kind.

I wanted to ask how he'd managed the alterations, but I wouldn't give him the satisfaction of refusing to answer. So I said, "Neat trick."

"It is to your liking?" he asked me. He waved his hands at the walls and ceiling. "It is necessary that you be comfortable."

"Well, a BarcaLounger would be nice—"

And I was sitting in a BarcaLounger.

I decided to *really* push my luck. "I haven't eaten today, whatever 'today' is. My grandmother used to serve up a nine-course Christmas dinner—"

And there it was: turkey, dressing, sweet potatoes, corn, peas, gravy, and apple, cherry, and pumpkin pies. Plus a silver coffeepot and pitcher of milk. And utensils. All on a table covered with a white tablecloth.

I leaned forward in the lounger, forked a piece of sweet potato, and ate.

"Delicious. I guess I won't worry about calories and cholesterol."

"I've eliminated those," Gandy said.

"Mind if I finish?" I *was* hungry.

"No."

For the next half hour I was busy chewing and swallowing. Compared with this meal, Grandma's tasted like cardboard. When I was done, I patted my lips with a napkin, leaned back in the lounger, and said to Gandy "I'd like to begin at the beginning."

"You are referring to the big bang. You are referring to the creation of the universe."

Was he asking or telling? Asking, I decided.

"Actually, someday I *would* like to find out about that."

"Someone of your kind should. Your scientists have gotten several points wrong."

"I'll be sure to let them know next time I run into them." Had he realized that I was joking? No matter. I continued, "For now, I'd like to talk about when we first met. The alley behind Omfrey's. You popped out of nowhere. Okay, for openers: What was the nowhere you popped out of?"

"I told you. It was a time stasis."

Score one for Gandy. He *had* mentioned this "time stasis" back there in Omfrey's alley.

"Then things started getting weird. The walls became transparent and I was seeing stuff that shouldn't exist. . . . More 'time stasis' action?" I sounded like I actually knew what the hell I was talking about.

"Yes," Gandy said.

"Then you vanished, or so I thought. Actually, you ducked into the ring—after rearranging the spatial-temporal energy flux within the ring's reality parameters, of course. I mean, really, anyone would've. But do you mind telling me why?"

"I was avoiding detection."

"Who was gonna detect you?"

"The others were going to detect me."

"Others as in other little blue men?"

"Yes."

"So they were *chasing* you?"

"They were not exactly 'chasing.' But English has no word for what they were doing, so 'chasing' will have to serve."

"Okay, you needed to . . . what? Get rid of the ring?"

"I required myself to give the ring to a human who might preserve and protect it."

"So you picked me . . . why?"

"You were present."

"You picked me at random?"

"Yes."

"Anyone would have done?"

"No. But I do not think you would understand the qualifications you possess."

"You *do* know how to make a guy feel special."

He remained silent. I should've saved the sarcasm for someone who would've appreciated it.

I stood, stretched, and said, "I'm gonna guess that you contacted me through the pictures I drew. True?"

"Yes. Telepathic contact between different species is

usually impossible, but with the drawings you provided a focus that facilitated it."

"We're different species, you and I? We don't *look* that much different. I mean, if I were short and blue and severely fashion-challenged, I could almost be your twin."

"You are seeing what your senses allow you to see."

"Not what you *really* look like?"

"You have never seen anything in its true form."

So maybe, I mused, the little heartbreaker who'd gotten me to Omfrey's in the first place, Sharon Klingerman by name, wasn't that hot after all. I was taking my comfort where I could. I was also being stupid.

An alarming thought suddenly occurred to me. "You were being chased or xtripreolfed or whatever."

"What is xtripreolfed?"

"The word I just made up to take the place of the word you said doesn't exist in English. Well, it does now. Anyway, who was chasing you? Not some intergalactic version of the cops, I hope. You wouldn't be a bad guy by any chance, would you?"

"I do not believe that I am."

"Let me rephrase. Why were you being chased?"

"Perhaps you should sit."

I dropped into the BarcaLounger. "Gonna take a while, huh?"

4

I'm not completely sure what happened next. Oh, I know, he told me a story. But *how* he told it to me—that I'm not sure of. I don't remember being told words, and I don't remember being shown images. Yet I have words and images to match my knowledge of the narrative. Did my imagination conjure them up later? If that's true, what conveyed the information to me?

Oh, well.

I leaned back, stared at the dome high above me, and . . .

The tale has a "once upon a time" quality—once upon a very *long* time. Back when the smartest creature on Earth was a fish who had sprouted what would eventually become legs—we're talking 450 million years ago, give or take a millennium or two—Gandy's folk, the Oans, had developed physics, chemistry, astronomy, biology, medicine. Not art.

That's an important fact: not art. And not much government; they didn't seem to need it. But they had almost everything else that constitutes "civilization." By the time the first mammals were appearing on Earth, they had visited all their celestial neighbors—their solar system had eleven planets and forty-three satellites—and were developing faster-than-light drive which, with the discovery and later creation of wormholes, would allow them to explore their entire galaxy.

And explore it they did. They visited a lot of life-bearing planets and discovered that, for reasons Gandy didn't share with me, the Oans had evolved much faster than any other life-form. This made them feel pretty special.

They were a curious bunch, and so they pretty much investigated everything that could be investigated. But they had one taboo: The Prime Cause of All Things was not to be known.

Why that particular commandment? Nobody knows anymore. The reason, if any, has been long forgotten. But the commandment existed, and almost everyone honored it. *Almost* everyone. The exception was a guy named Kronus, a genius who was both scientist and technician. Working alone, he built a device capable of looking back in time. He couldn't *travel* in time—that came later—but he could look, and he did.

Bad move. What happened next seems like something from mythology more than literal truth, but Gandy was presenting it to me as historical fact, and who am I to argue with Gandy?

I mentioned that I don't know what means Gandy was using to feed me this history lesson. But I seem to have a visual "memory," or reasonable facsimile, of Kronus staring at a round, slightly convex screen filled with images of stars. Kronus touches the screen—making an adjustment?—and then the stars seem to congeal and form a giant hand. Suddenly, there is a burst of searing white light and the screen shatters. Kronus covers his eyes with his forearms, staggers back, and—

The business of the giant hand sounded a bit fishy, I thought, but I didn't figure out why until later.

The visual memory, if that's what it is, goes no further, and I know the rest of the story as I know something I read in a textbook—the kind of textbook that's big on dates and place names and ignores the stuff that somebody might find interesting.

To put it simply: Things got bad for the Oans. First, there were inexplicable cosmic upheavals. The universe folded and warped and even split into duplicates of itself. Then even their home planet turned against them: floods of biblical proportions, earthquakes, volcanic eruptions that made Krakatoa seem like a hiccup in comparison. Then the Oans were decimated by an attack from a neighboring world, and finally, far worse, they began a series of civil wars that started on Oa and quickly spread to colonies on other planets. The mighty Oan civilization crumbled, and the Oans, once proud to the point of arrogance, were reduced to struggling for survival. A lot of them lived in caves and ate the Oan equivalent of worms.

But they did survive and, because even during the worst of the chaos some of them preserved their science and technology, they rebuilt. Within a century or so they were again bouncing around their solar system. But they couldn't forget the bad years, and they decided to take precautions. They needed to insure that their civilization would survive should the evil times ever return. But how to do that when even space itself might shatter and destroy them? The answer lay just beyond the gravitational pull of their sun in an anomaly created by a space warp. It wasn't a wormhole exactly, but it was a wormhole's first cousin. The difference was, instead of being a gateway to another part of the universe, this hole led to another universe entirely, one that somehow coexisted with our own. It was small and young, this alternate universe, too young for life to have evolved in it.

Pretty hard to wrap your head around, I know.

After a century or so of exploration, experiment, and debate, the Oans sent a hundred of their fellows through the gateway and into our sister universe. The explorers' mission was to establish a colony and preserve what the Oans thought was worth preserving in their culture, which was just about everything except art, which they didn't have yet. Then, if things went bad again, the Oans could be sure their civilization would survive.

I'd give a lot to know about the sister universe and the Oan colony there, but information about them was not on Gandy's curriculum. He did inform me that the colonists were supposed to check back home every couple of centuries, but the rift in space closed and the Oans didn't figure out how to reopen it until recently. *Very* recently, as these million-year spans go.

While the explorers were busy establishing their colony and maybe trying to understand a whole new kind of reality, the home folk were keeping busy. A lot of the bad stuff had been beyond their control, but some of it hadn't—the nasty business of being invaded by a race from another planet, for example.

The Oans were determined never to be conquered again. They adapted their faster-than-light technology into a strange kind of weapon, one that operated on the interface between matter and energy. Some of them were designated something that might be translated as "warriors" (though the word in Oan is a lot more layered and complex), and found that the best way to carry their weapons was in metal hoops placed around digital appendages. In other words, as rings worn on fingers or, in the case of life-forms that didn't have fingers, other bodily protrusions.

This next part is in my awareness as a memory, though, of course, I couldn't be remembering it because it happened in another galaxy millions of years before there were even human beings, let alone me. But I have images:

A vast outdoor arena beneath a clear orange sky. A thousand Oans, the planet's entire population (I somehow know), *standing in orderly rows. In their center an Oan is speaking—*

—and in my mind's ear I can hear what he says: "We do not understand the invaders. We should not (*a verb that combines the meanings of 'hostility' and 'self-demeaning'*) until we know of them."

Someone from the crowd: "They may return at any time and exterminate us. We must (*the verb again*) immediately."

"I disagree."

"How shall we resolve this difference?"

Then, they invented democracy—right there, on the spot. The Oan in the center asked for all those in favor of the retaliation to step to his right, and those opposed to step to his left. In a few minutes, the matter was decided. There were a dozen Oans to the left of where he stood, and everyone else on the right.

They wasted no time. The warriors, a thousand strong, immediately leapt into the sky and, with the few dozen left behind watching, dwindled and vanished.

I have no visual or auditory memories of what happened next, just bare facts, the kind of information you might get from an encyclopedia.

The Oans won.

But not without cost: A thousand went, a hundred returned.

Whether they completely destroyed the invaders, I don't know. But they did win. Oans hadn't yet invented things like victory parades, if they ever did, so there was no particular fuss, just the warriors dropping to the ground and reporting their victory to anyone they met.

The Oans assembled again and decided to retain the warrior corps—"corps" because the Oan word can't exactly be translated as "army." The task of the corps was to patrol Oa and other planets and the space between them.

Initially, these space-roving hall monitors were robots, charged with maintaining "order," whatever that meant, and averting potential disasters. Eventually, though, the Oans replaced the robots with living volunteers, again for reasons Gandy didn't share. The corps did a good job of patrolling Oa and its planetary neighbors and, in a thousand years or so, recruited other races into its ranks.

They made another, very odd, decision that day: They resolved to stop propagating. That's right—no more baby Oans. For many of us humans, that would be the equivalent of deciding to stop breathing. But continuing their kind had always been a rather cold, practical matter for Oans, with no strong emotion attached. They may not have even had a word for "love." I'm not sure exactly how they reproduced, but the fact that the race had only one gender meant that whatever they did probably wasn't much fun. This didn't mean that the Oans would be history in a few years, however, because somewhere, sometime, they'd discovered the secret of—excuse the oxymoron—limited immortality. Hit by a meteor, they'd die. But they were free of the effects of aging and illness. There were only a few hundred of them left after their war, and they thought that was plenty.

Eventually, what we call the Green Lantern Corps spread throughout the galaxy. It was a very loose organization with few rules, most of which I don't have concepts for. (Did Hal Jordan?) The rules I *do* understand go like this:

- *One is never to use the ring for personal profit.*
- *One is never to use the ring to gain renown for one's clan.*
- *One is never to use the ring to promote one's unique point of view.*

Those are the "thou-shalt-nots." There is only one "thou-shalt," and my comprehension of it is fuzzy at best, mostly because I can't come close to translating the most important word in it. It's something like "universal harmony/natural law," which would make the rule: "One is to use the ring to promote universal harmony/natural law." Evidently, the notion was so clear to the Oans that they felt no need to define it. Unfortunately, the rest of us galactic citizens are not so blessed.

But that didn't stop the Corps from being pretty much wholly successful and from proliferating.

The first Green Lantern to reach the Earth landed somewhere in Switzerland 370 years ago, had an accident—I have no idea what *kind* of accident—and lost a battery. It was found by a member of an arcane organization called the Order of St. Dumas and remained in the Order's care until I recovered it a few weeks earlier.

The Green Lantern who'd lost the battery managed to find the wormhole near Pluto and return to Oa. What he said about the inhabitants of this small planet, third from the sun in a rather ordinary system, apparently excited the curiosity of his fellow Oans. What particularly interested them was a local phenomenon called "art." In all their travels, they had never encountered anything like it before. Over the next couple of centuries, hundreds of Oans surreptitiously visited Earth's museums, theaters, and concert halls. They didn't understand what they were seeing and hearing, but they were fascinated by it nonetheless.

Finally, they tried to produce it. Soon, there were Oan painters and sculptors. I have "memories" of their work, and while I've never been into high culture—museums and galleries—it seems to me to be pretty good. Not great, not as good as the best of what we humans have produced, but pretty good. Their only total failures were theater and opera; they just couldn't get into acting, regardless of whether it was the spoken or sung kind. They were only slightly better with novels, movies, or short stories. Storytelling, of any sort, wasn't congenial to them. Neither, apparently, was music; they seemed to have a collective tin ear. But painting and sculpture—these they got damn good at.

They got so good at them that they decided to enlist their whole community, every Oan alive, in the biggest art project of all time. The goal was to recreate their planet—recast it in a more aesthetically pleasing form. And damned if they didn't do it. The Oa on which I found myself wasn't the original, except maybe at the innermost core of the planet. It was a world reshaped, reconfigured into an artwork of incredible complexity. Perfect air, perfect weather, perfect light. An adaptation of the technology that operated the ring allowed Oans to create, at will, any kind of structure they felt like inhabiting.

The teacher of the one art history class I ever took said that art should reflect the human spirit. Well, Oa didn't reflect *my* spirit; in fact, I found it a bit creepy. Then again, I'm not Oan and Oans aren't human.

But for some reason we fascinate them. They've been observing us, off and on, ever since the battery-losing Green Lantern told them about us. So, according to their system of logic, which isn't much like ours, it was only natural that they make humans the subject of their next artistic experiment. What they did was—

5

I was jolted out of my reverie, or dream, or whatever state I was in while Gandy was feeding me information. I was still in the BarcaLounger beneath the
dome, and Gandy was still standing a few feet away.

"That can't be right," I told him. What I meant was
that the last bit of data I'd received couldn't be right—
barely received, because it had brought me back to the
here-and-now, abruptly.

"It is," Gandy said.

"What you're telling me is that you Oans created
the Justice League."

"That is not an accurate understanding."

"Okay, correct me."

"We merely altered reality."

"Oh, is *that* all!"

"You are demonstrating the human phenomenon
of sarcasm."

"That *is* a distinct possibility," I said. "Okay, tell me
about altering reality."

"What we did cannot be expressed, except mathematically and as prorikib."

"'Prorikib'? You're getting back at me for 'xtripreolfed,' right?"

"Prorikib has not yet been developed by humans."

"Our bad, I guess. Now, about altering reality? The dummies' version, please."

"Infinitesimal forces exist. One, which humans express as 'N,' is a one followed by thirty-six zeros, measures the strength of forces holding atoms together divided by the force of gravity between them."

I was already lost.

"Another defines how firmly atomic nuclei bind to one another and how every atom was formed. This is expressed as zero-point-zero zero seven. There are others, such as the one humans designate 'lambda,' and which some of you have termed 'antigravity,' that we use in the rings, but they were not crucial to our terrestrial experiment."

"So you messed with 'N' and the other thing and . . . what?"

"Many volumes of print would be required to explain our methodology, which you would need a vastly enhanced education to understand."

"Tell you what," I said, trying to be witty. "Give it to me as a haiku."

"Physical forces
Altered: Thereafter super
Heroes can exist."

For a few seconds, I didn't understand that he had both created a haiku, though a very bad one, and answered my question. When I finally did understand, I was stunned.

"You're saying you Oans changed conditions on Earth so that guys like Superman can exist?"

"They did all appear within a few years of one another."

"Not Superman! I mean, he was the first, I guess . . . but you couldn't have created him."

"We did not create anyone. We merely generated possibilities."

"But Superman isn't *from* Earth. He came from another planet."

"The odds that a spacecraft bearing an infant could survive a journey from a planetary system thousands of light-years away and come to rest on one of the few planets congenial to its particular form of life are considerably greater than one over a number expressed as one followed by thirty-six zeros. Earlier in your history, it could not have happened."

"But there have always been heroes—"

"Not super heroes."

"We've got stories, mythology, dating back tens of thousands years. . . ."

"It was those stories that inspired us."

"So you screwed around with atoms and Superman landed and the others were . . . born, I guess."

"They altered into what they became."

"What about Wonder Woman? Didn't she come from a secret island that existed for centuries?"

"At certain levels of reality, time is malleable. Consider the unlikelihood of a complex civilization evolving on an island and remaining hidden."

I was expecting an elaboration, but I didn't get it. I might have saved myself some trouble later if I had.

"What about Batman then?" I asked when I realized that Gandy was done discussing Wonder Woman. "He's *human*, a hundred percent. Spooky as hell, but human."

"Batman is an enigma." Again I expected more, and again I was disappointed.

"Okay, I accept that for now, mainly because I have no choice. But what was the *point*?"

"Art is its own justification."

"This was more art stuff?"

"Certainly."

"You did it just to see if you could?"

"We did it to create. We took the substance of humankind and improved on it. Our endeavor was similar to that of your Greek sculptors, who perfected the human form. Instead of using clay and stone, we used life itself."

"I'm glad you guys don't admire Picasso," I muttered.

"I do not comprehend what he has to do with our discussion."

"Practically nothing." I gestured to the walls and ceiling. "Can you get rid of all this? I need some fresh air."

"The quality of the air is constant everywhere on Oa."

"Okay, I need some *psychological* fresh air."

And I was outside, in the pastel world on my feet instead of plumped down on a BarcaLounger. Gandy hadn't changed his posture.

"I assume that you told me all that for a reason, and I assume the reason has something to do with the disappearance of the Justice League," I said to him.

"You are correct."

"We haven't yet gotten to the part that I'm pretty sure I'm not gonna like—the 'what's next' part. Have we?"

"If you mean plans for our course of action, the answer is no, we have not."

"But you *have* a plan of action?"

"I have a belief regarding what must be done."

"I'll bet you have."

I walked around in a small circle, head bowed, staring at the ground. "Look, Gandy, I've had to swallow a lot in the past hour or so. If what you say is true, about forty percent of everything I believe is null and void. And I guess you must be telling the truth because . . . well, because I've stood on the surface of Pluto, if for no other reason. If that's possible, so is the rest. But I need time to absorb it all."

"We have need for haste."

"Why? There doesn't seem to be anyone around to bother us—"

And that, I suddenly realized, should not have been.

"Where *are* the other Oans?" I asked.

"They are either on Earth seeking myself or at the Creation Point."

"That's right. They were chasing you. Still are, I guess. This 'Creation Point' you mentioned . . . should I know about that? No, never mind. You haven't told me why you're being chased."

"The others wish to incarcerate me. They fear I will interfere with their plans."

"Can I ask what those plans are?"

"Yes."

Long pause.

Then I asked, "Okay, then, what are they?"

"I am aware of the instability of the human psyche," Gandy said. "I wonder if you can absorb the information you wish me to impart without damaging yourself."

"You mean, is it gonna drive me nuts! Well, we won't know until we try. So—impart away."

Another long pause. These hesitations, I realized, were how Gandy expressed the Oan version of emotion; his voice didn't change, and neither did his expression. He just shut up for a while.

"I'm waiting," I said.

"The task my brothers are involved in is the re-creation of the entire universe," Gandy said. "They are engaged in doing to the universe what we already did to this planet."

Now, I was the one who paused, trying to decide if I understood him. "What you're telling me," I said finally, "is that you Oans are making an artwork of the universe."

"Yes."

"Everything. Stars. Planets. Asteroids. Comets. All that other stuff. Making a big sculpture of it all."

"It is not a sculpture, though it has elements of sculpture. It also has elements of other arts."

"No drama?"

"We do not comprehend drama."

"Music?"

"We do not comprehend music."

"Okay," I said, "why are you opposed to this project? What are the consequences?"

"There are approximately fifty-eight thousand sentient life-forms, and trillions of subsentient life-forms in the universe. If we succeed, all but nine will cease to exist."

"Nine sentient forms, you mean."

"Nine life-forms in all."

"Every living thing on Earth is a casualty, I assume."

"That is not true."

For a second I felt a stab of relief. Then he said, "Certain filamentous freshwater algae of the genus *Spirogyra* will survive. You humans sometimes call it 'pond scum.' "

"Uh . . . how soon is this gonna happen?"

"Because of variables, it is impossible to determine when the project will be completed."

"Soon?"

"Perhaps it is imminent."

I hunkered down on the ground and rested my head in my hands.

"You do not wish to sit on the BarcaLounger?" Gandy asked.

"No." I looked up at him. "I know this is probably a stupid question, but . . . is there anything I can do? *We* can do?"

"It may be possible to halt the progress of the project."

"*We* can halt it?"

"If we do not do it, it will not be done."

I stood. "It's up to us to prevent the end of the universe, correct? No offense, Gandy, but I need some time alone. Can you give me maybe thirty minutes? I'd ask for thirty years, but I'm pretty sure you'd say no."

"You do not wish to be inside a structure."

"No, I'll just wander around out here."

I moved away from him, heading in no particular direction—assuming there *were* directions on Oa. Something about this world had bothered me from the moment I landed here and it seemed important to decide what.

I looked around at the greenish sky, the pink-blue-tan ground, the unbroken horizon. I sucked in a double lungful of the fragrant air. I knelt and ran the tips of my fingers on the smooth, ungranular ground. Then I rose and walked a bit farther. What was wrong? The answer, when it finally occurred to me, was stunningly obvious: Nothing grew on Oa. Nothing was natural. Nothing was alive. I felt as though I were standing on top of a giant beach ball. Compared with Oa, Pluto was the Garden of Eden.

The Oans didn't reproduce. They didn't have a

word for love. And this celestial monument to sterility was their idea of a perfect world.

Something moist was on my cheeks. A tear. But I didn't know who I was crying for.

I turned to Gandy, who apparently hadn't moved, and ran toward him.

"Okay, I volunteer," I said. "Consider me enlisted. How do we stop your friends?"

"First, you must learn how to use the ring."

"Don't I already know? I mean, it got me here, didn't it?"

"Yes. But it did so inefficiently."

I remembered the scuba tanks and had to admit that he had a point.

"Then show me efficiency," I said.

"We begin by altering your metabolism."

"Want to explain that?"

"Your body does not get maximum benefit from its fuel. Your brain does not focus your thoughts. These difficulties can be remedied."

"Did Hal Jordan have his metabolism altered?"

"Yes."

"And it didn't kill him? Or make him less human?"

"It did not."

"Or make him crazy?"

"His mental state was unchanged."

"All right, Gandy, do your stuff."

A diagram appeared in front of me, floating at eye level—balls and cubes joined by rods in an intricate pattern.

"Stare at the image," Gandy said.

I did.

It vanished. For a second, I felt a tingle in my head.

"Did something just happen?" I asked Gandy.

"Yes. I improved your ability to visualize and thus use the ring."

"Improved how?"

"It is much quicker. You need not actually create a mental picture. Merely intending to do so will achieve your end."

"Can I try it?"

"Yes."

I visualized myself airborne, and I merrily anticipated soaring upward, diving, swooping, looping loops, doing all the stuff I'd done back near Earth when I discovered how much fun flying without a plane could be. Okay, showing off.

I stayed on the ground.

"What happened?" I asked Gandy. "Or rather, what *didn't* happen?"

"I assume you were attempting to fly."

"Right."

"You didn't."

"And that would be because . . . ?" I let my voice trail off.

"You are questioning me?"

"Yes, Gandy, I am. I am asking you, as politely as possible, why I couldn't lift off."

"The rings do not work on the surface of the planet because a field of counterenergy nullifies them."

"Oh," I said, and a moment later, "And why is that?"

"It is a precaution."

A precaution? I mulled that for a second. "You're afraid somebody might stage an insurrection of some kind? Come down here and use the rings to kick some Oan butt?"

"Yes."

"Okay, so how do I practice flying?"

"Your flying skills are sufficient."

Had I just gotten my first Oan compliment?

"There is much else you must learn and practice," Gandy said.

"*How* much else?"

"You need months."

"Did Hal Jordan need months?"

"Yes."

"But didn't you tell me that we're in a hurry? I mean, do I *have* months?"

"We can compress time."

"We can?"

Gandy got professorial. "Time is largely a factor of entropy combined with consciousness. There are other factors, but those are crucial to our task."

"Which is?"

"We must make of you a true Green Lantern."

"By having me train for the months we don't have."

"There is little entropy on Oa. Some is inevitable, but we were able to slow the entropic process considerably."

"So I can shrink months into days?"

"We do not have days. We have hours."

"Then let's get started."

"There is still the matter of your consciousness. I would like your permission to tamper with it."

"You need my permission?"

"It is necessary for the process to be completely successful."

"Okay, Gandy, permission granted. What do I have to do?"

"Simply will yourself to stop resisting. I shall establish a parasynchronistic link."

"I am putty in your hands. Parasynchronistic-link away."

Gandy didn't use his hands, not as far as I can tell. He used his mind, and mine. How? I'll probably go to my grave not knowing. However, my memories of the next few hours are clear. What I did was work at using the ring.

Gandy began by reviewing basics, some of which I knew and some of which I didn't. I learned that the ring was a distant relative of a computer with certain functions hard-wired into it: Other stuff had to be supplied by the wearer's will, acting sort of like computer software.

The most important new information concerned recharging the ring with the lantern. It seems that earlier models of the ring, like the one Hal Jordan used, required a recharge every twenty-four hours. The ring on my finger operated more like a car's gas tank: As it was used, it gradually emptied.

"So how do I know when I need more juice?" I asked Gandy.

"When I altered your metabolism I instilled in you the ability to sense how much power is left in the ring."

"So I just sort of . . . what? *Feel* when the ring needs a refill?"

"Yes."

Well, I doubted it until I tried it. I focused my attention on the ring and had a feeling of fullness like the feeling I got after a big meal. Only *this* feeling was in the center of my head instead of my belly.

A few days into the training process, I realized that something was bothering me, and a few days later, I realized what it was: The ring shouldn't have been working on or near the Oan surface. When I asked Gandy why it was, he replied that we were operating in a cerebral reality shift, and that I should be quiet and not worry about things that did not concern me. Having absolutely no idea of what he had really said, I decided to obey him and concentrate on my training.

6

So I trained. I practiced flying in the Oan atmosphere and in space. I formed objects with my ring, and then I formed more complex objects, and then objects more complex yet, and then I formed objects without thinking of them. I came to do certain things reflexively: shield myself when I went into space, form bubbles of breathable air, do what's necessary to use the ring underwater, deflect missiles hurled at me by Gandy, and hurl missiles back.

Yes, I'm afraid so. I practiced using the ring as a weapon. Gandy would form ring energy "enemies" and I'd overcome them: all kinds of enemies— mounted Cossacks, World War Two–vintage tanks, knights in armor, spacecraft straight out of a George Lucas flick, street punks with knives, commandos with submachine guns, dragons, giants, other monsters I couldn't name. I handled them all, no problem. It was a lot like playing a video game, but not as much fun at first and later no fun whatsoever.

A lot of it was boring. I've heard martial arts guys talk about doing the same move ten thousand times. Well, I wasn't counting, but I must have practiced some ring stunts almost that much. Weeks and weeks of repeating the same drills. The better I got, the more tedious the drills became.

But they worked. I became quick and adept and confident. A Green Lantern. A warrior. *Me*, a warrior?

Not exactly. Not if a warrior is a guy who likes war. If anything, the Green Lantern training made me really think about violence and realize how much I genuinely despised it. But I acquired a lot of skills, some of them certainly adaptable to combat situations. I was still, basically, a wuss, but a wuss who could kick butt—with help from the ring. Without it, I was just plain wussy.

I didn't spend every moment honing my warrior skills. There was classroom work, too, with Gandy as the professor. I've never been a big fan of classrooms, but I have to admit that Gandy wasn't as boring as a lot of teachers I've had. Having said, or written, that, I've got to admit that I remember very little of what he taught, and some of what I do remember I can't claim to understand. How the ring enabled me to fly without wings, for example, and to travel in a vacuum where wings would be useless: It had something to do with bending the fabric of space, and something else to do with the antigravity Gandy had mentioned, and that was one of the functions hardwired into the ring.

I *can* both recall and understand his explanation for the rules governing the ring's use. He stood in front of a desk and blackboard, both formed with ring energy, presumably to make me feel at home, and adopted a professorial air:

"One is never to use the ring for personal profit," he said. "This is commanded because to use the ring for personal profit would potentially upset the normal societal balance of the user's civilization. You understand."

"I do," I said. "I think."

"One is never to use the ring to gain renown for one's clan," he said, reciting rule number two. "This is commanded because whatever benefit might be gained through competition between groups would be lost if only one side had the ring, which would confer an unfair advantage."

"Got it," I said.

"One is never to use the ring to promote one's unique point of view," he said: rule number three. "This is commanded because a diversity of points of view can be useful to a society."

"I couldn't agree more," I said. Actually, I didn't exactly agree: I'd never given thought to what Gandy had just said, but it *sounded* right.

I squirmed around in the school desk he'd created for me, the kind with the seat attached to the writing surface like the ones that I'd squirmed around in throughout my school days. "I have a question," I said, fighting the urge to raise my hand (which, in my school days, I'd done only when I needed to go to the bathroom).

"Yes?"

"Why the costume?"

"It is a uniform that identifies you as a member of the Corps."

"Okay, fair enough. But why the mask? Hal Jordan wore one, and for some reason I've included one in my version of the costume."

"It has a number of uses," Gandy replied. "The first is practical. If you are not using the ring for personal gain and the glory of your clan, it is best to hide your identity, lest you be hounded by those who would try to enlist you in their cause."

"In other words, the price of fame."

Gandy ignored me. "The second was inspired by your art. It is symbolic. It expresses the idea that the individual identity and its ego are not important."

"Okay," I said. "Are you gonna give me a test now?"

"Resume your combat training," he said.

I did. More drills, more flying and shooting and dodging and vanquishing of enemies large and small.

On the final day of what I now think of as my Green Lantern boot camp, exhausted to the point of stupidity, I ring-formed an Earth-type house, a nice little two-bedroom bungalow complete with Sears furniture, nice yards in the front and back, and—what the hell—a white picket fence. I went through a kitchen smelling of Lysol into a bedroom furnished with a queen-sized double bed, two night tables, a chest of drawers, and—what the hell again—a Norman Rockwell print on the wall. The place was a big improvement on my basement apartment-cum-futon. I flopped onto the bed and immediately went to sleep.

"Darling?" Someone was shaking me.

I opened my eyes. Jennifer Tulone's face was a foot from mine. "Whazzit?" I mumbled.

"Saturday. The kids' picnic, remember?"

"Kids?" I sat up in bed and looked at Jennifer. Her round face had acquired a few wrinkles, especially around the eyes, and her hair, messy at the moment, was cut very short. She was wearing a bulky, floral-print robe.

"Yes, kids. You've had 'em for years. Sometimes, you even like them. Now, rise and shine before I get rough with you."

"I wish," I said, and we laughed together, as we'd done often over the past dozen years.

I'd been dreaming. Red Nightshirt, the ring, Pluto, Oa—it had all been a crazy dream. I'd been married to Jennifer Tulone for twelve years. She designed software used by scientists, and I worked in the art department of the local paper. Our children, Meg, Beth, and Larry, were in fifth, sixth, and eighth grades, respectively. I was filled with relief. The dream . . . exciting and yet ugly and frightening.

If man ever did travel in space again, I remember reflecting, he'd be well-advised to give Pluto a miss and stay at least a galaxy away from anything resembling Oa. But man should learn to be as content as I was. We belonged here, on the good, green Earth and—

1

"Waken!" This time nobody was shaking me. Gandy didn't have to shake. His voice could cut through tungsten when he wanted it to.

I didn't need to sit up. I was standing on the surface of Oa, not lying in bed. I'd been dreaming. Jennifer, the kids, the house—it had all been a crazy dream. Or was I *dreaming* that it had been a dream?

Suddenly, I was struggling not to weep. I wanted the house and Jennifer and the rest to be real. I wanted what was normal. I wanted the Earth.

"Okay, okay, what's next?" I asked, turning from Gandy.

"Years of further training. But since that is impossible, we are finished."

"No kidding. How long have I been at it? Couple, three months?"

"As you reckon time, forty-three Earth minutes."

"I'm really not in the mood for jokes."

"I do not joke."

Didn't he? I wasn't sure.

"You compressed all that into forty-three minutes?"

"Your own mind compressed all that into forty-three minutes. You've done what few humans have ever accomplished—integrated the subjective and objective."

"With your help. You jumped into my mind once in a while, no?"

"No."

"Come *on*. You answered questions!"

"No. If questions were answered, you answered them."

"No way. I didn't know the answers."

"If questions were answered, you answered them," he repeated.

"Let me test that. The reason for the mask"—I pointed to it—"is to check my ego and remind me that my identity isn't important. True or false?"

"That is partially true."

"Damn," I muttered. Then: "You said I was the only human who'd ever . . . how'd you put it? . . . 'integrated the subjective and objective.' What about Hal Jordan?"

"Hal Jordan had months of training that were administered over a span of years."

"So I'm the only Green Lantern who managed the time compression stunt," I said, feeling cocky.

"The only human," Gandy amended, and my cockiness evaporated.

"This time compression . . . did that have something to do with the ring working on the planet surface?"

"Integrating the subjective and the objective necessarily activates a cerebral reality shift," Professor Ganthet told me.

"I assume my training is complete then."

"Your training is complete, yes. However, in order for you to function fully as a Green Lantern, we must achieve an alteration."

"In my costume?"

"In your physical form."

I didn't like the sound of that. Not at all.

"If you're gonna make me look like Tom Cruise—hell, I'll settle for Brad Pitt—well, full speed ahead. Anything else, I'll need more information."

"You must be able to live outside a planetary atmosphere, whether real or artificial."

"Artificial, as in breathing masks and pressurized cabins?" *And,* I added silently, *scuba tanks,* and winced.

"Yes."

"How does that work?"

"I shall try to explain it in terms you can understand."

"That'd be swell. Try and hold the words down to one syllable."

"You inhale a combination of oxygen and other gases. You exhale a combination of carbon dioxide and other gases. All are made of arrangements of atoms, which in turn are made of smaller particles. Rearrange the particles, and you alter the atoms. The substance they comprise changes into something different."

"They call you Mr. Science, I bet."

He ignored the gibe—for which I can't blame

him—and continued: "When we have accomplished our task, your physical form will rearrange the atomic components of the carbon dioxide compound, altering it into the oxygen compound."

"Without any help from me?"

"I do not understand."

He didn't understand? That was a switch.

"I won't have to do anything to make this change," I said.

"Your physical form will accomplish the alteration. Your physical form is you. Therefore, you will be accomplishing the alteration."

"Won't the atoms and molecules and whatever . . . *dissipate* after a while?"

"No. Gases are matter and matter is energy, as your human Albert Einstein explained. Energy is eternal."

"Gotcha. Or not. Anyway, how do we alter my physical form?"

What happened next didn't feel *authentic* somehow—more like a magician's misdirection, though why Gandy might have wanted to con me I don't know. He materialized a diagram in the air between us and told me to stare at it as I pressed my ring to the center of my forehead. Then he went behind me, touched a spot between my shoulder blades, and—

I blanked out, for no longer than a couple of seconds, and when I woke, I threw up.

Charming.

"You have undergone a metabolic alteration," Gandy explained.

"Now I can breathe in space?"

He moved to stand in front of me. "Yes. However, you cannot survive in space. Your physical form will still succumb to cold and lack of exterior pressure."

"In other words, I'll pop like an overinflated balloon."

"Yes."

"I still need to surround myself with a green bubble."

"Yes."

"So now we'll be going back to Earth. Maybe we can skip the stopover on Pluto."

"No."

"We have to visit Pluto? Okay, Gandy, if that's what it takes—"

"You will not return to Earth until your task is done."

My task. My task was . . . what? I'd started out to learn what happened to the Justice League and, if possible, undo it. Was that *still* my task?

"My 'task' is to rescue the Justice League, assuming they're not all dead. Or am I wrong?"

"You are wrong. Your task is to halt the alteration of the universe."

He had a point. Important as the survival of the League was, the survival of everything else was obviously even more important.

"This cannot be accomplished on Earth," Gandy continued.

"Then where?"

Long pause: Gandy was experiencing an emotion of some sort.

"We must go to the computer and destroy it."

I vaguely remembered his mentioning a computer earlier. "Where is it?"

"Nowhere."

"That'll make it kind of hard to find."

The ground shook. I assumed that Gandy was disapproving of my attempt at humor—just trying to lighten things up, folks. I, in turn, wasn't in the mood for any ring energy–induced earthquake. Or Oa quake. "Stop it," I said.

"They are near."

"Who?" But I knew who "they" were. Although I hadn't known it until that moment, ever since I'd left Earth I'd been preparing to do battle with a faceless enemy: Gandy's mates. Now, they were about to stop being faceless.

The ground shook again. I had no idea what to do. Stand? Hide? Attack? My time-compressed training hadn't included a course on tactics.

"They are entering the atmosphere," Gandy said.

"How do you know?"

"The tremors are an alarm. I calibrated it to detect Oans."

He stood as still as a pillar, concentrating. "They have brought with them other Green Lanterns," he said after a full minute.

"We're outnumbered?"

"Yes. We must flee."

"Into space?"

"No. They would be able to overtake us."

A chasm opened at our feet: a vast, circular hole with no visible bottom.

"Let me guess," I said. "You want me to jump into that."

"Protect yourself with a shield. The pressure will be great."

The enemy would have to remain faceless for a while.

I formed a bubble around myself and jumped.

I don't know how hot the drop was, or how much pressure there was as I approached the center of the planet. Plenty, probably. I had a sense that Oa was a lot smaller than Earth, about the size of our moon, maybe, but still, any area that far beneath the surface had to be hot and dense.

I seemed to be in a smooth-walled tunnel that went straight down; yellowish light came from somewhere below. Like everything else about Oa, it was unnatural; nature does not provide absolutely straight lines. Would I come out the other side, in some Oan equivalent of China?

Or would I be incinerated?

I remembered from my crash course in self-education that the Earth's center was a huge globe of molten iron. Would Oa's center be the same? I glanced around, scanning for Gandy. He was several feet to my left, encased, like me, in a green bubble and falling at the same speed. I guessed that he wasn't in the process of killing himself, so I decided to follow him.

Of course, I thought, *I could be wrong. Maybe he's committing suicide and wants company.*

Suddenly, I slowed. My plunge became a gentle

waft. Good or bad? Something Gandy engineered or a sign that our pursuers had caught us?

The tunnel became brighter. I looked toward its source and saw a perfectly round chamber filled with a perfectly round globe of yellow light. Not exactly how I'd imagined a ball of liquid iron.

I wanted to ask Gandy what was happening, and wondered if my voice would carry through the two green bubbles. I'd taken a deep breath, preparing to shout, when my green bubble touched the globe and I slid through it into—

Well, I shouldn't have been surprised. I was inside a perfectly round yellow globe. But not *standing* inside it—floating. And Gandy was floating beside me. He wasn't wearing his bubble, so I willed my own to vanish. I sniffed: The air was no different from what I'd been breathing on the planet's surface.

"We're hiding?" I asked.

"We will not remain concealed for long," Gandy said.

"Is it of any use for me to know exactly what we're inside of?"

"No."

"Then is it okay for me to ask what's next?"

"We will eject ourselves into space. You will instruct your ring to go to the transit. We will meet on the surface of Pluto."

"If we've gotta . . . Hey, couldn't we try talking to whoever's chasing us? I mean, maybe they'd listen."

"They would listen and they would not change their minds."

"I know people like that." I could have added, Mostly girls I've asked out on dates.

"Prepare yourself for space travel."

I was surrounded by my good ol' green bubble, or its direct descendant, without having to command the ring; hooray for boot camp.

I don't know if we left by the tunnel we'd traveled earlier or by another, or somehow oozed through the planet's matter. But leave we did, and fast. One moment I was bathed in yellow light, and the next I was in the darkness of space, speeding away from Oa; if the ring hadn't cushioned me, G-forces would have reduced me to jelly.

I couldn't see Gandy, but that meant nothing. He might already be on Pluto, or on the other side of Oa, or . . .

No point in speculating. "Take me to the transit," I commanded the ring.

I stopped accelerating. And didn't start again. I hung in the void, going nowhere.

"Take me to the transit," I repeated.

My bubble now seemed to be a darker shade of green. I peered through it and, silhouetted against Oa, maybe a half-mile away, saw a blob with a green rod jutting from it.

"Huh?" I think I said that aloud.

The rod began to shorten, pulling me toward the blob. Then, I realized that the blob had to be a Green Lantern, though certainly not a humanoid one, and he/it/they had caught me, was/were in fact hauling me in like a fish on a line.

I had no idea what to do. I should fight, I supposed. But how? Obviously, my first job was to free myself from Blobbo's beam.

I willed the ring to take me in the opposite direction. It didn't. Did Blobbo's ring have more horsepower than mine? Was his will stronger?

What the hell kind of creature *was* he?

He had surrounded my bubble with one of his own. That gave me an idea. I told the ring to expand my bubble. I mean, really *expand* it. I mean, expand it to the size of Australia. And do it fast, before Blobbo could compensate.

My bubble burst his. Score!

Now, I had to fight. Despite my training, I was not a fighter. At least not until now. Reading Rip Riley novels was as close as I'd ever gotten to combat.

Okay, Kyle, the problem is to deliver a telling blow to Blobbo's body—assuming that what I'm seeing is, in fact, a body. How is this to be achieved? Rip Riley would unsling his trusty machine gun and feed the s.o.b. hot lead. But I'm not sure what a machine gun looks like, much less how to ring-form one.

I went primitive. No gun, just a boxing glove, green, as big as a bungalow, which was a lot bigger than the one I used on the wannabe bicycle thief outside Omfrey's. I hit Blobbo with it, hoping he'd survive, because I wasn't prepared to be a killer. Blobbo not only survived, he didn't seem to mind a bit.

He aimed a beam at me.

I formed a big pair of scissors and snipped his beam to pieces.

I'd become curious about my opponent. I wanted a closer look. I ring-formed a magnifying lens and a spotlight, which I shone on him, and peered through the lens.

He was a purple blob. Just a blob the size of a whale. No mouth or nose, no appendages, certainly no fingers on which to stick a ring. He had a green stone embedded in his mass and from within it he was shooting another beam at me. I snipped it to pieces.

It was pathetic. Here I was, doing what no human had ever done before (with the exceptions of Hal Jordan and whoever first met Superman): encountering a sentient alien. We should have been facing each other across a conference table, or whatever passes for a conference table on his (its?) world, learning how to communicate, and then, once we could talk to each other, having a discussion. We should have been comparing science, religion, art, philosophy, learning what we have in common and maybe from that deducing what is truly real and important.

Instead, we were fighting.

I didn't know why. I wondered if he did.

Pathetic!

I noticed that he was not surrounded by a bubble, meaning—duh!—that he could survive in a vacuum. That gave him an advantage. But I had a hunch he was handicapped, too. I've never been much of a believer in intuition; it's always seemed a fuzzy-minded excuse for wishful thinking. But I now think that it exists and that it's nothing more than the subconscious reasoning from things the conscious is not aware of.

Anyway, I had this hunch, which was that Blobbo had not only never fought before, but that maybe fighting was unheard of where he came from.

Now, as mentioned earlier, I'm not exactly an ass-stomping, horseshoe-eating, macho kind of guy. But anyone who grew up near a television set in the America of the late twentieth and early twenty-first centuries has at least been exposed to scenes of battle—mostly phony, enacted by people no tougher than I am, maybe. But those scenes *did* get across the idea.

Which was, bash whoever's in front of you.

Or, in this case, *what*ever's in front of you.

None of my cognition was really necessary. I'd been through Oan boot camp, after all. Having decided to engage in combat, I needed only to trust my training.

Blobbo formed a hexagon a mile high and left it floating in front of me. I guess on his world the sight of a hexagon is paralytic, but it didn't impress me much.

I attacked. Flew straight through the hexagon at Blobbo, full speed, the bubble around me shaped like a bullet. But at the last microsecond—and who knew I could react that quickly—I slowed. I didn't want to *kill* him/it. I just wanted to make him/it let me alone. So I slewed my bubble-bullet sideways and hit him/it broadside.

Score!

Blobbo went flying toward Oa, obviously out of control, no longer a threat. I'd won the first fight I'd had since Donny Saldern called me an old poopy-head in the first grade.

Who's bad? Mr. Kyle *Rayner*'s bad, that's who!

Now, where was I? Oh, yeah, on my way to Pluto.

"Take me to the transit," I told the ring.

I began to accelerate. And then stopped.

About a dozen green beams were sticking to my bubble.

I pivoted inside the bubble. It was as I feared: The green beams were coming from green stones that were attached in various ways to creatures. Blobbo had friends. It was just barely possible that I was in trouble.

I'm not particularly proud of what happened next. I kicked alien butt, but only because my Oan training and conditioning had been amazingly thorough, and because I am of a race whose genetic survival traits include aggression and anger and violence. Oh, and art. Art was an element too. Blobbo's race didn't have these qualities, and neither do a lot of others.

Although it won't be particularly edifying, I'll describe the fight briefly.

I opened the bottom of the bubble and slid through the hole, leaving the beams attached to something that no longer contained me. I was unprotected in space, but only for a fraction of a second. I immediately surrounded myself with a second, much smaller bubble. I ring-formed four hard, blunt missiles, and sent them toward my four nearest opponents. Three hit their targets. The fourth was somehow deflected. Five beams sped at me from five directions. I got out of the way with a sinuous bob-and-weave that would have done any pro wide receiver proud, and returned the attack with five of my blunt missiles. This time, all five hit.

I'd eliminated eight opponents. Only four to go. Maybe. I didn't really have any clear idea how effective my missiles had actually been.

I could see three figures, barely visible in the glow from Oa, about a thousand yards to my left—"left" being purely relative and almost meaningless, as all directions are in space. I decided to fake them out. I began accelerating away from creatures, and when a glance backward assured me that they were following, I immediately reversed and hurled toward my pursuers.

As I was nearing them, I ring-formed three sabers and slashed at their middles. That distracted them from the three boxing gloves I used to smack their heads, or where heads would be on humans.

Score, score, score.

Eleven down. (Maybe.) One to go.

But where was he/it? Had I miscounted?

A large, flat object with curved ends materialized a dozen yards away and came toward me in little spasms. An alien weapon, obviously, and for all I knew, a ferocious one. But again, I wasn't impressed. I ring-formed a fly swatter and smacked the alien weapon in the direction of the nearest star. Then I formed a big butterfly net and tangled my opponent inside it.

I caught a glimpse of something thrashing around as I swung the net in a circle, and flung it in the same direction I'd sent his weapon, with my attacker still snared within it. He'd gone a mile or so before he

broke loose and came back at me. I was possibly dealing with genes as aggressive and hostile as my own.
Which was fine with me; I was getting into this combat thing. I formed a bear trap half the size of Mount
McKinley, and clamped him in its jaws and—

The bear trap melted. How'd he do that? Another
flat spasmer appeared and came at me. I dodged. Per-
sistent little devil. Or big devil? I needed to know
what I was fighting. I formed the magnifying glass
and spotlight, but before I could get a good look at
him/it, the glass and light melted. I did manage to see
that, like Blobbo, my foe was not bubble-encased. I
got an idea. Maybe he *had* to live in space. Maybe he
couldn't function in a planetary atmosphere.

I dove toward Oa, glanced over my shoulder, and
saw that he was following me. Once more I was
sucked through the barrier and plunged through the
orange haze. Whatever had stopped my fall earlier
stopped it again. I landed on the planet's surface and
looked up. He was dropping straight toward me.
"He" looked a lot like the thing he'd been throwing at
me—flat, rectangular—but two stalks were growing
from his center, and there were a dozen tentacles
sprouting from various parts of his body. One was encircled by something that could have been a larger
model of my ring.

He landed and immediately another weapon materialized and jerked toward me. Okay, I'd been wrong:
My opponent *could* function in an atmosphere. I decided, *No more Mr. Nice Guy!* I'd hit him with a barrage—missiles, boxing gloves, pistons, whatever else I

could think of. I willed the ring to form weapons and . . . nothing happened. I tried again. Nothing.

Déjà vu; I'd been through this before. As I'd learned earlier, for some reason the ring didn't work on or near the surface of Oa.

"Time out?" The stupidest thing I've ever said.

My huge, rectangular enemy was moving toward me. His ring apparently wasn't working either; he was going to finish the job the old-fashioned way. Okay. A race then. I'd bet on me. After all, he/it was large, flat, and awkward, and I was a young, slim, pretty damn fleet guy who sometimes had to run a whole block to catch a bus.

So I ran. No idea where I was going; I just ran. I looked over my shoulder, expecting to see my pursuer forty or fifty feet away. Wrong. More like *three* feet. How the hell could he/it move so fast?

Then I stopped running because the spasmer had caught me—the big, awkward bastard had *outrun* me—enfolded me, and begun to contract.

This wasn't a video game. The screen wouldn't go blank and then brighten, with me hale and whole. The end would *mean* the end. I tried to struggle, but my arms and legs were already immobilized. I couldn't breathe.

I was dying, billions of light-years from home. I'd never believed in an afterlife. Now, I wished I did. It would have been at least something. . . .

8

Something hard was beneath my back, and something bright was shining on my closed eyelids. I opened my eyes and was looking at the sun, or at least *a* sun. Then I sat up. I was on a stone bench a few steps from a gravel path, surrounded by grass and trees. The path sloped downward toward a burbling brook. No kidding—a genuine burbling brook. The sky was a gentle blue, the air warm.

I'd been mistaken about an afterlife. This was obviously heaven.

Death wasn't so bad.

I stood, stretched. I was wearing the Green Lantern costume, but my fingers looked bare. I willed the ring to appear. It didn't, but not because it wasn't there. I could feel it, but I couldn't see it. Just out of juice, I guessed. No power, no switching from invisible to visible. Oh, well. I probably wouldn't need it in paradise.

I began to walk down the path, hearing the gravel

crunch beneath my boots. I stopped to smell some flowers, smiled, continued walking. After I'd gone about a quarter mile, I saw someone standing on the riverbank and I broke into a trot. Running felt good, especially since no ill-tempered alien was chasing me.

He must have heard me approaching, because he turned and waved. He was a tall man, six feet-plus, dressed in a white polo shirt, tan chinos, loafers. His thick hair was a dark brown with distinguished gray temples and, at the moment, was being mussed by a breeze. He seemed familiar, yet I would have sworn that I'd never seen him before.

I stopped a few feet from him.

"Hello," he said in a mellow baritone. "Nice day."

"Yes. Pardon the dumb question, but . . . where are we?"

He smiled. "I don't think we've ever given the place a name. Didn't seem necessary."

"Let me rephrase—and I'm warning you, this one is *really* dumb. Are we on Earth?"

"You mean, the third planet from a yellow sun? *That* Earth?"

I nodded.

"Far from it. But we like to think that this is just as nice."

I couldn't argue with that.

"How'd I get here?" I asked.

"I'm not sure. I was sleeping when you arrived."

"Do you have any idea how long I'll be staying?"

"You won't be in any hurry to leave." He smiled again. Up close, he was movie-star handsome. He reminded me of Robert Redford playing Sundance, or Harrison Ford as Indiana Jones.

"Do I have a room somewhere?"

"A house. Actually, a cottage, but you'll find it quite comfortable."

"And it is . . . *where*?"

"Not far. Come on, I'll show you."

We began walking, side by side, on a narrow dirt lane that bordered the brook.

"I'm warning you—this next one is really, *supremely* dumb," I said. "Am I dead?"

He chuckled. "Do you want to be?"

"Not particularly."

"Then you're in luck, because you're not."

"The last thing I remember is being squashed in some sort of alien weapon."

"Sounds bad. Not fun to lose, especially for a Green Lantern. You *are* a Green Lantern, aren't you?"

I nodded. "How'd you know?"

"The suit."

Of course. I was still wearing the costume.

"It didn't happen to me often—losing, I mean," my companion said, "but when it did . . . well, as I said, not fun."

"Is that how you came here? You lost a battle?"

"Oh, no, no."

"Excuse me, but . . . you *are* human?"

"So I'm told."

"But this isn't Earth."

"Nope."

We turned off the lane onto another gravel path that

led to a cluster of small green-and-white dwellings at the top of a small hill.

We passed the first three and stopped at the fourth. "Home," my escort announced. "Why don't you get acquainted with your new digs. I'll check in with you later. An hour, say?"

"Sure."

I entered the cottage and explored. There was a living room furnished with throw rugs and a couch; a bedroom nearly filled with a king-sized bed; another, much smaller room that had a chest of drawers and a closet; and a bathroom, complete with everything bathrooms usually contain, including soap, shampoo, and conditioner. I'd never used conditioner in my life. Maybe I'd start.

I did everything you do when you first arrive in a hotel room—that's what I was thinking of the place as, a glorified Holiday Inn. I turned on the taps, wet my hands and face, bounced on the bed. I looked in the chest and the closet. They were filled with a lot of summer clothing in my size, but nicer and more expensive than anything I had in Mr. Gloinger's basement. I did not switch on the television because there was no television, nor did I check the contents of the refrigerator for the same reason. No radio or telephone, either.

I went back into the bathroom and washed my hands and face. They weren't dirty, but it seemed like the thing to do after a journey of . . . How far *had* I come? A billion light-years? Could be. I decided to call it a billion light-years because the figure was impressive, and I really didn't understand any number bigger than eleven anyway. I looked in the mirror above the sink and saw the Green Lantern costume. It seemed silly.

In the small room, I changed into jeans—*pressed* jeans, they were—a blue knit polo shirt, and running shoes sans socks. Call me Mr. Casual Chic.

I still had a few minutes before I was due to meet the tall, dark and, I had to admit, handsome stranger. I strolled outside and circled the cottage. It was in a glade, trees all around. Lush, full trees. Olive trees. Apple and palm and maple trees. Their leaves stirred gently in a breeze that also stirred the short, perfectly cut grass and some kind of shrubbery speckled with sweet-smelling, red-and-purple blossoms whose fragrance scented the air. Despite what the stranger had told me, I wondered once again if I'd died and literally gone to heaven. If this wasn't paradise, it was a damn fine facsimile.

I wandered back to the front of the cottage and saw the stranger waiting by the door.

"Like it?" he asked.

"Oh, as Edens go, it's okay."

"Feel like walking some more?"

"Okay."

We moved deeper into the woods. More perfection. Every leaf, every blade of grass, perfectly sized, perfectly symmetrical. Yet something seemed to be missing, though I couldn't figure out what. Not that I'd spent much time playing Henry David Thoreau. I was pure city boy. I really didn't *like* woodsy scenes. In my experience they tended to be full of things that itched and buzzed and occasionally bit. . . .

Suddenly, I knew what wasn't there. Bugs. Insects. Flying nasties.

My companion broke a long silence with a strange question. "Are you content?"

"You mean, right now? Or in general?"

"Right now will do."

"Well, yeah. I mean, who wouldn't be? Not that I've had a lot of experience with contentment."

"Most humans haven't."

"You sound like you know what you're talking about."

"My friend, I am an authority on malcontent. Or I was."

"Which means you *are* human? Oh, right . . . you said you were. Sorry."

"Apology not necessary, but accepted."

We lapsed back into a silence broken only by the whisper of the greenery and the soft sound of our shoes on the carpet of grass and leaves. The sky had darkened and the reddish rays of the sun were slanting through the trees.

"We'd better go back," the stranger said. "Unless you'd prefer to spend the night here."

"Would that be safe?"

He chuckled. "Here, *every* place is safe. You'll just have to get used to the idea of there being absolutely no danger anywhere."

"Gee, *that'll* be tough."

"Actually, it will be. We humans are programmed

to react to danger, and where there isn't any, we tend to manufacture it. It's part of why our distant ancestors were able to climb out of the slime and last long enough to become us."

"So you're a philosopher? A scientist?"

"*Me?*" He laughed. "No, no. I am, or *was*, what we call a 'man of action.' Swashbuckler. Knight in armor. Daredevil. Some days, when I was forgetting manly modesty, I would have admitted to being a hero. I *breathed* John Wayne and Clint Eastwood."

"Robert Redford and Harrison Ford?"

"Before they got sensitive and actory, yes. I saw every movie Bruce Lee made at least a dozen times."

"Ever read a Rip Riley book?"

"Once, when I was stranded in an airport during a storm and there was nothing *else* to read."

"Like it?"

"I'm no literary critic, but the writing seemed pretty bad. Good plot, though."

"My feelings exactly," I said, not truthfully. Rip Riley was beginning to seem stupid to me.

We emerged into a glade.

"Now what," I asked. "Indoctrination lecture?"

The stranger smiled. "No need. You're indoctrinated."

"When did that happen?"

"It began the moment you arrived. I'd say it ended . . . oh, ten minutes ago, when I saw you grinning."

"Look, there's still a lot I have to know—"

"*Have* to know? Let me ask you: Are you in pain?"

"No."

"Hungry?"

"No."

"Thirsty?"

"No again."

"Too cold? Too hot?"

"No and no. But still—"

"But still there are things you think you *ought* to know. Right or wrong?"

"Right," I admitted after a while.

"But you don't *have* to know them. All you *have* to know is that, right now, you're not hungry, thirsty, hot, cold, or hurting."

"Did you belong to the debate team in school, by any chance?"

He looked at me with raised eyebrows. "No way. Debaters were sissies. I was a fullback. Did you play ball?"

"Neither literally nor figuratively."

"Beg pardon?"

"Never mind."

My walking partner planted himself in front of me and said, "Pretty soon, you'll forget to ask the questions that seem most important, and later you'll forget them entirely. Meanwhile, you'll live very comfortably."

"When do I turn into a pig?"

He raised his eyebrows.

"Odysseus' men hung out on some island having a good time, not a worry in the world, when all of a sudden . . . instant oinkers."

"That's mythology?"

"Of course." I sounded more sure than I was. I vaguely remembered the story from the weeks I was trying to give myself a crash course in what I'd missed in school, which was practically everything.

"If you say so," the stranger said, with just a hint of condescension. "Don't worry, Kyle. You won't be turned into a pig."

"I wasn't really worried."

"I know. You like to joke."

We'd reached the door to my cottage.

"Hungry?" the stranger asked.

"I guess I could eat something."

"Want company or would you rather dine alone? I could see if my friend wants to eat."

"Your friend?"

"Want to meet her?"

"She's a girl?" That just sort of tumbled out of me. Except for the dream of domestic bliss I'd had on Oa, I hadn't thought of females since I'd left Earth—which was, in itself, amazing.

"Matter of fact, yes. Though to be politically correct, she's a 'young woman.' "

"Okay."

"You'd like to meet her?"

"Why not?"

He pointed to one of the cottages. "She lives there."

We walked the short distance to the cottage. The stranger knocked on the door.

"Di?" he called.

"Back here." The voice, a nice contralto, had come from behind the cottage.

We walked to the rear of the small building and saw her: a girl—excuse me: *young woman*—of about twenty. Dark hair, dark eyes, about five-eight, nice figure if you like them lean and athletic, and I do. She was dressed simply, in a short-sleeved white shirt, tan shorts, boat shoes.

I was relieved. I has half expecting some kind of alien weirdo, and instead I got an extremely attractive human female. She was jumping rope, or trying to. Holding on to each end of the wooden handles, she raised a loop over her head and brought it down and hit her calf. She tried again and somehow tangled the rope in her ankles and fell onto the grass.

"Ooops," she said, getting up and really seeing us for the first time. Her eyes widened and I'd swear she gasped when she saw me.

"Company, Di," my companion said.

Di tossed the rope over her shoulder and came toward us.

There was something familiar about her, but I couldn't decide what. She might have been the daughter or younger sister of someone I knew. Were she and the stranger an item? I didn't think so: no hello kiss, no affectionate arm-touching.

The stranger said, "Di, I'd like you to meet Kyle."

We shook hands. Hers was warm and soft.

"Hi," she said. The voice was somehow familiar too.

"Hi," I answered, which, I admit, was not exactly a sparkling comeback.

"Kyle has joined our little group," the stranger said.

"Welcome," Di said.

At least she wasn't the kind of woman who'd bore you with a lot of chatter.

"Join us for dinner?" the stranger asked Di. She nodded assent. No, definitely not the talkative type, our Di.

"What are you hungry for?" the stranger asked me.

"I'm easy to please," I replied—not a lie, since I'd often made a meal of potato chips. "Can I have pancakes?"

"Maple syrup?"

"Why not?"

"Eggs?"

"I'll pass."

He turned to Di.

"I'd like a tuna salad on rye toast," she said. She was becoming absolutely loquacious.

"And I'll have my usual," he said. It occurred to me that he wasn't speaking to either Di or me.

"My place okay?" the stranger asked, and Di nodded.

We strolled to the cottage at the far end of the glade, about two city blocks away, and went inside. It was the same size as mine, with pretty much the same furnishings, as far as I could see, with a few exceptions: On one wall there was an oil painting of a jet plane—a fighter-bomber, I think—and facing it on the other wall was an American flag. Below that there was a long, wide table covered with model airplanes, and in the center of the living room was another table, the dinner variety, set for three and heaped with goodies.

I'd been right when I'd guessed that the stranger hadn't been speaking to Di and me. Someone lurking nearby must have heard him, beat us to his cottage, and prepared dinner. The "lurking" part spooked me, but I had to admire the efficiency involved.

We sat and ate. Di was quiet, no surprise, and so was the stranger, which was fine with me. I've never been a whiz at dinner table chitchat. For the record: Di and I had what we'd asked for—a tuna sandwich on rye for her, a stack of syrupy pancakes for me. The stranger's "usual" turned out to be a real man's man meal: a well-marbled steak at least a half-inch thick, a baked potato with sour cream, a small heap of green beans, and apple pie. In the center of the table were a pitcher of ice water and a silver coffeepot, which we all shared.

"I think I'd like another piece of pie," the stranger said, patting his lips with a napkin. "Anyone else?"

"Not for me," I said.

"I'll join you, Hal," Di said.

Hal?

Two pieces of pie appeared on the table, and I remembered the Thanksgiving feast I'd had on Oa that Gandy had conjured from nowhere. So this place was equipped with the same bag of tricks. . . .

Hal?

A lot of random information and half-guesses suddenly formed a pattern.

"Excuse me," I said to Hal, "but is your last name Jordan, by any chance?"

"You found me out," he—*Hal*—said.

It was as though the father I'd never seen and knew to be dead had climbed from the grave, shaken the dirt from his clothes, and joined me for a snack.

"The Green Lantern Hal Jordan?" I asked, stupidly.

"One of the Green Lanterns," he said. "There are about thirty-six thousand of us . . . I mean, of *them*. I'm no longer a member of the Corps."

"Can I ask why not?"

"Long story."

"I'd like to hear it."

"We wouldn't want to bore Diana here."

"Not at all," Di said. She sipped at her water and somehow managed to drop the glass on the floor when she tried to replace it on the tabletop. The glass didn't break and the liquid vanished immediately.

"Excuse me," she said, unconcerned. To Hal: "Your story?"

If she hadn't heard Hal tell his tale before, they probably weren't involved. Life was filling up with possibilities.

"Let's go outside," Hal suggested.

Di and I followed him to the brook and across a small wooden bridge to a gazebo. Di stumbled halfway across the bridge, but managed not to fall.

The moon was full and high, the air sweet. In other words, a perfect night. I'd expected nothing less.

9

Inside the gazebo, we found padded benches and a low table on which were three tall glasses and a pitcher of icy lemonade.

We sat and sipped and listened to the chirp of crickets. For a while, I occupied that pleasant area between wakefulness and sleep. Finally, I leaned forward and said to Hal, "You were going to tell us your story."

"I was hoping you'd forgotten."

"Never happen."

"Oh, it will, eventually. You won't really forget, but things won't seem important enough to ask after."

"If you say so. About your story . . ."

"All right," he said, and sighed. "Well, as you know, I was Earth's Green Lantern."

"Yeah. How'd you get the job, by the way?"

"I was chosen—I've never been quite sure how. But, in effect, the Guardians of Oa recruited me. How about yourself?"

"Happenstance," I said. "Right place at the right time—or wrong time, depending on how you look at it."

We sipped lemonade while I waited for him to continue. "You were Earth's Green Lantern, you were saying," I finally prompted.

"Part-time," he said. "My day job was being a test pilot. Did a stretch in the Air Force and afterward went to work for a California outfit called Ferris Aircraft. I pretty much made my own hours, so being a Green Lantern wasn't often a problem."

"Wife? Kids?"

"Nope. Had a few relationships, though. Long one with Carol Ferris. She ran the company. Inherited it from her old man."

"Sounds like she was rich."

"She was. Still is, probably. Real pretty, too. But in the end, we couldn't make it work. My fault more than hers."

"I heard about Coast City," I said, trying to steer him in the direction I wanted him to go.

"From whom?"

"Superman."

"The old Man of Steel himself!" There was admiration in his voice, and even a bit of affection. I couldn't imagine anyone feeling *affection* for Supes: admiration, awe, envy, yes, but not affection. Of course, in his day, Hal was nearly Superman's equal.

"How is he?" Hal asked.

"That's kind of a long story, too," I said, "and I'd rather you tell yours first."

"Not much to tell. After I tried to restore Coast City, and failed, I got kind of hostile. Pissed a lot of people off—while still trying to do something about Coast City. Finally, I gave up. By then, I was persona non grata virtually everywhere on Earth, and on a few other planets, too. The Guardians were nice enough to let me come here."

"Getting in a little rest-and-recreation, huh?"

"That's not how I think of it."

"What do they expect from you? From *us*? What do we pay as rent?"

"Nothing at all."

"How do we get what we want or need?"

"Ask for it. Simple as that."

"No catches?"

"Nope."

"How long do you plan to stay here?"

He seemed surprised. "Till I die. Why would I want to leave? Why would anyone?"

I turned to Di. "How about you?"

"I was born here," she replied slowly, thinking about it, choosing her words. "This is my home."

"Are your parents here?"

She looked at me with a startled, deer-in-the-headlights expression, and then dropped her gaze to her lap.

"She doesn't know about her parents," Hal said quickly.

I finished my lemonade in a gulp and put the glass down. "I should feel tired," I told Hal and Di, who were still seated. "I don't, but I should."

"You can sleep," Di said: a simple statement.

"You'll find getting shut-eye easy to do around here," Hal said.

"I'm sure. I'll see you guys in the morning."

"Good night, Kyle," Di said.

" 'Night," Hal said, nodding and giving me a two-finger salute.

I walked back to my cottage, trying to enjoy the moon, trees, air, and not quite succeeding. As I neared my cottage, I knelt by the side of the path and plucked a blade of grass. I rubbed it between thumb and forefinger, expecting it to feel phony, to be some kind of artificial turf. But it felt like grass. I put it into my mouth and bit, tasted the greeny vegetable taste, and was flooded with memories of being a child and playing in my grandparents' backyard. Those were the most recent memories I had of tasting grass.

I entered the little house, dropped my clothes on the floor, a slob even in paradise, and flopped down. Almost immediately, I yawned and felt myself drowsing. I got up. I didn't want to sleep, not yet. I wanted to think about my situation and about Hal and Di. I went outside and sat on the porch. Nothing had changed in the last five minutes; the night was still beautiful.

Okay, stop staring at the moon and think.

Hal: once a sharp knife, now a knife without an edge. He'd been helpful, friendly, courteous, kind . . . a real Boy Scout. But he hadn't asked about how I'd come to this place, what my plans were. . . . He'd shown no curiosity, no energy, no zest. The events he hinted at, those that Superman told me about, would certainly dull anyone. Maybe he was shell-shocked, or suffering a kind of exhaustion a man doesn't recover from. My guess was, he'd lucked into a good deal here and chose to be satisfied with it. Fair enough.

And Di? The prettiest blank page I'd ever seen, but a blank page nonetheless. She seemed to have virtually no personality, like the women in that movie *The Stepford Wives*. Di's only distinguishing trait, apart from her beauty, was her clumsiness, which was kind of endearing. The worst thing about her was, I still couldn't decide who she reminded me of.

Would either of them help me, once I'd chosen a course of action? Not a good idea to bet on it.

But maybe they could tell me who else was sharing our garden of bliss, if anyone, and whether there were any Oans around. Gandy was still the only one I'd met. If I was to know my enemies, which was probably a good idea, it might help to get a look at them.

I got up, yawned again, and turned to go inside.

Sometime later, I awoke. How *much* later, I couldn't say: My watch had stopped somewhere between wherever I was and Earth, and there were no clocks in the cottage. Whoever had erected my little Eden apparently thought I'd have no need of a timepiece, and may have been right. Judging from the position of the sun, it was about nine o'clock.

I was hungry. I said, "Pancakes, syrup, a cantaloupe, coffee." Then I visited the bathroom for a while, and when I emerged from it, my breakfast was waiting for me in the living room. You could *not* beat the service in Eden. I ate, only vaguely aware that the food was superb—I was getting used to being treated like royalty—and went out into the sunshine, the breeze, the scented air, all that good stuff. No sign of Hal, Di, or anyone or anything else.

Time to explore. I glanced at my watch and remembered that it was no longer working. No problem. I wouldn't be going far, probably, and if I needed something, I guess I could just ask for it.

I picked a direction at random and began walking. I entered the woods and busied myself trying to notice anything exceptional, anything I wouldn't have seen on Earth. But it was all pretty familiar, or at least as familiar as it *could* be to a kid who'd lived his whole life on pavement. No purple bunnies, or three-headed giraffes, or talking pebbles. Just beautiful trees and grass and flowers.

The sun had moved a few degrees in the sky when the trees began thinning and I saw, directly ahead, a clearing and a scattering of the familiar cottages. I began to head toward them.

Someone was coming around the nearest cottage, a tall, dark-haired man. . . .

Hal?

Yeah, Hal. Coming from the cottage I recognized as his. Di's and mine were behind it, and behind them I could see the brook and the gazebo. I would have guessed that I'd come upon a duplicate settlement except for the presence of Hal Jordan.

So I'd entered the glade at the end opposite from where I'd started. Had I made it all the way around the planet? If I had, it was pretty damn small, and if it was that tiny, its gravity wouldn't be strong enough to hold me on it.

"Out for some exercise?" Hal called.

"More like some exploration." I slowed and fell into step beside him. "Weird thing. I thought I was going in a straight line away from here, and in an hour or so, I'm back where I started."

"That'll happen," he said affably.

When he didn't elaborate, I asked, "How's it work?"

"I've never tried to figure it out. Some kind of trick of the Guardians. Maybe something like a Möbius strip, only flat on the surface of the land."

I refrained from saying what I felt like saying, which was *Huh?* Didn't want my new pal to think me dim.

Together we sauntered along companionably, crossing the bridge and going to the gazebo.

"Thirsty?" Hal asked.

"Let me do it," I asked, and before he could reply I said, "Lemonade," and there they were, two frosty glasses waiting to be emptied.

After my first gulp, I asked, "Where's Di?"

"Haven't seen her."

"You guys, like, engaged?"

He chuckled. "No, no. Just friends."

Good news. Di wasn't exactly Ms. Personality, but she *was* gorgeous and besides, she was the only female around.

"This is going to be tricky to ask," I said, rolling my glass between my palms, "but, well, how smart is she? She doesn't say much. . . ."

"Not much for small talk, true," Hal said. "But smart? Hell, you've never met anybody smarter. Next time we run into her, I'll show you."

We sat and sipped. Already this day was beginning to resemble the previous day. So what was wrong with that? Compared with this place, Club Med was the Black Hole of Calcutta. But I'd run away and ended up where I started from, and that bothered me. I had a hunch that I was in the nicest prison in the galaxy, maybe in the universe, and some part of me was insisting that somebody who lived in a prison was a prisoner. Which I did not want to be, not even here, though I couldn't say why.

Hal seemed content to sit in silence. I couldn't allow that: I was beginning to believe that he was going to get me out of here, whether he wanted to or not. I thought maybe I should try to shock him.

As casually as I could, I said, "I hear you had something to do with the disappearance of the Justice League."

He turned, looked at me quizzically, and sipped some lemonade.

"That true?" I tried to sound like the meanest cop in town.

"I don't know anything about it," he said mildly. "I wasn't aware they'd disappeared."

Come on, I urged silently. *At least ask me when!*

"How long ago did it happen?"

Hooray.

"As I reckon time, about three weeks."

"How'd it happen?"

I told him the story and, while I was at it, I gave him a lot more: Omfrey's, Superman, Batman, Gandy, Pluto, basic training on Oa, the fight with the aliens. Partly, I wanted to watch his reactions, and partly—mostly—I just desperately wanted to tell someone the story.

"You must be a real badass," he said when I was finished. I needed a second to understand that he was referring to the fight with the aliens.

"I'm not. At least, I never have been."

"What kind of tactics did you use?"

"I don't know about tactics. I just . . . visualized things and used them."

"Different kinds of things?"

"Yeah." I paused, remembering. "Sabers, scissors, a boxing glove—"

"That's your secret then. Same as mine."

"Want to explain?"

"Most alien GLs only know one use for the ring. Seems that not too many nonhuman cultures have art forms. Gives us Homo sapiens an edge."

"How so?"

"We use the ring to form different shapes. Stuff they've never seen. Confuses 'em."

"So we're smarter than they are?"

"Naw. We just have an edge when it comes to fighting with rings. No big deal. But something to keep in mind next time you're in combat with an extraterrestrial."

"Let's hope that never happens."

He raised an eyebrow.

"Look, Hal," I said. "I know what I've done is strictly minor-league compared with what you've done. You're the Green Lantern of Earth, the real deal, a hero. I'm just a guy who has the ring. But I guess I was expecting more than 'oh' and 'interesting.' "

"Sorry to disappoint you . . . Kyle, is it?"

At least he remembered my name, sort of.

"My heart's broken, but I'll survive."

"You like to joke."

"Shame I'm not better at it."

"Kyle, I'd like to get excited about your news. I really would, because I don't like to see you pissed off—"

"I'm not—"

"Then you're doing a good imitation. But remember what I told you yesterday?"

I did, but just barely. "Yesterday" seemed like a million hazy years ago.

"Remind me," I said.

"Pretty soon, you'll forget things that seem important now. They just won't matter. The more you relax, the sooner it'll happen."

"That's where you're at?"

"That's *exactly* where I'm at, and I've never been happier."

There was still one bit of information I hadn't relayed to him: the Oans' big, lethal art project. Would even *that* fail to shock him out of his complacency?

Hal raised his hand and I started to tell him that,

yes, he could go to the bathroom, but before I could, he looked past me and called, "Di. Over here."

I turned to see Di approaching. She was wearing a two-piece bathing suit, and as my grandfather would have said, *Hubba hubba*.

"I was thinking a swim would be nice," she said.

"You up for a dip?" Hal asked me.

"Do I have a suit?"

"There'll be one at the pool."

Pool? I hadn't seen a pool yesterday. But I followed Di and Hal and, yes, there it was, between the cottages and the woods, exactly where I'd met Hal earlier: a standard, suburban park–type swimming pool, complete with deep and shallow ends, bathhouse, beach chairs, and even a red-and-white striped cabana.

"Before we go in the water, there's something I'd like to ask you," Hal said to Di. "What's the sum of nine hundred and sixty-three plus two hundred and forty-seven plus eleven thousand eight hundred and sixty-eight plus four thousand and four."

"Seventeen thousand and eighty-two," Di said immediately.

"Your turn," Hal said to me. "Give her a multiplication problem."

"Okay . . . multiply five thousand eight hundred and ninety-two by, oh . . . six hundred fifty-four point three."

"Three million eight hundred fifty five thousand, one hundred and thirty-five point six," Di replied.

Obviously, I didn't know if her figures were accurate—as I mentioned earlier, any number higher than eleven baffles me—but I was impressed anyway.

"Told you she was smart," Hal said, winking. He could have been a suburban dad boasting about a brainy daughter. He and Di then trotted off toward the pool.

I went into the bathhouse and found a pair of blue trunks in my size on a wooden bench next to a shower. There was also a pair of goggles, which I ignored. Who did the Oans think they were dealing with anyway—a sissy? It was a bathhouse exactly like a half-dozen others I'd been in, but with something missing. As I was changing, I tried to decide what. Finally, I got it: the smell—that unmistakable swimming pool odor of chlorine, sweat, disinfectant. The air in *this* bathhouse was as sweet as the air everywhere else on the planet, assuming it *was* a planet.

The Oans didn't get *everything* right. That was a comfort, somehow.

The concrete didn't burn my bare feet as I walked to the pool—another thing the Oans had gotten wrong. The others were already in the water, Hal dog-paddling and Di doing lazy, graceful breaststrokes— superbly, I might add. In the water, there was no trace of her clumsiness. In the water, she was a goddess.

They looked up at me and when Di's gaze met mine I was suddenly, acutely aware of my pallor, my awkwardness, my general scrawniness. Di smiled and continued swimming.

"C'mon in," Hal yelled. "The water's fine."

I'm not much better at swimming than I am at

most athletic stuff, but what the hell? Di had already seen me in a swimming suit; how much worse could it get? I held my breath, shut my eyes, and jumped.

The water was, indeed, fine. No, better than fine: It didn't fill my nostrils with that mediciney chlorine reek, nor was it host to any little green scummies. Clear, sparkling, perfect water. Of course. What else?

I bobbled up, shook droplets out of my hair, blinked my eyes. Hal was paddling and Di was stroking. I thrashed and splashed and walked on the pool bottom while moving my arms and pretending to swim. I don't think Di was fooled, and I know damn well Hal wasn't. But it was fun anyway.

Eventually, Di swam to the ladder, started to climb out of the pool, somehow slipped, fell back into the water, tried again, and succeeded. I stared, and not just because she was a gorgeous woman wearing not a hell of a lot. Something about the way she held her shoulders, the curve of her middle back . . . I wondered if she was aware of male eyes gazing at her, of the admiration she was generating in me, and probably in Hal, too.

Then I knew who she reminded me of, and suddenly I was *very* interested in her.

She sat in one of the lounge chairs and turned her face to the sun and again, seeing how the light hit her cheeks and forehead, I was struck by the resemblance. I heaved myself up onto the concrete, trotted over to her, and sat in the lounge chair next to hers.

"I don't remember if I asked you about your last name," I said. "Did I?"

"Prince," she said. "Diana Prince."

"Are you related to Wonder Woman?"

"I don't know. I don't believe I have *any* relatives."

Hal had left the pool and joined us. "The Guardians said that Di provided the model for the person who became Wonder Woman," he said.

"You mean Wonder Woman is a clone of Di?"

"Nothing that simple. It has something to do with what they call 'establishing a morphogenic energy matrix.' "

"Which means?"

"Hey, Kyle, I'm just a jet jockey; the scientific stuff is way beyond me. As I understand it, it's something like creating a blueprint that reality follows. I know, I know—none of it makes much sense, at least not to us."

"But in effect, Di and Wonder Woman are the same?"

"More like Di is a rough draft of Wonder Woman."

I realized that we'd been discussing Di as though she weren't present. I said to her, "I'm sorry to talk about you in the third person. . . ."

Her expression was blank. Not uncomprehending, just blank. I turned from her, stood, and jumped into the pool. I didn't know what else to do.

The rest of the afternoon was a lazy blur of heat, pointless talk, covert glances. I felt myself relaxing into the situation. None of my problems seemed as important as the glitter of the sun on the water. Occasionally, I tried to make small talk with Di. She listened politely, attentively, but we weren't really communicating on any level. She wasn't interested in me, but she wasn't *uninterested*, either. She was just *there*. Instead of being frustrated, as I would have been on Earth, I found myself accepting her attitude as I accepted the trees and sunshine.

At dusk we dressed, then ate dinner in the gazebo. Hal excused himself and wandered away. Di and I stayed to have a second glass of lemonade each. For a while, we sat and watched the sky darken. She said she wanted to sleep and I offered to walk her back to her cottage.

On the path, I brushed my arm against hers, hoping she'd think it was accidental—the old adolescent dating maneuver. She didn't pull away, but she didn't edge closer, either. So the question implicit in the gesture went unanswered.

She stumbled only once.

At her door, we experienced the Inevitable Dating Moment. Will we or won't we? Should I or shouldn't I? What the hell—one more rejection wouldn't kill me.

I kissed her.

I feel idiotic writing that, and even more idiotic when I add that her lips were soft and giving. But they were. Sue me.

"Was that a kiss?" she asked.

She had to *ask*?

"I think so," I said. "As close as I can come to one. Sorry, I didn't mean to offend. . . ."

"It was nice."

"It was? Thanks. I'm glad. Okay, 'night, Di." I was

moving away. "Maybe we can do it again sometime."

Call me Mr. Smooth.

But she didn't say, "No, absolutely not, that was disgusting and vile, not to mention repulsive." Plus, she'd used the word "nice."

Swell word, "nice." Has a ring to it. You might even say, a *nice* ring. My hormones, I firmly believe, were at that moment doing the hokeypokey on my libido.

No way I was going to sleep, not for hours.

Time to focus on my situation. Okay, here I was someplace where everything I wanted was instantly provided. For companionship, I had a faux big brother-cum-father figure and a gorgeous and apparently friendly young woman. There would apparently be no rivalry between Hal and me for Di's affections, though I remembered what my uncle Charlie had once said, something to the effect that where women are concerned, you can begin to trust a man about ten minutes after he's buried. Anyway, I had no reason to believe that I couldn't take the relationship between Di and me anywhere I wanted it to go, at any speed. She was young, extremely beautiful, quiet, and with apparently no mind of her own; I know some guys who would call her the perfect female—the American dream girl. Hell, she didn't even need airbrushing.

All that on one side. On the other: Well, there was this little matter of the wholesale slaughter of lifeforms throughout the galaxy. Yes, indeed. But was I sure that would happen? I had only Gandy's word for it. (And where *was* Gandy, anyway?) Assuming that it was going to happen, could I do anything to prevent it? Probably not. And if it did, I might very likely survive—I was in a place created by the Oans, and wouldn't they likely spare their own property? *And* . . . if I *did* perish, it wouldn't hurt. If I understood what Gandy had said, it would be as though I had never existed.

Finally: The Oans, in their own strange way, were altruists—they wanted to make the universe perfect.

Their version of perfect, of course.

I'd been walking while thinking under a perfectly clear sky dotted with perfect stars and glowing with the light of a perfect moon—perfection was the order of the night, no doubting it—and discovered that I'd again gone around the world. In, I estimated, about fifteen minutes. Eat your heart out, Flash.

I passed Di's cottage, briefly considered knocking on her door, hesitated, and in the end continued on to my own room.

I slept. Perfectly.

Had a perfect breakfast alone in my cottage, then joined Hal and Di for a perfect swim—well, at least their swimming was perfect. Mine was terrible, as always. But they didn't seem to mind, and if they didn't, I figured, why should I? I guess, by then, I'd decided not to fix something that wasn't broken.

Sometime during the night, I realized that I could never hope to improve on my situation. Which was perfect. So maybe there would be wholesale extermination elsewhere. Not my business, really. And all those creatures, including humanity, would have to perish eventually anyway. At least the Oans would make their ends painless.

Di was stretched out on the lounge, her lovely face to the sun, eyes closed. I climbed out of the pool and joined her. Suddenly, I had an urge to draw her. Something in me wanted to preserve this beauty— and maybe to somehow own it by reproducing it. However, I had neither sketch pad nor pencil. But as soon as I said aloud, "Sketch pad and pencil," they were lying on the concrete next to Di's dangling ankle as though they'd always been there.

"Mind if I draw you?" I asked her.

"Draw me?" I'd forgotten how uninformed she was. I did a happy face and showed it to her. "See, this is a drawing," I said as though I were speaking to a child—which, in a way, I was. "Only it'll look like you. I hope."

I consider myself a beginner when it comes to drawing people the way they really look, but I had taken the odd life drawing class now and again. (In a way this whole bizarre trip began in a life-drawing class, the one where I became enamored of Sharon Klingerman.) So I thought I could probably do a decent likeness of Di, and began to sketch.

Hal was doing laps in the pool, a good forty feet away. I could have a relatively private conversation with Di, and I surely knew what I wanted to talk about.

"Last night," I said as a I moved my hand. "Your first kiss?"

"Oh, yes."

"Okay, this is gonna sound dumb, but . . . how'd you know it as a kiss?"

"I've read about kisses and seen them in films."

New information: Books and movies *were* available. I just hadn't requested them. Good: I've always wanted to see the director's cut of *Blade Runner*.

"You said it was nice. The kiss."

"It was."

I'd been wondering if Di was, well, normal, since she wasn't born in the normal way. Apparently she was. I should have been overjoyed. But I wasn't, and I didn't know why.

I sketched. Didn't like what I'd done. Said "Eraser" and without looking reached out, knowing an eraser would be there. It was. I erased part of Di's hair and redid it. Still no good. Had I always been this lousy?

"Damn," I muttered.

"What's wrong?" Di asked, scooting forward. "May I see?"

"I'd rather you didn't." She was reaching for the pad as I was pulling it back, and she lost her balance. The lounge tipped and she fell to one knee. She yelped.

I knelt and examined the knee. The Oans had been a little too realistic when they'd created the concrete; it was hard enough to have broken Di's skin. There was a small gash with a drop of blood leaking from it.

"Band-Aid," I said, then reached out, got a Band-Aid, and applied it to Di's mini-wound.

"You don't want me to see the picture?" she asked when I finished.

I flipped the page. "This one's pretty bad. Let me have another shot at it."

I started again. My second try was no better than my first. Part of the reason was that my gaze kept going to the Band-Aid on Di's knee, which was absolutely fascinating.

Because it was the only thing about her that wasn't perfect.

I dropped the pad, sat back, stared at the strip of off-white that slightly marred her flawless skin, and felt enormous love surge through me. Love not only for her, but for all humanity. This was amazing, because I'd never loved anyone before—not myself, not any of the girls I'd dated, nor Mr. Gloinger, nor Batman, certainly not Gandy or Hal. Love was not a part of my vocabulary. Lust, yes. Love, no. Not until that moment, when, suddenly, I loved everyone.

It was pretty damn scary.

I've never figured out exactly what was happening in my mind and—allow me the word—*soul* at that instant, and maybe I never will. But whatever it was, it changed my thinking.

I'd stop the Oans.

Now I had to figure out how.

Hal trotted up. "Accident?"

"Yeah, I'm sorry. She'll be okay. Hal, you and I have to talk."

"Sure. You seem excited. Want some lemonade?"

"Only if it's sour."

"Huh?" He smiled. "Oh. Another of your jokes."

"Yeah. Uproarious, right? All together—ha ha." I

was being pretty annoying to someone I'd just decided I loved.

"Go ahead and talk," he said, either ignoring or choosing not to hear my attempt at humor.

"Give me a few minutes. I've got to think of what we'll talk *about*."

"Take your time. I'm not going anywhere."

Still clad in damp swimming trunks, I left the pool. I hadn't gone far when I turned back. I'd been wrong. I didn't need to think.

"That didn't take long," Hal said as I approached him.

"Some questions."

"Okay."

"First, where are we? I know you said this place doesn't have a name. But what *planet* are we on?"

Hal shrugged. "I asked the Guardians for help and the next thing I knew, here I was."

"Could it be Oa?"

"Could be. Or *an* Oa."

"What does *that* mean?"

Hal shrugged. "Probably nothing. Just that once or twice I've gotten the idea that the Guardians may have more than one home world."

"Why?"

Hal smiled and shrugged again. "Maybe 'cause they're Oans."

Okay. Maybe there were two Oas—for all I knew, there were a *dozen*. But what I was standing on had to be one of them, the one on which Gandy had trained me. Why had I ever thought otherwise?

When I'd been sent to la-la land by the spasmer, I was on the Oan surface. Gandy had demonstrated that the planet was as malleable as Silly Putty and infinitely accommodating; shapes, forms, artifacts—anything could be ordered up. Creating this Eden would be no problem at all. Maybe it, like Di, was some sort of rough draft. Maybe those arrogant little blue bastards had set out to create a perfect Earth and then said, *"Hey, we're the high-and-mighty Oans! A mere Earth isn't good enough for us! We'll do a whole freaking universe. 'Cause we're the* Oans!*"* Then they used their cute little Eden as a dumping ground for washed-up super heroes and failed Wonder Women and as a fancy-shmancy prison for a wannabe artist who was annoying them.

"Hal," I said, "I'm about to lay some pretty heavy stuff on you. I'm not sure Di"—I nodded at her—"should hear it. And I'm not sure she shouldn't."

"Hard to give advice without knowing what you plan to say. But I trust her. She's the most honest, straightforward person I've ever met."

But could she keep a secret? Probably made no difference; if the Oans wanted to learn my plans, they almost certainly would need no help from Di. Besides, she was a million miles from my idea of a snitch, much less a Mata Hari.

"Okay, get comfortable. This may take a while."

I said aloud, "BarcaLounger," and one materialized beneath me.

I settled back and began at the beginning. Though Hal had heard some of the story, I told him and Di about Omfrey's, Gandy, my meeting with the Justice League, the League's disappearance, my trip to Oa, my Green Lantern training, and finally, the Oans' plan for the universe. I watched their faces as I talked. Di frowned and craned her head slightly forward, like someone struggling with a language she wrote but did not speak, and Hal frowned. The frown deepened as I went on. By the time I finished, the crease between his brows looked as deep as the Grand Canyon.

"Uh-huh," he said.

"You don't seem surprised," I said.

"I can't say I am."

"Care to elaborate?"

"I've always been a little bothered by the Guardians' . . . smugness. They never seemed to care about any opinions or values except their own. I used to worry that one day they'd ask me to do something they thought was right and I thought was wrong. It never happened, but I guess it could've."

"What would you have done?"

"Damned if I know. Tossed a coin? I mean, they *are* smart, and they were planet-hopping while our ancestors were still sucking mud. But you know . . . my hunch is, even an immortal can be wrong. And sometimes I think that immortality worked against them. They got set in their ways."

"What would have happened if you'd disobeyed them?"

"Not too much. They're pretty nonviolent. Worst-case scenario, they'd have kicked me out of the

Corps. But that wouldn't have been a small thing, not to me. Man, I gotta tell you, I *loved* being a Green Lantern, for the same reason I liked being a pilot. The freedom I felt flying around, the power, the sense of being special . . . major kicks."

"But you quit."

"More like I was kicked out, finally. But not exactly. In the military, they'd call it 'put on administrative leave.' It was after I tried to reconstruct my hometown. But when I couldn't do anything for Coast City, I was ready to call it quits anyway. What was the point in being powerful if I couldn't save all those people with my power?"

He squeezed his eyes shut and breathed deeply. "Man, that is the longest speech I've given since I had to tell Carol Ferris why she wasn't getting an engagement ring for Christmas. Pardon me for blowing off."

"Hey, don't apologize," I said. "It was interesting."

And it had given me an idea.

"What's your current status?" I asked him.

"I'm a lazy slug enjoying the good life."

"I mean with regard to the Green Lantern Corps."

"Still on the Guardian equivalent of administrative leave, I guess."

"Do you still have your ring?"

He rested his chin on his right fist. "Yeah. In a drawer."

"How about your battery?"

"It's around someplace." He looked directly at me. "I see where you're going."

"You'd have to—you're a bright guy. Question is, how do you feel about it?"

Hal got up, walked to the edge of the pool, and stared into the water. Di was leaning forward, eyes half closed, anticipating his answer. Me too. Anticipating and fearing.

He turned and walked slowly back to us. "Yeah," he said, answering a question in his own mind. "The Guardians are smart, but they aren't God, though they might not agree. It's not their universe. It's ours as much as theirs, and I didn't give them permission to change it."

"Then you'll help?"

"If I didn't say so, I should've."

He spun, an Air Force officer doing a classic about-face, ran to the pool, jumped in, and began swimming furiously. After a while, Di joined him. I didn't. I just leaned back in the BarcaLounger and basked in the sunshine. The sun hadn't changed position in the sky since we'd arrived at the pool. Of course not. It had already been positioned perfectly.

Eventually, Hal and Di joined me and we all got dressed and went back to the cottages.

"We've got plans to make," Hal said as we approached his place.

"Yeah," I said. "My first prison break."

Hal waved a hand at everything around us. "You call this a prison?"

"Matter of fact, I do."

"You're right."

Di had, as always, been quiet.

"What about you?" Hal asked her. "You understand what's going on?"

"Not exactly. You want to leave home."

It was odd, hearing our faux paradise referred to as "home." But Di had no other word for it.

"Yeah, in a nutshell," Hal agreed. "I'm not sure how yet. Could be dangerous. I'll understand if you want to opt out. Hell, I'm *urging* you to."

"I'm with Hal," I said.

"I would like to stay with you," she said to him, and I suddenly understood one of the consequences of what we wanted to do: Di would be sentenced to a life—an eternity—of loneliness, unless Hal chose to stay with her after we left this world and resettled somewhere. I hoped he would, for both their sakes.

"Hal," I said. "You better do the planning. I imagine you've had more experience with this kind of thing than us. Closest I've ever come to a prison break was sneaking out of detention in high school."

"Let's eat first," he said. "I don't think too well on an empty stomach."

We went into his cottage. I won't bother describing the meal we ate except to note that it was—let's have a fanfare—perfect.

Hal pushed himself back from the table. "Okay, people, now we get down to the hard tacks. Mission is to get at least one of us off-world."

"I've been thinking," I said. "Why shouldn't that one be you? Makes a lot of sense. You've got the experience—"

"But not the stomach for it," he interrupted.

"Hal. I'm like a buck private. You're a general—"

"Generals don't go to the front lines and fight the enemy. They let the privates—the young guys—do the fighting. Besides, this thing is likely to take you back to Earth. I'm not welcome there, and to be honest, I don't know that I could handle seeing the place again. No, Kyle, I'm afraid this is *your* show."

"Okay." I'll admit that when I suggested Hal as the hero of our little venture, a small part of me had been thinking of a long, easy lifetime with Di. But I wasn't upset when he refused the job. I was beginning to *like* being a hero.

"How'd you say you got off-planet last time?"

"Gandy took me through a hole. We went down a long way—to the center of the planet, I guess—made a turn, and then I was in space."

Hal got up and went to stand in front of the flag on the wall. "Not likely we'll find one of those holes," he muttered, obviously thinking aloud. "Might not be a good idea to use one in any case."

"We're getting ahead of ourselves," I said. "We're talking about using the ring, or rings, and in case you've forgotten, they don't work."

"True," Hal said. "Not on the surface of Oa, which is where we think we are."

"Any idea why not?" I asked.

"Yep, I got an idea. But just an idea, not a certainty."

"Go on."

"Well, if I were a Guardian, I wouldn't want to take

a chance on somebody misusing a ring on my home turf. Maybe I'd establish some kind of field that blanks out the ring power a certain distance from the planetary surface."

"Yeah," I muttered, more to myself than to him. "That squares with what Gandy told me. My ring went on the blink. So did the Spasmer's."

" 'The Spasmer'?"

"An alien. Kicked my butt. Put me here." I nodded toward Di. "Not that I'm complaining."

She nodded back and smiled, imitating me.

"Apparently, the field is calibrated only to blank out the rings," Hal said. "Otherwise, this place"—he waved at the room around him—"wouldn't work. Our problem is getting high enough to be free of the field, if that's what it is."

I leaned back and scanned the room, looking for nothing in particular. My gaze fell on one of Hal's model jets. I stood, walked to the table, picked up the toy plane, and examined it. For a minute or two, the room was quiet.

"This is gonna sound dumb," I said finally, "but I have a plan. We fly out."

Hal whistled. He'd gotten it immediately. "All *right*!"

We talked for the better part of the next hour. We began by recapitulating what we knew, which was that Oa, using the same technology that powered the rings, could produce anything we requested. When *we* made stuff with the rings, we could make only what we could visualize or knew well. I couldn't

conjure up a computer back on Earth because I had
no notion of how a computer worked. The more I
knew, the more I could do with the ring. So—we
were hypothesizing now—somewhere in or on the
planet was a giant database that knew virtually
everything.

Or, if not everything, at least the workings of a jet
aircraft.

We hoped.

"To summarize," Hal said. "We order up a jet. We
fly it to the outer limits of the atmosphere, charge the
rings, and carry on from there."

"Sounds like a plan," I said.

Di nodded. I wondered if she knew what she was
agreeing with.

Hal led us outside.

"What kind of plane we gonna order?" I asked.

"I've been thinking about that. Our best bet is a
Ferris Aircraft X45 Cloudbuster. We built it as a high-
speed attack fighter for the Navy, and later sold a
bunch of 'em to the Marines after we added an au-
toignition feature. Twin jets, kind of like the Navy's
Tomcat, but smaller and faster. By the way, calling her
'Cloudbuster' was Carol's idea. I thought it was way
too cute. Still do."

"But you can fly it?"

"Hell, kid, I helped *design* it."

"I didn't mean to insult you."

"You didn't."

Hal turned away from us and said to the air,
"Okay, let's have a Ferris X45 Cloudbuster. Marine

configuration. Fully prepped, fuel tanks topped off. You can skip the armament."

And there it was, in the area between the cottages. I never got used to how Oa provided what we requested. Stuff didn't just *appear*, like a magician's trick gone big time; it was as though the stuff had always been there, only you hadn't been aware of it earlier.

I'd have noticed the cloudbustin' X45. Must have been fifty feet long, tapering from two jets about six feet in diameter to a pointed nose. Wings swept back and surprisingly short. Gleaming silver. Plastic canopy over two seats. Impressive. Reminded me a little of Flash Gordon's spaceship—the comic strip ship, not the wheezy, clanky one in the old movie serials that I always thought must have been steam-powered.

"Forgot something," Hal said. Then: "Runway."

Why the *heck* hadn't I noticed the long strip of concrete or asphalt or something that ended near where the trees began? Silly me.

"Ready, son?" Hal asked.

Hal must have seen the reply in my face, which was: I wasn't. I never would be. Oh, I was sure I could handle a ride in an airplane, all right. But what would follow . . . ? Taking on a whole alien race? Going to the end of the universe? Me? Uh-uh.

Hal planted himself in front of where I stood. "Look, Kyle, you don't think you can do it, but you're wrong. You can. You're young and determined and you're combat-savvy—you kicked major-league butt a couple of days ago, took on GLs with decades more experience and handled 'em. You're ready, kid. Me, I feel sorry for anyone who gets in your way."

If I'd ever had a father, I'd have wanted him to be Hal.

"Thanks," I said, feeling sorry for not saying anything more.

"Okay, let's get going. Couple more things to take care of."

We followed Hal back into the cottage. He went to the bedroom and almost immediately emerged holding a power battery in one hand and a ring on the flat palm of the other.

He grinned. "These look familiar to you?"

"I may have seen something like them before."

"May I see them?" Di asked. I'd almost forgotten that she was in the room.

"Don't see why not. Do you, Kyle?" Hal gave Di the ring and placed the battery on the table.

"Of course not." Unless, I added silently, she was an Oan spy who planned to destroy them.

But she wasn't and she didn't. She slipped the ring onto her middle finger and gazed at it like a bride gazing at her wedding ring. I realized that she might never have worn jewelry before; she might never have even *seen* jewelry before. Then she walked around the battery, looking at it from all sides.

Hal was leaning against a wall, arms crossed, watching her, a small smile on his face.

"All right," Di said finally, sitting. She removed the ring and set it next to the battery.

"Might as well get started," I said.

"I'm wondering," Hal said. "Maybe we should wait till nightfall."

"I don't think time of day will make any difference," I said. "Anyway, day and night probably aren't real here. Who knows if the planet really faces the sun during our 'daytime.'"

"Absolutely right," Hal said, slapping me on the shoulder. And to Di: "Didn't I *say* he's smart?"

"No," Di replied.

"Well, I should've."

"I want to get something," I told Hal and Di.

I went to my own cottage and changed clothes, dropping the chinos and polo shirt I'd been wearing onto the bed, and put on my Green Lantern suit. I've never been big on ceremonial garb—I think military uniforms generally (pun intended) look silly, and I wore shorts and a tie-dye T-shirt to the only formal wedding I've ever attended. (And there went *that* friendship.) I believed that clothes make the man only if the man is a mannequin. But now, I wanted to look the part, maybe to con myself into believing I *was* a space-roving hero/warrior-type guy instead of a wannabe illustrator who lived in a basement.

I returned to Hal's cottage, stuck my head in the door, and said, "All set."

Hal eyed my costume. "Looks sharp."

"Sure."

Hal, Di, and I went to the Cloudbuster. Di stood a little apart, as though acknowledging that she could not be a part of whatever we did next.

I put my hands on her shoulders. "Look, there's

only room in the plane for two. But Hal will just be gone a few minutes and then he'll come back for you."

Hal nodded confirmation.

"You won't be back?" Di asked.

There it was—the question I'd been dreading. "Someday soon," I said, wondering if I were lying and hoping I wasn't.

I kissed her. Everything that was nice about the first kiss was nicer about the second, and that, emphatically, is that.

Hal was climbing up a short ladder on the Cloudbuster, holding the battery. I followed, and lowered myself into the seat behind Hal's. He did something to his control board and the plastic canopy slid into place over our heads. I was prepared to put on one of those nifty pilot's outfits, a rubbery suit with all the flaps and pockets and little metal rings and the big helmet with the little microphone, like the one Tom Cruise wore in *Top Gun*. But apparently Hal thought that what I was already wearing was enough.

"Buckle up," he said. I figured out the safety harness, which was about twice as complicated as the ones on commercial aircraft, and secured myself to the seat.

A wheeze was followed by a rumble and the plane began vibrating. A couple of yards in front of my face, Hal was busy with switches and buttons and levers.

I looked out the plastic canopy. Di was standing on the grass by the runway, watching. I waved to her.

The rumble became a whine and then a roar.

"Here we go," Hal said, his words almost lost in the sound of the jet engines.

We lurched forward.

I saw the trees beyond Hal's head at the end of the runway rushing toward us and then slide down out of sight as my belly slid with them. We were going almost straight up, in a hurry. The sky was rapidly darkening, from robin's-egg blue to azure to indigo. Then, abruptly, the color changed again, to the orange of the Oan atmosphere; until that moment, I hadn't even been sure we were still *on* Oa.

I remembered the multicolored barrier. I looked past Hal's head and saw that we were approaching it. I started to yell a warning, but before I could, we erupted through to the other side. Apparently, the Oans intended the barrier to keep things *out*, not *in*.

We were in space. It was oddly familiar, and comforting in an utterly bleak way, this vast expanse between the stars. Almost like home.

The vibration of the engines stopped. We were in free fall.

Hal pushed the battery over the top of his seat.

"You first," he said. "Better hurry. We don't have much oxygen."

Some problems never go away.

I pressed the ring, which I could feel but not yet see, against the battery. I tingled. A green glow surrounded the middle finger of my right hand and the ring became visible. Welcome back.

"My turn," Hal said. I handed him the battery and watched him charge his ring, mumbling something as he did. I'm pretty sure what he said was:

"In brightest day, in blackest night,
no evil shall escape my sight!
Let those who worship evil's might,
beware my power—Green Lantern's light!"

I cupped a hand to my ear. "What?"

"Just a little verse I say when I'm recharging. Helps focus me."

"You'll have to teach it to me."

"Someday, maybe."

I looked first to the left and then to the right and saw no hostile Green Lanterns, or anything else except the distant stars and, below, the rim of Oa.

"Guess we better go our separate ways," Hal said.

"Yeah."

"Once we're outside the plane, we won't be able to communicate."

" 'In space, no one can hear you scream,' " I quoted.

"That from a movie?"

"Ad for the original *Alien*. Released in 1979."

"Anyway, if you have anything more to say, better say it now."

I thought I had at least a *dozen* things to say, but none came out of me.

"Okay, then. The drill is, once outside the plane you form a bubble, dip into the planet's atmosphere just long enough to fill it with breathing air, and then head out."

Hal did something and the canopy slid back. I surrounded myself with a green bubble and lifted from the plane as Hal did the same. I thought of what I wanted to say then: I wanted to thank him for helping me escape from Oa and for showing me around our little Eden and for giving me at least a taste of what having a father or a big brother would have been like. I wanted to tell him to take care of Di and to tell her that I loved her—because, no kidding, I did—and to wish him well. And a lot more. But in space, no one can hear you scream. Or say thanks.

Hal grinned, saluted me, pivoted, and dived toward Oa. I watched him vanish into the barrier and knew that in a minute he'd be with Di and a minute after that, they'd probably be sipping lemonade.

The Cloudbuster wasn't high enough to be free of Oa's gravity. I watched it fall and vanish, and then I was alone in the vast nothing.

As Hal had ordered, I dipped just below the barrier that surrounded Oa, opened my bubble, closed it, and went through the barrier again.

Where to next?

Gandy's final instruction had been to ride the ring to the transit, and from there to Pluto. The first time I'd tried to obey, I found myself fighting aliens. Maybe the *second* time would be the charm.

"Take me to the transit," I told the ring, and looked around for possible attackers. There were none. Instead of fending off green energy in various forms, I was again moving, watching Oa dwindle as Pluto had dwindled, waiting for the almost imperceptible shift that would indicate a transition to another part of the universe.

Presumably, I'd meet Gandy on cold, nasty Pluto,

which, however far it might be from Earth, was at least in the same solar system. When I got there, I'd probably think I *was* in my own backyard.

I traveled, I guess. For a while, at least.

It seemed to be taking longer to go from Oa to the transit than it had to go from the transit to Oa. But I couldn't be sure. My watch wasn't working any better than it had on Oa, and there was no other way to measure the passage of time: no sun, no stars.

But there *were* stars. I was seeing them outside my greenish bubble, and I shouldn't have been. During my other really, really fast journeys, what was outside the bubble had been either a blur or nothing at all. These were stars, definitely—not in any configuration I'd ever seen, but stars, I'd discovered, looked like stars anywhere in the universe. And that's what these were. Which meant I wasn't moving. Unless the Oans were playing a trick on me.

"Take me to the transit," I told the ring.

Outside the bubble, stars.

I was going nowhere.

Now what?

"The transit does not exist anymore," a familiar voice explained. The voice belonged to Gandy, who was suddenly sharing an enlarged bubble with me. He hadn't changed, which was not surprising because he probably hadn't changed in tens of thousands of years.

"Where the hell have you been?" I asked, and immediately answered myself: "Hiding in the ring."

"Yes."

"Hey, I could have used some help getting off Oa. Why didn't you volunteer? Too busy in there?"

"When the ring lost its charge, I was trapped."

"Then why didn't you show yourself when I *charged* the ring?"

"You were performing satisfactorily."

Coming from him, that was high praise. Hal would have been slapping my back. Of my two ersatz father figures, the human one was definitely nicer.

"Why'd you hide in the first place?"

"If I had not concealed myself, I would have been apprehended as you were and separated from you."

"And the thought of being apart from wonderful me just filled your little heart with sorrow."

"I do not have a heart." Whoa—*that* was news. Little dude was weirder than I'd imagined.

"But you need me," I suggested.

"Yes."

"What happened to the transit?" I was slipping back into the student-teacher mode, begging for information.

"It ceased. This may mean that the Oan plan to remake the universe is far advanced."

"The world . . . the *universe* as we know it, could end any second now? Or at least soon?"

"Soon," he agreed.

"So we charge up San Juan Hill, pistols firing, sabers slashing."

"I do not understand San Juan Hill."

"Spanish-American war, Teddy's Rough Riders . . . Never mind. I meant, we attack."

"We must." His voice was, as always, a flat monotone, but I thought I detected a note of uncertainty in it.
Probably my imagination. But the Oans had had one
war in all their long existence. Part of the reason for the
Green Lantern Corps was to do the dirty work. The
Oans weren't warriors. Yet they *were* used to getting
their way.

Because nobody ever argued with them? I wondered.

"Take me to your leaders," I told Gandy.

His silence indicated that he didn't understand.

"Your posse, the other Oans," I continued. "I want
to meet with them, talk to them."

"Why?"

"To reason with them. To maybe argue them out of
doing what they're doing."

"You would fail."

"How do you know?" *"You arrogant little jerk,"* I
wanted to add, but I didn't.

"I am of them."

"And I'm not, and that may be a help. I can bring a
new perspective. I can think of arguments that you
can't."

"You would fail," he repeated.

"Hey, Gandy, something just occurred to me. Did
you ever lose an argument?"

Long pause. Then: "No."

"I'll bet I know why, too. Because you guys don't
argue. You don't discuss. You probably haven't for
eons. You're out of practice. Whereas we humans . . .
we'll argue over whether or not to argue."

Silence.

"Kind of hard to admit there's something you haven't thought of," I suggested.

More silence.

"Can you take me to your brothers?"

"No. But we can speak with them."

"That'll do."

"I will need to return to the inside of your ring," Gandy said, and then he wasn't there anymore.

Then, five seconds later, he was. "They will arrive in the form of projections," he said.

"Like holograms?"

"Yes. But not using concentrated light. The principle—"

"If you're gonna give me a scientific explanation, don't bother. I wouldn't understand it anyway."

"That is true."

"Where's this meeting going to take place?"

"Here."

I looked around at the green-tinted stars and yawning nothingness and my mind began to whimper and crawl inside itself. The environment was just too damn alien and hostile to what millions of years of evolution had made me. To fully function, to *think*—which wasn't my strong point to begin with—I wanted air and soil.

"Can we do it on a planet?" I asked.

"You wish to return to Oa."

I mulled for a moment and said, "No, not Oa." If I saw Di again, I might not be able to leave her, and if I were close to her—on the same world, say—I'd probably weaken and see her. So no Oa.

"There is an Earth-type planet nearby," Gandy said.

"How 'nearby'? No, don't tell me. Just get us there."

Gandy vanished into my ring again, reappeared, and then there was only a blur outside the bubble. We were moving.

We must have approached another wormhole and entered it because I felt the telltale shift, and then I saw stars outside the bubble. We were elsewhere. But we still had some distance to go. One star was a bit brighter than the rest; it reminded me of how the sun had looked from Pluto. I'm guessing that the wormholes aren't formed near the center of a star system—maybe they can't be.

Gandy said something in a language I didn't understand—Oan?—and the ring responded by moving us. There was the interval of blankness I'd experienced on the trip from Earth to Pluto, and after some time had passed—I have no idea how much—I felt the tug of gravity pulling me to one side of the bubble. Through the green membrane, I saw that we were approaching a bright, blue-white-green sphere: a planet.

"What now?" I asked Gandy.

"Enter as you would enter the atmosphere of the Earth."

Easy enough. I certainly knew *that* procedure.

10

A few minutes later, I dissolved the bubble and placed my feet on the soil of a world—yet *another* world. Kyle Rayner, slacker, loser, C-minus student, who had never even been as far as Chicago and had never planned to be, was stepping onto the *third* alien planet he'd visited within the month.

We were standing on a flat plain near a crater filled with boiling liquid that reminded me of pictures of Old Faithful in Yellowstone Park. There was not much in the way of vegetation, just what looked like moss on the occasional flat, blackish rock that dotted the tan soil. In the distance, I could see jagged mountains. The sky was blue and streaked with thin clouds. Not Earth, this new place, but definitely Earth-like. I sucked in as much air as my lungs would hold. It had a thin, ozoney smell, but it was quite breathable.

"Does this world have a name?" I asked Gandy.

"No."

"Tell me about it."

"It is as your Earth was three hundred and sixty million years ago. There exist a few vertebrates that dwell primarily in water but no mammals. Vegetation is also primitive, though evolving rapidly. Do you wish to know more?"

"That'll do for now."

I walked around the boiling crater, feeling the dirt shift beneath my boots, hearing it crunch, smelling sulfurous fumes.

So this was Earth, minus 360 million years. Not exactly hospitable, but a man could make a life here, given time and a few resources. I let myself imagine what it would be like to remain where I was, for eons, and watch the planet change, watch those watery critters evolve into fish and dinosaurs and birds and mammals and eventually men. Cities would rise and crumble. Voices would be raised in song and shrieks. Children would be born, age, die. Men and women would love and laugh and suffer and probably forget where they came from, who they were, and worry about who they weren't and what they could be.

But not unless I could convince the Oans to abandon their plans.

I returned to Gandy.

"Where are they?"

"Do you understand that 'they,' by which I presume you mean my brothers, will not be physically present?"

"So you said. Holograms, right?"

"Projections."

"Project away, then."

"The projections will occur shortly."

That was okay by me. I was perfectly willing to explore Earth-minus-360-mil. Let the Red Nightshirts be as fashionably late as they wanted. Let 'em arrive next week, for all I cared.

Unless their late arrival meant they were blocking wormholes, or whatever they were doing to permanently cancel the future.

"They are present," Gandy said as the air around him briefly shimmered, turned red and blue, and finally congealed into a couple of dozen Gandy duplicates. It was like Captain Kirk beaming down accompanied by a whole company of ensigns, all disguised as funny-looking short people.

"Hi, guys," I said. "Welcome to my world."

Well, why not? It was as much my world as anyone's. I'd have to remember to write my name in the soil before I left. *Kyle's World*. Nice.

"What do you wish from us?" This from the Oan to Gandy's immediate left. I expected the voice to be tinny, like sound from a cheap speaker, but it was as normal as Gandy's—flat, monotonic. As normal as Oan voices get, I figured. Whatever kind of "projector" they were using sent both images and sound, from billions of light-years away. I'd forgotten how astonishing their technology was.

I hadn't planned what I was going to say, which was typical of me. For a moment, I felt as I had when I'd stood on the edge of the swimming pool, all my gawkiness exposed to Di's scrutiny. I mentally reviewed my options and immediately discarded one: coming on strong. There was nothing I could possibly threaten them with. Okay, second option: sweet reason.

"Look, you guys," I began. "Let me be sure I understand what's going on. What you plan to do is refashion the universe, right?"

"Perfect it," an Oan said.

"Right, perfect it. But in so doing—correct me if I'm wrong—you'll wipe out most of the universe's life, like ninety percent of it."

I waited for a reply and when none came, I asked, "Well?"

"Ninety-nine-point-nine nine nine nine nine nine percent," another Oan said.

"Including every living thing on Earth but some pond scum."

"Nothing on Earth will survive."

I looked at Gandy. "They have revised their plans," he said.

Oh well. I was never that fond of pond scum anyway. On the other hand . . . if the pond scum went, everything else would go with it.

"Okay," I continued, "let's discuss this. Let me ask you—and I'm asking this with the utmost respect— why you think you have a right to do that?"

"We were here first."

"Beg your pardon?"

"Our species evolved intelligence long before any other. On Earth, you have a legal concept called 'homesteader's rights.' It means that whoever occupies land first has dominion over it. Thus it is with us. We occupied the universe before anyone else. Therefore, it is ours to use as we wish."

Well, that took all the prizes on the shelf for arrogance, and it was probably false and illogical. But I couldn't say why. I'm a bad arguer and a worse debater—in other words, not the guy you'd want to do what I was doing, which was trying to dissuade immensely powerful beings from obliterating virtually every living thing.

Where was Perry Mason when we needed him?

I wanted to slink away and say to hell with it. Maybe spend the last few minutes or hours or days left on Oa, getting to know Di. But I couldn't, or wouldn't, at least not until I'd tried everything I could think of.

"Okay," I told the assembled universe-wreckers, "let's go at this from another angle. *Why?* Why do you want to commit wholesale slaughter. Is life so bad?"

"Yes," an Oan on the far right replied.

Silence.

"Care to elaborate?" I asked after a while.

"Life causes suffering and suffering is messy."

Messy?

"That offends you?"

"It offends us profoundly."

"Go on," I prompted.

"Life involves change and makes the achievement of perfection impossible."

"Why?" I was actually getting interested. Maybe *they'd* convince *me*.

"If perfection is achieved and life exists, the life will change the perfection and cause it to be imperfect."

Hard to argue with that, especially when the would-be arguer had only the faintest idea of what it meant. One thing I was sure of—it couldn't possibly be as stupid as it sounded. I mean, these were the wise-and-mighty *Oans*!

"We have Earth to thank for this truth," one of them said.

"How so?"

"We learned of art from observing your civilizations, and from art we learned of perfection. Your painters and sculptors created the human body as it should be, shorn of all blemish and asymmetry, and devised means of preserving their work for centuries."

There *had* to be an answer. Didn't there?

"You're talking about painting and sculpture," I said, beginning to feel desperate. "They don't move. What about art forms that *do* move. Drama. Movies. Hell, even music."

"They are similarly preserved, albeit only recently. But that is of no consequence. They are inferior and so beneath our consideration."

"Meaning you don't understand them."

Apparently, that didn't even merit a reply.

"So you guys are going to create this perfect universe and . . . what then? Just sit around and admire it?"

"We will be among the life-forms that will perish."

I was certain that I hadn't heard him correctly. "Say again?"

"We will not survive the perfecting."

"You're going to kill yourselves? All of you?"

"No. We will simply have never existed."

"After the . . . *perfecting*—no more Oans?"

"Yes."

I'd thought of them as arrogant, but I'd been wrong. I didn't have a word for what they were, not at first. I'd have said they were insane, but insanity suddenly seemed to have no meaning. Then I realized that I *did* have a word for what they were: tired. They were millions of years old and they'd lost the knack of dying. They were tired and they were bored and they couldn't admit it, the stupid bastards. So they created this idiotic notion of universe-as-art to allow themselves to pass from existence without the messy business of actually doing themselves in. That was their word: "messy."

But I didn't need Perry Mason. I needed some kind of cosmic psychotherapist, Freud times Jung times a million.

I didn't even have Perry. I had only me. Humanity's last chance.

With little hope of convincing them, I said, "Look, can't you eliminate this messiness some other way? Couldn't you just *tweak* instead of *obliterate?*"

"It is not possible," an Oan replied.

"Have you *tried?*"

No answer, which I was pretty sure meant that *no*, they had not tried, and *no*, they weren't about to.

Their little old—and I do mean *old*—minds were made up.

Clearly, I knew, I should switch tactics. But switch to what? To buy myself a few moments while I groped in my head for another way to go, I asked, "How far along on this project are you guys?"

The Oan said something I won't even try to reproduce phonetically; if I did, I'd have a word with about a hundred consonants and no vowels.

Raising my eyebrows, I looked at Gandy.

"He spoke in Original Oan," Gandy explained, and then translated: " 'Time is an arbitrary mental construction that has no absolute meaning.' "

"Hell, *everybody* knows that," I said. "But humor the dumb human. Tell me arbitrarily, in stupid Earth terms, how long before the big kablooey. Talk to me about years, months, minutes, nanoseconds, whatever's right."

I think it took them a few seconds to comprehend "kablooey." Finally, one of them said, "It will occur in four Earth days."

"Till the end? Just four days? Ninety-six hours?"

"Yes," one of the little monsters deigned to reply.

"We have to discuss this further," I said, hoping I didn't sound as desperate as I felt. "Don't you realize that all life is sacred?"

Again, a string of unintelligible Oan. Were they being jerks deliberately? Having a bit of fun with the doofus from the cosmic sticks?

Gandy translated: " 'Life is as accidental as everything else in this arbitrary . . .' " Gandy hesitated; apparently even a mighty Oan intellect could have occasional difficulty going from one language to another. " '. . . happenstance universe,' " Gandy concluded, probably not too accurately.

"Maybe. But that doesn't mean it isn't important."

"Yes it does," a smug little Oan said.

"Once it exists, it has meaning," I insisted.

Unintelligible Oan, Gandy-translated as: " 'The only meaning life has is the meaning it assigns itself.' "

My turn to be silent.

Suddenly, the Oans weren't there anymore, except for Gandy: "That went well," I told him.

"You are not correct."

"I was being sarcastic."

"You were indulging in humor."

"Your massive Oan intellect has arrived at the truth. Congratulations."

"You are being sarcastic."

"Absolutely. I assume your pals are gone? Like, they're not gonna reappear and admit that I'm right?"

"They have returned to their tasks."

I needed to get away from him. He'd proven that he was on my side—*our* side, the side of life—but he was one of *them*, and I couldn't stand the sight of him.

"Stay here, please," I told him, and wandered away.

I went past the seething crater and onto a rock-speckled prairie. Decision time. A while ago, I'd shot off Oa, determined to be, let's face it, the greatest hero ever known. Not enough for me, the saving of mere fair maidens, or tribes, or cities, or even whole planets—no: I'd save the whole, glorious, star-spangled *universe*! Sure I would. Instead, I'd allowed myself to be stymied by a bunch of short blue snots who hadn't even bothered to debate me, really. I'd wilted and they'd left without even a polite farewell, the rude bastards.

So now what? It seemed to me that my choices came down to two: return to Earth and spend my last hours among my own kind, or return to Oa and perish in the company of the two people I felt closest to.

Except I wouldn't perish. I would simply *never have been*. Somehow, I didn't find that comforting.

But back to my choices. On Earth, I had no family except for the California cousin, and I couldn't remember what he looked like. He was probably married by now, with kids, and would not welcome some half-forgotten relative raving about The End of It All. Who else? Batman? Didn't really know him, didn't like him, couldn't find him anyway. That left Mr. Gloinger, a landlord whose first name I'd never bothered to learn—nothing to be proud of there—and who would not enjoy hearing about The End of It All any more than my cousin would.

I turned and trotted back to where Gandy was standing; he still hadn't moved.

"I'm going to Oa," I said.

"You can thwart the Oan design from there." His inflection didn't rise—Oans never sounded like they were puzzled—and so I needed a few moments to understand that he had asked me a question.

I started to answer, but stopped before I'd spoken the first word, struck by the implications of what I'd just heard. Which were: *Gandy wanted his brethren stopped, and he needed me to do it.*

Of course, it should have been obvious all along, but I hadn't recognized Gandy's need for me until that moment. I mean, he was an Oan with a mighty intellect who'd lived thousands of years and mastered superscience and so on and so forth and so forth . . . but he needed *me,* a kid from a race in its early infancy who wasn't even a prime specimen of his kind. He was *depending* on *me.*

I asked him why.

"Your genes command survival, and such a command wakens in you traits that lie dormant."

"So I'm . . . I don't know . . . stronger and smarter than usual? When these dormant traits are awakened?"

"You express the concept crudely. But you are essentially correct."

"You don't have this survival thing?"

"We lost it when we gained immortality."

Well, that figured.

"Any other reason?" I asked.

"It is difficult for me to reason when I am separated from my family."

He'd never used the word "family" before.

I had a final question. "Why are you on the side of survival?"

Gandy took a while to reply. What he said was, essentially, that when the Oans began their lives as immortals, they had virtually identical bodies and minds. For thousands of years they monitored themselves to remain that way. But they got lazy and overconfident and while they weren't looking, some of them changed. If they were human, you'd guess genetic drift was to blame, but I'm not sure Oans even *have* genes, so maybe the changes were caused by something else. In any event, Gandy was one of the ones altered, and he found himself disagreeing with his brethren, especially about the desirability of things forever staying the same. He concluded, "It is the nature of reality to change, and because that is so, change must be accepted as the highest good." The other Oans disagreed.

During my brief foray into self-education, I'd read that a philosopher or two came to the same conclusion as Gandy. I mentioned this to him and then I asked, "Aren't you lonely? Cut off from the rest of the Oans?"

"We do not experience loneliness."

"Good for you."

I, on the other hand, *was* experiencing loneliness, which puzzled me. I mean, on Earth I was the quintessential loner, sequestered in my subterranean cave with no family, close friends, or significant other. But, I guess, I was always aware of the presence of people—in the building, just outside my window, everywhere—and of the possibility that I'd someday manage to hook up with someone who'd rock my world, or at least be my pal. I'd always thought that sooner or later I'd work through my grouchy recluse phase and become the life of somebody's party.

Wasn't gonna happen. In just ninety-six hours—more like ninety-five now—the universe would be sterile, and I would never have been even a gleam in my daddy's eye.

Something acrid filled my throat, and I wanted to touch Diana's hand.

"We'd better get going," I told Gandy. "To Oa."

I was lying to Gandy by letting him believe that I had a plan to use Oa against his fellows, of course. The honorable thing to do would be to tell him why I wanted to trek to his home planet. But if I did, he might not want to accompany me, and I was afraid that I might need him.

The drill was getting to be pretty familiar. Use the ring's power to rise, will a green bubble around us, then head for the nearest wormhole.

"I shall enter the ring," Gandy said.

"Hold on a second."

I allowed myself a minute to gaze all around us. Though the stars weren't in any formation I recognized, they looked like stars seen from the surface of Earth. They were beautiful. But would they be beautiful after all living beings ceased? No. Because who would see them? Suddenly I realized that beauty really *was* in the eye of the beholder. Where else?

"Go," I told Gandy, and he vanished into the ring, and we went through a rift in space to another part of the galaxy, and then we sped toward Oa.

11

And there it was, just as I'd first seen it, a glowing round kaleidoscope of brilliant color. I willed the ring to stop and suddenly I wasn't moving anymore. I hovered above the barrier at about the place where Hal and I had exited the jet, where I had waved good-bye to him for, I thought, the last time.

Okay, now what?

The next part of the program was, I conjure up a daring, ingenious, decisive plan to stop the Oans. Or at least an adequate one. *I should mull*, I thought. *I should be giving this problem some really serious mulling.* So I mulled. And had no success whatsoever.

I was an American male, barely out of adolescence, and the only thing I knew about dealing with enemies—*real* enemies, as opposed to the various jerks I'd met—was what I'd learned from movies and television. And what was that? Hit something! Attack. Assault. I guess I'd been assuming I'd deal with this situation as I'd dealt with the aliens: kick butt. Which was profoundly stupid. Now that I was in the moment, now that I had to *do* something, I was stymied. Scenes from John Wayne and Clint Eastwood flicks darted across my consciousness, scenes of problems being solved with a fist or a gun. But I had nobody to punch, nothing to shoot. My foes refused to present themselves, and instead of wielding weapons, they were manipulating elements of the universe that were almost intangible.

How do you strike something that's an abstract mathematical entity represented by a digit and thirty-six zeros?

The little guy hiding in my ring couldn't do it, and not only was he a lot more intelligent than any human who ever lived, he had about a million years of evolution on me.

Why did he think I could do what he couldn't?

Why did *I*?

When in doubt, move. I circled the planet, and circled it again, hoping I'd see something in the swirl of color I was passing over that would give me an idea. I didn't.

Finally, I returned to the point I'd started from and admitted defeat. I had no plan; no hope of creating a plan. I was finished. I had failed, and countless creatures would perish because of it. Sure, I hadn't asked for the task, wasn't qualified for it, couldn't possibly be expected to do it.

None of that was a comfort.

So I had three days before I would cease to have

ever been, mine to use as I chose. In an odd way, I felt privileged. Not many people, if any at all, know the exact time of their end and that it won't hurt. In fact, I realized, I wouldn't die, not really, because I would never have lived.

I did not doubt, for a single second, what I'd do next.

Somewhere on the other side of the bright barrier surrounding Oa were Hal Jordan and Diana Prince. I'd go to them and tell them lies.

I'd tell them I'd beaten the Oans, or that they'd changed their collective mind, and assure my friends that all was well. We'd begin living a three-day life-time together. I'd let them think they had decades to bask under the warm sun, swimming and drinking lemonade and gorging on nonfattening feasts. I'd de-vote my energies to making them happy. I'd be funny and accommodating and willing to please.

I moved toward the barrier, flattened myself and my bubble, and slid along its perimeter, waiting for it to suck me through into the planet's atmosphere.

Nothing happened. I stayed on the barrier's sur-face.

What the hell!

Oa was smaller than Earth, but still big enough to qualify as a full-grown planet, and as far as I knew the barrier totally surrounded it. I had a lot of surface to explore if I decided to keep looking for a place where I'd be sucked in.

I could be direct and use the ring, maybe form a huge drill and bore through the barrier, but I'd be playing with a lot of unknowns. I had no idea how the barrier would react if force were used against it. Explosions or worse didn't seem to be out of the question.

"*Gandy!*" I yelled, and suddenly I had company in the bubble. I explained the problem to the Oan and waited for him to supply a solution.

"I do not know," he said.

"Don't know what? Why we can't get past the barrier or what would happen if I used force?"

"Both."

"Any suggestions?"

Silence. Gandy may have been an abnormal Oan, but he shared with the rest of them a reluctance to admit ignorance about anything. Their attitude seemed to be, *If I keep quiet, maybe the question will go away. . . .*

I was debating with myself whether to plead with Gandy or threaten him or devise some other method of making him suggest a plan when suddenly I glanced at the barrier, let my gaze sweep past it to the stars, and then stopped and looked at it again.

It was no longer swirling with color. It had become a dull gray.

"Use force," Gandy said.

I visualized a hammer as big as a mountain and a chisel the size of the Empire State Building, placed the chisel against the barrier, and had the hammer whack it. The barrier cracked and a baseball diamond–sized chunk went spinning into space.

We sped to the hole and looked at Oa. I think I

made a noise then, something between a gasp and a scream.

The planet was shrinking. As I watched, the horizon dropped and became curved and then became an arc and then a sphere completely surrounded by the orange sky, the sphere growing smaller and smaller until another sphere appeared around it—the yellow globe at Oa's center that Gandy and I had entered just before we'd left Oa.

Hal and Di were somewhere down there. What was happening to them? Were they, too, diminishing? Or had they already suffered something final?

I forgot about Gandy, forgot about everything except my need to save them.

I shed the bubble and willed the ring to speed me downward, dimly aware that when I'd entered the Oan atmosphere earlier, the ring hadn't functioned, and not caring because now it *was* functioning and I was hurtling through air that was shrieking around me.

The planet continued shrinking until it seemed to be swallowed by the yellow globe, and then there was only the globe, tiny, far away, a minute yellow speck in a vast sea of orange. I lit on the globe and, as before, slipped into it.

It was empty.

Only dimly aware of what I was doing, I willed the ring to carry me in the direction from which I'd come. I passed through the globe without effort and continued away from it, moving toward the hole I'd made in the barrier, buffeted by hurricane-force winds rushing through the hole into space. I put a bubble around myself, trapping some of the air inside, and then the winds didn't buffet me anymore.

I had no idea how long it had been since I'd started chasing the vanishing planet, nor even any clear idea of how long it had been since I'd left Earth. Years? Days? Time was becoming elusive and almost meaningless.

The hole in the barrier was enlarging and other holes were appearing. The entire thing was cracking, fragmenting, the pieces drifting into space, pushed by what was left of the Oan atmosphere.

Gandy was where I'd left him. Maybe he could explain what I'd witnessed, but at that moment I didn't care.

I felt a great weariness. I didn't just want to sleep—I wanted not to be. That was the Oan plan for me, and for everyone else, and I thought, *Okay, Nightshirts, bring it on.*

I went away. Not physically. My body stayed where it was, floating in the void, limp as a dishrag, eyes staring at stars, but my mind was like a slate that had been wiped clean. I'd experienced a lot since leaving Earth, and I didn't understand most of it, partly because I'm an uneducated doof and partly, I think, because at this point in our evolution, there are things we humans *simply can't comprehend*. We lack the proper mental and physical equipment. But despite my inadequacies, I'd managed to assimilate most of what I'd gone through, maybe because I was too dumb *not* to.

But I'd just watched a planet, a whole planet, disappear. That was too much—more horrifying than the thought of the mass extinction the Oans were planning, because it wasn't an abstraction: I'd *seen* it. So I went away.

I don't know how long I stayed away—time was becoming even more meaningless, and I couldn't be sure time existed in whatever part of the galaxy we were inhabiting. But I did come back, and immediately wished I hadn't, because the slate was no longer blank—it was filled with huge, ugly blotches of failure. I couldn't save the universe, and I couldn't save Di and Hal, and I was good for absolutely nothing.

Gandy hadn't moved; if there were Nobel prizes for patience, he'd be a winner.

I enlarged my bubble to enclose us both and said, "There's no point in talking."

"Your plans are thwarted."

"Gandy, I didn't *have* plans. I just wanted to see Di again. I wanted to die . . . to *stop ever having been* among friends."

"That is what befell Oa."

So that was it. Despite the bleak place I was in, I found myself getting interested.

"Everything—every*body*—on it also stopped being, I guess."

Silence. I knew what that meant.

"You don't know, do you?" I asked.

More silence.

"Di and Hal might have escaped," I said.

Well, why not? Hal had the ring and the battery

and he could have easily conjured up another jet. He and Di might have somehow learned what was about to happen and taken off before Oa winked out of existence. Or Hal might have gotten sick of being nothing more than a lump in paradise and fled earlier. Fled with Di; he wouldn't have left her behind. I couldn't remember if he and I had discussed the Oans' plans, but we *might* have.

The slate was still covered with blotches of failure, but I was ignoring them. Or, to extend the metaphor and make it even dumber, covering them with a gloss of hope.

"Why didn't the yellow globe stop existing?" I jerked a thumb toward where I thought the globe was, though it was too far away for us to see it.

"It is serving as a transmitter," Gandy said. Meaning, I surmised, that it was built to be something else and later adapted.

"A transmitter of what?"

We have a translation problem again here. I knew what Gandy meant—I understood the concept, anyway—but I don't know how because I sure as hell didn't understand his *words*. I'm not sure if he spoke English or Oan or both. But I did somehow grasp his meaning—something like: *The waves of dark energy generated by the Oan's big computer were sent to the yellow globe and the globe, in turn, sent them to every infinitesimally tiny subatomic particle in this part of the galaxy and so began the process of altering reality.*

I wouldn't blame anyone who was unable to make any sense at all of that. I'm not sure I did myself, then or now. But that didn't stop me from asking, "If we destroy the globe we stop the . . . whatever it is—*reality altering*?"

Gandy replied that destruction of the globe would, at best, inconvenience the Oans; there were other receiver-transmitters scattered throughout the universe, some of them in the hearts of stars, all aiming dark energy at the empty hearts of atoms.

"Like cell phone relays?"

"The energy is not broadcast," Gandy said. "It is linked with the energy in the computer."

I wasn't going to even *try* understanding that. "But these things, like the globe—they're necessary to the Oans' plans?"

"Yes."

"How many of them are there?"

"Twelve million."

Okay, even if they weren't buried in atomic furnaces, I'd never find them all in time.

"I can't think floating out here like smoke," I shouted, suddenly furious at Gandy for no apparent reason.

"You have the ring," he reminded me.

I nodded, and willed the ring to create a version of my apartment in Mr. Gloinger's basement on Earth. The ring must have dug around in my memory, and did a pretty good job of reconstruction, if I ignored the fact that everything was greenish.

I flopped down on the futon, but I couldn't stay there. I didn't understand gravity well enough for the ring to create it, and we *were* in space. I allowed myself to waft gently around the room as Gandy and I continued our conversation.

"Is there any way we can get to the computer, Gandy? I mean, do you know where it is?"

"At the Creation Point."

"Which is where?"

"Where our reality is becoming."

"You're not enlightening me. Pretend I'm just a doof from Earth and say it very simply."

"Our universe is expanding into what we think of as nothingness. At the edge of the expansion is the Creation Point."

"Because our universe is creating itself as it expands?"

"Yes."

"Back to my original question . . . can we get there?"

"I do not know."

"Are there any wormholes that'd put us in the vicinity?"

"No."

"How about instructing the ring to go real fast?"

"We could not exceed the speed of light."

"Of course not," I said, and hoped I sounded like I knew what I was talking about. "But couldn't we get *close* to light speed?"

"Yes."

"Then, going as fast as we can, how long does it take us to reach the Creation Point?"

"Eleven million years."

Stymied again. Eleven million years was a bit longer than we had.

"Okay," I said after a while, "do *you* have any bright ideas?"

"No."

I stared at the greenish ceiling and tried to recall what I did when I cogitated on Earth. Then I remembered: On Earth, I *never* cogitated. Silly me. But in fairness to myself, there had never been any real need to cogitate longer than was needed to decide on a pizza topping.

"Tell me about the yellow globe," I said, after I'd opted against cogitation.

"What do you want to know about it." I was getting used to Gandy's monotone; I recognized instantly that he'd asked a question.

"Well, when we escaped, we went through the globe. Exactly what happened then?"

"I willed us to be away from the planet."

"Willed? Like I will when I use the ring?"

"It is a different process. The globe is a tachyon generator."

Well, of course. How dopey of me not to recognize a tachyon generator when I saw one.

"I don't mean to be critical, Gandy . . . but couldn't you have sent us a *lot* farther? Like a parsec or two?"

"Yes."

Meaning he could have but he didn't because he didn't think of it. So I got to fight a lot of aliens.

Then I had an idea. "How far could the globe send us?"

"Do you want the distance in light years, parsecs, miles—"

"Never mind. Just tell me—could it get us to the Creation Point?"

Silence. He didn't know?

"I hate to be insistent—," I began.

"We could integrate our matter with the transmission beam and proceed to its origin."

I thought about that for a second and said, "We could hop onto this beam and ride it back to where it came from?"

"Yes. We could do so unless my brothers have mastered synchronicity."

"And if they have?"

"We could not."

"There has to be a risk," I said, hoping he'd contradict me.

But he didn't. Instead he said, "Yes."

"Care to elaborate?"

"We could unincorporate."

I wasn't sure what that meant, but it didn't sound good.

"But maybe not?" I asked.

"Yes."

"We'd achieve this . . . how?"

"Achieve what?"

"Hopping onto the beam."

"We would proceed to the center of the globe—"

Okay, been there.

"—and I could will us onto the beam," he concluded.

"We wouldn't have problems going in reverse? I mean, it wouldn't be like swimming upstream?"

"Such terms are without meaning in both the microcosm and the macrocosm."

"Just in the *middle*-cosm, huh?"

"Yes."

Apparently, he knew what I meant. Good, because *I* sure didn't.

"Well," I said, "I guess we should just shoot on down to the globe and be on our way."

"What will you do if you arrive at the Creation Point?" Gandy asked monotonously.

"Destroy the computer."

"How?"

Well, now *there* was a good question. A *fine* question.

"Aim the ring and . . . shoot great big stuff," I said after a while.

Silence. This time, I was afraid, the lack of response didn't mean that Gandy didn't have a reply; it meant that what I'd said was idiotic.

"Won't work, huh?" I asked.

"Yes." Meaning it wouldn't.

Then what would? I needed to be clever, *really* clever and smart and daring and determined and maybe a few other things. The problem was, I wasn't. Gandy had the brainpower, but with all due respect, he seemed to lack almost everything else.

Somewhere, a gigantic cosmic clock was ticking.

I was certain I was too damn dumb to solve what needed solving, but I was equally certain that if I didn't, nobody would. And everything would be different and . . . less. No life, no change. No me, no

Gandy, no Hal or Di—assuming they were still alive—no human race, no alien beings, nothing but eternal perfection with nobody to appreciate it.

So I had to try. I remembered what I'd read about logic.

Syllogisms: *If A is to B as B is to C then C is to A as A is to B. . . .*

Law of the excluded center: *A thing cannot be both A and B. . . .*

Useless.

What else? Go back to the origin of the problem and seek a solution there? No good. The origin of this problem was buried far, far back in antiquity, in the collective childhood of the Oans.

But: While that was true, I mused, maybe I should narrow my focus and look at how I got involved—the origin of *my* problem. This whole trek began when the Justice League satellite vanished, a mystery I still hadn't solved. Solved? Hell, I hadn't even *thought* about it much since I'd left my own solar system.

I went to sleep about then. Well, why not? I really hadn't slept since I'd left Hal and Di—unless you count the brief blackout I'd experienced after I'd watched Oa do its vanishing act—and sleeping in free fall made sleeping on a water bed seem like sleeping on rocks.

I drifted through dreamland and saw the Oans' big computer: At first it looked like a big—and I mean *big*—PC, then it morphed into a big iMac, and then it became one of those faceless gray cabinets with flat spools—mainframes, I think they're called—that I've seen pictures of. The mainframe in turn morphed into an old-fashioned alarm clock, the kind with two dome-shaped bells jutting from the top. The bells were ringing, and somehow I knew they were ringing so loudly that they could be heard in every corner of the universe by every living being. And then I woke up and said: "It's about time."

Gandy hadn't moved.

I floated off the futon, stretched, and said, "This whole thing's about time."

Gandy was silent. Big surprise.

"I mean, maybe my brain's been packed in dry ice. Or maybe I'm even dumber than I gave myself credit for not to have gotten it before now. Way, way back you told me that you Oans created the Justice League and all the rest of the superguys and gals by altering an earlier reality. That *has* to mean that you can travel in time."

"Certainly," Gandy said.

His attitude seemed to imply that anyone who was *anyone* did a bit of time-hopping now and then. Did I mention that the Oan smugness was annoying? But maybe I'd been unfair to Gandy; maybe he wasn't smug, but rather just used to being instantly understood and to sharing the same information pool with everyone he knew. People who've been married for three or four decades often finish their partners' sentences; imagine living with the same people for *tens of thousands* of years.

"I apologize."

"For what do you apologize?"

"Never mind."

I'd floated to a wall. I pushed myself away and wafted to the futon and said, "Okay, I'm gonna need a lot more on the hows and whys of time travel, but for now correct me if I'm wrong: The Justice League satellite didn't disappear, it went elsewhere—" I stopped, realizing that my vocabulary wasn't sufficient. I'd have to coin a word, and I did: "—went else*when*. Some other year. Or century."

"Yes."

I waited for him to elaborate, which, I should have known, was futile.

"You're not making this easy," I said, and reminded myself that he wasn't being deliberately difficult. "For openers, do you know where . . . *when* the Justice League is?"

"I do not know how to express in language the exact year."

"Okay, give me a ballpark. Eighteenth century? Fifteenth? They hanging with Columbus? Earlier?"

"They exist in what in English you refer to as the 'Precambrian' Era.' "

"Pre . . . *cambrian*? Like, the era that *ended* almost six hundred million years ago?"

"Five hundred and seventy million."

"Oh."

My turn to be silent. I'd need to stretch a very long way to reach back 570 million years.

"Are they alive?" I asked finally.

"I do not know."

"Is there any reason they *shouldn't* be? I mean, would the trip have killed them?"

"I do not know."

"Your best guess," I prompted.

"The journey would not have killed them."

"Has anyone ever survived a trip like that?"

"We Oans have."

"Anyone human? Any Homo sapiens?"

"No."

I tried to console myself with the thought, *Well, they are super. If anyone can survive, they can.* Then I got irritated with myself: *Why worry about the Justice League? They're either dead or they aren't. And if they aren't, they will be, along with everyone else, unless I can stop the Oans.*

"Okay, I assume your brethren sent the League back—" I stopped, not sure where I wanted the sentence to end.

"They did not," Gandy said.

"They *didn't*? Then who?"

"I did."

I struggled with that for a minute. "You mean . . . I don't know . . . symbolically or something. Like, you're an Oan and the Oans did it? Or something?"

"I personally transported them to the Precambrian Era."

For a second I felt an adrenaline surge and I wanted to do him some serious harm. Instead, I blurted, "Why the *hell*?"

I wanted a nice, simple, one-line answer, like, *"Because it was Thursday,"* or *"Because it was there,"* and I didn't even care if it made sense. I didn't get it. Gandy told me that, like so many things I'd encountered since leaving Earth, his motives would be hard to describe in English and even harder to explain. But I listened to him, as attentively as I've ever listened to anyone, and a lot *more* attentively than I'd ever listened in a classroom. When he finished talking, I thought I had the gist of his meaning, but I wasn't sure. At that point, I wasn't sure of anything.

Here is what I *think* Gandy said:

The creation of the conditions that allowed superbeings to arise on Earth had been an experiment, and part of what inspired the Oans to attempt their grand, life-destroying art project. When the Oans did embark on their project, those conditions already existed in and around the planet, so the Oans didn't have to meddle with that particular piece of the universe; it was already meddled with. By then, Gandy was determined to stop his brethren, so he used the Oan time-travel technology to send the Justice League back to the dim, distant past. This slightly altered the aforementioned conditions, and slowed the progress of the project.

That's it, stripped of terminology nobody but an Oan could understand, and reduced to extremely simple, Kyle Rayner–sized terms.

"They—the other Oans—got wind of what you were up to and came after you," I said when Gandy had finished. "How *did* they find out what you were doing?"

"They did not have to find out. When I was not with them, they thought as they would have thought in my circumstance, and knew what I was thinking."

A mouthful—easily the longest single burst of speech I'd ever heard come from Gandy. But not exactly elegantly phrased. Still, I understood him.

"They followed you to Earth?"

"They went to Earth knowing I would be there."

"I stand corrected. Okay, so you arrived on Earth with your brothers hot on your trail and . . . what? Picked me out at random?"

"I did not exactly choose you at random. Before I spoke to you I scanned your energy patterns and determined that they were not inappropriate."

Not inappropriate energy patterns. Wow. Guess I'm pretty special! I wonder if girls notice "not inappropriate" energy patterns.

"Something else bothers me. That weird stuff behind Omfrey's—the transparent walls . . . the other stuff . . . snow and horse-drawn carriages and people in funny clothes—what was *that* about?"

"It was a time stasis," Gandy said, exactly as he'd said it in the alley behind Omfrey's.

"In English?" I prompted.

"I did speak English," Gandy countered, being infuriatingly literal.

"Paraphrase?"

"There was a brief dissolution of the gap between what you might term 'eras' when we arrived on Earth."

"You came from the future? You traveled backward in time?"

"If one is at the Creation Point, all travel is backward."

To my amazement, I understood him, though I'm not sure I could explain what he'd just told me.

I had a sudden thought and asked, "Did we travel forward in time to get where we are here and now?"

"Yes."

Ask a silly question . . . But I wanted elaboration, so I asked another silly question—silly-*sounding*, anyway: "At this moment, I'm not existing in the early part of the twenty-first century, right?"

"Yes."

"When we passed through the first wormhole—we traveled in time as well as in space, right? How far into the future *am* I?"

"In Earth reckoning, forty million and twenty-three years."

"Which certainly makes me eligible for social security."

Okay, dumb wisecrack, but how does a man react upon learning he's forty million and twenty-three years old? For me, it was either crack wise or scream. I knew if I allowed myself to really understand what I'd heard, to really believe it in my bones, I'd be lost in a vast, endless, and pretty damn melancholy reverie.

"So what are we stewing about?" I asked before that could happen. "I mean, worrying about something that'll happen so far into the future—what's the point? Is there even an Earth *left*? And if there is, I'll bet nobody *I* know is walking around on it."

"If my brothers succeed, there will never have been life on Earth."

Oh, yeah. Forgot that part.

What I needed, about then, was more information and a lot of time to digest it—a *lot* of time. Months. Years. Decades, centuries, millennia. And for all I knew, Gandy could provide it: manipulate the spatial-temporal coordinates and do the hokeypokey and turn himself around and give forty-million-and-twenty-three-year-old me all the time I could possibly want. But I'd had enough. I couldn't process any more.

My sense of reality had already been shredded and stomped on, and I couldn't think. I had to *do* something. And I had to do it alone, unless I counted on Gandy, and I wasn't sure I could. For all our conversations and face-time, he was still too damn . . . well, *alien*. I knew I'd never really be able to understand him. Maybe somebody smarter than me could. Maybe Superman . . .

Or Batman. Or the Atom . . .

I needed the Justice League. If anyone could demolish the Oans' giant, economy-sized monomania, the League could.

Gandy had sent them back to the Precambrian Era. Could he retrieve them?

I asked him, and he said yes. But we'd have to return to the point at which they'd departed, 22,500 miles above the Earth.

I asked him if we could do that.

Apparently, we could. But it would be dangerous because the Oans had already begun their universe alteration, which meant a lot of things might happen, such as a wormhole ceasing to exist while we were in it, causing us to cease existing too. Great big cosmic stuff like that. And while we were negotiating the tricky business of time-traveling and hero-rescuing, the process the Oans had begun would continue. If and when we finally succeeded in finding and retrieving the League, we might be too late to stop that process.

Had I really once worried about being mugged outside Omfrey's?

It was better to do something here and now.

"Let's go to the globe and bounce on out to the Creation Point," I told Gandy. "We'll figure out what's next when we get there."

"Yes."

I dissolved the imitation room and we were, again, floating in space. I took a moment to look at the stars, orient myself, and figure out where Oa had been and where the yellow globe was now. If I'd stretched my left arm straight out from my body, it would be pointing at where I wanted to go.

Suddenly, Gandy wasn't there, but I wasn't worried; he'd obviously ducked back into the ring.

I moved, slowly at first, until I was sure I was going in the right direction and then, when I saw something yellow glimmering in the distance, I willed the ring to greater speed and, for the hell of it, stretched and flattened my body until I must have looked like a bodysurfer.

A while ago, before Oa had vanished, I would have been passing through its artificial atmosphere and then smashing into the planet; now, I was merely hurtling through emptiness toward a yellow globe that seemed to hang suspended against the stars. It grew larger and larger until my outstretched hands were within inches of the shimmering surface.

I hesitated, floating right above the globe, twisting my body until I could look back at where I'd just been, a certain point in space, and the stellar array all around me. These alien constellations, so far from everything I knew in both time and distance, were suddenly familiar and friendly, and I didn't want to leave them. I guess that if you have no idea where you're going, wherever you're leaving seems like home.

Then a star vanished. More Oan mischief? No, nothing that grand, just something blocking my view of the star. Waiting to see what it was gave me an excuse to hesitate longer.

The thing between the star and me grew larger, assumed a shape, and shot at me. But I'd recognized it—*him*—and was able to ring up a shield.

"Welcome back, Spasmer, my old sparring partner," I murmured. I braced myself for a fight. He'd beaten me earlier only because my ring had run out of charge. The rematch would end differently. I'd kick his ass, assuming he had an ass, and if he didn't I'd find something else to kick.

I remembered a scene I'd witnessed outside a bar at about one in the morning a few months (or a few million years) ago. Two beer-bellied, balding guys, swaying, their fists cocked in a bad caricature of a boxing stance, the less steady of the two yelling, "You want a piece of me? Huh? Do ya?"

Pretty stupid. But I wasn't like those doofs! Was I?

I deflected another beam and shot back one of my own. Trading green blasts wasn't the way to win, of course, but it would keep him nervous while I thought of a devastatingly effective strategy.

But my mind wouldn't strategize. I wondered if the Oans had sent Spasmer after me and immediately doubted it; the Oans were at the Creation Point. So the Spasmer must be holding a grudge because I'd hassled him. Unless he wasn't. Unless—

A planet had vanished and I was where it had been. Like a guy in a detective story standing over a freshly deceased body holding a weapon. If I'd been the Spasmer, what would I conclude?

My shield shattered—literally shattered, pieces blasting away in all directions. The Spasmer was single-minded, I knew; if what Gandy had told me about him was true, he wouldn't have learned any new tricks, so he must have found a way to increase the power of his ring.

I could go inside the globe and express myself to the Creation Point. But that would be running away. And I didn't want to run away. Why didn't I want to run away? Because at heart I'm a wannabe macho human male who'd recently acquired some warrior moves, and no twitching slab of an alien was going to make *me* chicken. Even if I *were* standing over the body with the smoking gun in my hand.

You want a piece of me?

I ringed a giant slingshot and used it to hurl a lot of stuff at the Spasmer, including a 1935 Cord convertible, the head of Teddy Roosevelt from Mount Rushmore, the Washington Monument and, yes, a BarcaLounger. As I'd hoped, a lot of it hit him, and he went backward.

Again, I was hesitating, debating with myself whether or not to pursue and do him further harm, when suddenly Gandy appeared between us. Not the Gandy I was familiar with, the dwarfish guy in the red nightshirt. Oh, the nightshirt was there, all right, though it wasn't red—more like deep scarlet—but nobody would call *this* Gandy dwarfish; he must have been at least eleven stories tall and appropriately wide. I shouldn't have been surprised. He had to be capable of changing size to fit inside the ring: If he could make himself smaller, why not larger?

Facing the Spasmer, his body shimmered—was this communication? Probably yes, because he turned to me and held up a flat-palmed hand, clearly indicating, *Stop!*

The Spasmer and I were a couple of unruly schoolboys whom Teacher caught fighting at recess, and Teacher would have none of it!

Gandy shimmered again, and the Spasmer drew closer until, in the glow from the globe, I could see him clearly for the first time. He was the same ol' lovable Spasmer—flat, rectangular, sprouting stalks and tentacles. His color was a blue so deep it was almost black, with streaks of crimson running through it and a few white specks he'd kept me too busy to notice before. I couldn't see anything I recognized as eyes, ears, a mouth, or nose. Obviously, his senses didn't operate anything like the way humans' did. He was utterly *different:* nothing like the TV show aliens who *were* people with funny noses and ears. I probably had less in common with him than I did with a chrysanthemum.

Gandy gestured to the globe. I willed the ring to send me to it and the Spasmer must have done the same, because we both moved to the gleaming, glowing yellow surface and slid through it, the three of us now inside the big ball. I looked for a machine of some kind, or some other artifact—this was the source of the ring's power, wasn't it? And wasn't there supposed to be some kind of tachyon thingy that would send us to the Creation Point?

Apparently, we weren't inside the ball.

We were traveling. But I have no idea how. We weren't moving, not in any way I could detect. We didn't seem to be inside anything, but we weren't *outside* anything either.

I'm finding this hard to describe.

Try this: It was like being six and riding in your grandfather's big car, with the leathery seats and the radio playing strange grandfatherly music, the air filled with a combination of new-car smell and grandfather smell, going along a two-lane country road on a bright, breezy June afternoon. Except there was no car, seats, radio, smells, road, or June afternoon. No brightness. No breeze. No grandfather, either, unless you count Gandy, who was certainly old enough for the role. (But then, so was I. Forty million and twenty-three is old enough.)

It wasn't like my trip to Pluto, when I was traveling at near–light speed and there was a big Nothing around me. I had a distinct sense of place; I just couldn't describe the place I had a sense of. What was happening, I think, is that my brain was unable to process the data it was receiving, so it provided me with a remembered mood instead. Someday, if we humans don't exterminate ourselves and manage to continue evolving, we may be able to actually experience this kind of space travel. But not now.

I wasn't alone in the big car that wasn't. There was Spasmer—I was mentally calling him "Spaz" by then—and Gandy. But not the short blue dude in the red nightshirt—not *that* Gandy. I'm not sure he even had a body. He was more like pure energy. I felt him like you feel static electricity; you damn well know something's there, but you can't see it.

I have no idea how long, in Earth time, the trip lasted. At one point, I felt like I was back on Earth living a life that hadn't exactly been mine. Oh, I was still Kyle Rayner, wannabe artist. But I didn't live in a medium-sized city in a basement; I lived in big, bad New York City and I actually had a girlfriend. Her name was Alexandra and one fine day I came home and *found her murdered . . . stuffed into a refrigerator!*

It wasn't like the dream I had on Oa, the blissful, domestic scene with Jennifer and the three kids; it was ugly and gritty and real and it went on for years and years . . . this alternate Kyle Rayner life. . . . Or seconds. Or nanoseconds. I had a powerful feeling that it went on even after I'd stopped participating in it and returned to Gandy and the Spasmer. . . .

The part of my brain that marks the passing of time had shut down for the duration. Nonetheless, the journey wasn't a blank, by any means. There was the episode of my alternate life and other visual fragments, like isolated moments from movies devoid of context and therefore meaningless, and occasionally, bursts of sustained thought. I can remember ruminating, for instance, thinking:

I'm passing through another gate—a metaphorical gate, that is. Who knows what I'm really passing through? Been doing this a lot lately. How many metaphorical gates have there been? Does the trip from Earth to Pluto count as a gate? Sure, why not! And the first wormhole, and the barrier that covers—covered!—Oa. And the skin of the yellow globe—did that one twice!—and the second wormhole, and now this tachyon thingy, and maybe something I've forgotten. Not bad for a slacker who used to have trouble prying himself out of his apartment. Pity, in a way—it's wasted on me. I'm too uneducated and dense to understand most of what I'm seeing. This stuff should be for scientists, philosophers, even poets. Even saints. They'd comprehend it and, better yet, they might have some idea of what to do when and if we reach the other end of the line—what Gandy calls the "Creation Point."

The Justice League, the real Justice League: Superman, Batman, Diana . . . Wonder Woman, the Flash, even Plastic Man and the snotty Atom—oh, and Batman, who might be snotty but nobody can tell—they're equipped to handle cosmic menaces. Me—I'm not equipped to handle milk money. . . .

Then something odd happened. I got mad—at me. I was bone-weary of thinking of myself as a slacker, a loser, a doof, and I was thoroughly frosted at myself for doing it. After all, I *had* survived a lot. I'd made mistakes, sure—I'd never forget the smell that came from the burning pickup truck—but hey, read a little history: *Everybody* screws up. I mean, the damn ring didn't come with an instruction manual, and as a mentor, Gandy wouldn't exactly win prizes. I'd done as well as I could and, all things considered, that was pretty good. As well as most, maybe. Better than some.

At the very least, I could boast of having "not inappropriate energy patterns."

Okay, resolved: No more self-deprecation. All in favor, say nothing. Resolution carried.

Somewhere along the way, or along the *when*, I must have communicated with Gandy because by the time we reached our destination, which we'll get to shortly, I had acquired a bit more information. Not much—just enough to help me understand what we were about to experience.

The computer—which I'll call "Big Momma," because that's how I'd begun to think of it—was, among many other things, continually rebuilding itself using the energy that fills the universe. It is one of the things that causes change, which may be the thing that is pushing the universe outward.

The excess is funneled—this is a mind-bender—out

of this dimension entirely and into another. I didn't get how it could work then and I don't now, but the idea wasn't new; it pops up in science fiction pretty often.

Gandy wasn't the only one I conversed with. I talked with Spaz, too. I've since learned, through experimentation, that the ring has a translator function. It has a database that encompasses every known language in the universe. Tens of billions of languages. A big database.

So maybe the ring translated Spaz's talk or—here's a nifty possibility—maybe I *simply* learned his language. That would have taken a while—say, a dozen Earth years? But maybe I *had* a dozen Earth years to do it. As I remarked earlier, time was becoming almost meaningless. Another way to say that is, it was malleable. Stretched, compressed, bent every whichway. That might mean that my memory wasn't functioning normally, assuming that anything in the universe could properly be called "normal." So maybe the trip to the Creation Point took long enough for me to learn to understand Spaz, but my memory wasn't able to register all those passing moments, perhaps because they didn't really pass?

This stuff is not easy to write about. Half the statements I want to make come out as questions. Don't they?

Anyway, I got to know Spaz. His race communicated with their tentacles, partly through a kind of sign language and partly through sounds they made by rubbing together bulbs that were on the bottom of their appendages.

I guess we maybe whiled away a lot of long, leisurely afternoons just shooting the breeze. He may have versed me in his race's religions, philosophies, sciences, even mating rituals, assuming large, flat slabs mated. If he did, I don't remember.

What I *do* remember is this:

He hadn't attacked me, back there in the vicinity of the yellow globe. He'd approached because he wanted to ask us some questions and, stupidly, I'd assumed hostile intent and attacked *him*. (Oops—I did it again. Called myself "stupid." I wasn't. I'd merely used the best information I had. It was lousy information, but that's not my fault.)

Spaz and the other alien Green Lanterns, the ones I'd fought earlier, were looking for their leaders. They hadn't seen or heard from the Oans for months. That was unusual, and so they went to Oa to ask what was happening and to mount a rescue operation, if one was needed. The beam that had latched onto my bubble had been meant to pull me into the group, not harm me. But neither Gandy nor I knew that and so we'd fought. Our bad. (No, the *information* was bad.)

We had to guess, then, Spaz, Gandy, and I. We guessed that the Oans had disbanded the Green Lantern Corps and neglected to inform the members, either because they'd forgotten—they *were* really, really old—or because in their arrogance they didn't bother. Bet on the latter. Most of the GLs hung around, literally, for a while, and then went home. But not Spaz. Spaz didn't *have* a home. His world had been clobbered by an asteroid while he was away on Green Lantern business.

"If you ever get to Earth, there's a couple of movies you'll be interested in," I told him, thinking of three flicks in which the Earth was almost destroyed by interspace flotsam but wasn't because we humans are so intrepid and cool. Then I realized I'd been thoughtless and had maybe hurt his feelings. And then I realized I shouldn't worry because he didn't know what I was talking about anyway.

I'm not sure Spaz had anything we could call an "emotion" at all. He was certainly free of self-pity. He was the last of his kind in the whole of creation, and he showed no trace of sadness about it. Maybe I just couldn't read his emotions, or maybe his race had never evolved them—or had evolved *past* them.

I couldn't say the same for myself. Spaz's story reminded me that, in all likelihood, *I* was the last of my kind. I was over four million years old. Humanity, as I knew it, was undoubtedly long gone. So Spaz and I had something in common.

Also: We both wore power rings.

Two things.

Also: We were on our way toward the end of the universe.

Three things.

Also: We were sentient beings formed from atoms created during the big bang who existed in the same space-time continuum. . . .

Okay, we had a lot in common.

But we'd never be pals. We'd never be as chummy

as Kirk and Spock or Han Solo and Chewbacca. But we weren't enemies, either.

In fact, we were allies. Gandy explained to Spaz where we were going and why: the Oans art project, Big Momma, and all the rest of it. Then he gave Spaz a choice: Spaz could return to the yellow globe—apparently, we were on a two-way street—or he could accompany us to the Creation Point and join in the attempt to scrap Big Momma.

Spaz seemed to be asking Gandy a lot of questions, and although I could understand the *words*, the meaning eluded me. Technical stuff. High science. Spaz wanted a full briefing on Big Momma and related matters, and Gandy was obliging.

Obviously, Spaz had more smarts than I'd given him credit for. Lots more. I was beginning to believe that he was Gandy's intellectual equal, at the very least.

In the end, he chose to come with us.

"Welcome aboard, Spaz," I said.

Spaz waved a few tentacles and then became still. He wasn't much of a conversationalist.

Of course, on his own world, he may have been a blabbermouth . . . make that blabber*tentacle*.

I relaxed into whatever was happening—enjoyed the ride, so to speak—and eventually Gandy said, "Erect shields."

Gandy wasn't much of a conversationalist either. By "shield" I assumed he meant my green, ring-formed bubble.

"Why?" I asked him.

"When we emerge we will be immersed in lethal energies."

Which told me that the ride was almost over.

I surrounded myself with a bubble, and so did Spaz and Gandy. Then we waited.

But not long. Suddenly, we were elsewhere/elsewhen. The journey from the yellow globe had been notable for its lack of sensory input. That changed.

We were in space, I guess, but not the black, star-spotted emptiness I was used to. We were in the middle of something I can't describe. I *can* say this: It wasn't black. There was every color imaginable, bursting, streaking, swirling—a cosmic fireworks display. But whatever was causing the show emitted no light. No light at all, just these utterly beautiful colors. As I just noted, it's impossible to describe, because I'd seen nothing like it before, and I'm sure that nothing like it even exists on Earth.

I knew my ability to perceive was limited by my crude physical senses. On Earth, I could see only a relatively small part of the electromagnetic spectrum. So whatever this was, this thing that surrounded us, was probably a million times more magnificent than I could appreciate. What I'd seen on Oa was pale water compared with what I was seeing now.

For a moment I thought that if this was the Oans' art, maybe the extinction of sentient beings was a small price to pay. But only for a moment.

I stared, almost hoping I'd die while surrounded by this glory. I was so enrapt that I didn't notice Gandy and Spaz melding their bubbles with mine.

I heard something I'd never heard before: Gandy, speaking my name.

I turned to him and asked, "Did your brethren do this? Is this part of the big art project?"

"No."

"Then what is it?"

"Incidental energy emitted by the computer's operation."

A glorified electromagnetic field, then. A *seriously* glorified one. But an accident, not the realization of some artistic vision.

I would have been happy to continue staring, maybe forever, but Spaz wriggled and "said" something I didn't catch. All his tentacles except two were pointed in the same direction, though—Spaz's version of pointing a finger—and when I looked there I saw a swarm of green capsules, like the ones we'd seen near Oa, moving toward us.

"More incidental energy?" I asked Gandy.

"No. We are under attack."

Oh. Well, *that* was bad. But how dangerous could green capsules be? I sent a ring beam through the bubble and met the lead capsule head-on.

The explosion was tremendous. Of course, I didn't hear anything, and I felt very little, but our bubble was suddenly moving away from the lightless fireworks display. We'd literally been blown back by something that was as powerful, I guessed, as a small nuke.

"What the hell?" I said.

Spaz wriggled and rubbed: The capsules were

what the Oans had created to replace the Green Lantern Corps. In effect, they were robots of ring energy programmed to protect things. So "said" Spaz.

Made sense. Why mess with sentience, which often carries opinions and independent thought with it, when you can have obedient green capsules, each with enough oomph to level a city.

When Spaz had finished "speaking," I said, "Look, guys, that was more fun than anything else. We've got to get to the computer, right? Let's just charge into the capsules, and if they blow up, so what?"

"Our shield withstood one explosion," Gandy said. "It could not withstand a dozen explosions."

Stymied. Again. Gandy and Spaz were about a thousand times smarter than me—I'm not putting myself down, just stating a fact—but their intelligences were not suited to solve the kind of problem a high school football coach solves every weekend. *They've got this really big line, see, and our quarterback weighs a hundred ten and has a sore toe and we gotta get the ball to the end zone . . .* So it was up to me.

After a few minutes of mulling, I had an idea.

"Gandy, you understand gravity, right? I mean, you told me the ring lets me fly by bending space. That's gravity, no? Well, do you really *understand* it or can you just talk about it?"

"I understand it."

"Great. Then this might work."

Using the ring, I sketched a diagram in the air between us of what I had in mind —the first drawing I'd done since that day beside the swimming pool with Di.

Gandy spoke a few sentences of high science, amplifying my basic idea.

"We ready?" I asked.

Spaz wriggled understanding and agreement. Gandy was silent, which indicated assent. I was beginning to comprehend his silences, which was like reading a book with blank pages.

We accelerated to near–light speed, and in a few seconds were back at the fireworks display. Then, as the capsules sped toward us, we put my plan into action.

We separated, and Spaz and I ringed a big box in the space between us and the advancing capsules. Then Gandy added energy of his own.

The box bulged for a moment and then shrank a few meters and we retreated, again at near–light speed.

The capsules converged on it.

And we continued to retreat—fast.

The capsules nearest the box struck it and exploded, and then the farther capsules shot toward it, picking up speed as they went until they, too, vanished.

I'd say that what we'd done was simple, except that it involved an understanding of physics human scientists can only dream about. In effect, we'd built a big lump of gravity that Gandy somehow programmed to reach full potency only when we were clear of its pull. According to Gandy, none of us could have accomplished the job alone.

We'd cooperated, as humans have always done to accomplish the really impressive stuff, from building the pyramids to landing on the moon.

We merged our bubbles and I said to Gandy and Spaz, "I hereby dub you honorary Homo sapiens."

Gandy was—guess what?—silent. If Spaz had been capable of forming an expression, it would have been blank. But *warmly* blank.

Spaz. My buddy. The Huck to my Tom, the Tonto to my Lone Ranger, the E.T. to my whatever-that-kid's-name-was.

We disintegrated the box and moved back into the fireworks display. I allowed myself a few more moments of gaping, and then I remembered our mission: We had to save the universe, and soon; we might already be too late. Our latest caper, capsule-bashing, had been exciting, and probably necessary, but the important job was yet to be done.

I asked, "Where *is* the computer?"

"It is on the other side of the energy."

"The other side of *that*?" I gestured to the magnificence outside the bubble.

"Yes."

"What are we waiting for?"

Wriggling and rubbing his tentacles, Spaz joined the conversation: *Our shields cannot withstand the energy at its most dense part.*

"So, in effect, the computer is surrounded by an impenetrable wall."

Gandy spoke and Spaz tentacled and both said yes.

"So we've come all this way for nothing."

"We have come to destroy the computer," Gandy answered, without supplying information.

I had an idea. "Where are the rest of the Oans?"

"I can only offer a hypothesis."

"Offer, then."

"They are inside the computer."

"How'd *they* get past the wall?"

"They placed themselves there before the wall became impenetrable."

Stalemate. But maybe not. "Is there some kind of rear entrance? What's *behind* the computer?"

"It is the end of the universe."

Of course. The nothingness into which the universe was expanding. The Creation Point.

"We can't get there from here?"

"We cannot exist outside existence," Gandy said. Which made sense, in an utterly nonsensical sort of way.

It was, indeed, the end of the universe. Unless Spaz had a contribution. I asked him if he did, and he communicated with Gandy for a while. More high-science stuff, the import of which I thought I understood— and, as a matter of fact, events proved that I did. The import was this: If something could absorb the energy the computer was emitting, even for a second, we could penetrate the wall.

"Where are we gonna get an energy-absorber like that?" I demanded. "Here, at the end of the universe?"

I had another idea. "Could the rings do it? Maybe if we worked up another gravity box?"

"The task is too great," Gandy replied, and I must have had a hunch about where we were going because I shuddered.

I let myself gaze at the colors again for a moment,

and when I returned my attention to what was happening inside the bubble, I saw a green glow flowing from Gandy to Spaz, and I knew that Gandy was infusing Spaz with some of his own energy. I also knew what they were planning, but I wasn't ready to admit it.

"I feel left out here," I complained. "C'mon, guys—share!"

Spaz wiggled and rubbed: *My body can absorb enough energy to disrupt the wall.*

"Won't that hurt?"

Silence from both of them. It occurred to me that maybe Spaz's race didn't know pain.

"Let me put it another way: Won't that do permanent damage? To your body, I mean."

This time, I knew their silences meant *yes*. Big, big permanent damage. The biggest.

"There has to be another way," I protested.

"What is it?" This from Gandy.

"Hey, *you're* the smart guys. Think of something."

From Spaz: *We can conceive of no other possibilities.*

"Do you *want* to die?"

From Gandy: "He has no survival instinct."

A bunch of questions flashed through my mind, such as, *Then how the hell did his race last long enough to develop intelligence?* But I kept them to myself.

I watched Spaz leave the bubble—I'd forgotten that he could survive in space—and glide toward the energy wall.

"We must act as soon as the wall is disrupted," Gandy said.

Spaz was a tiny, rectangular speck in the distance, growing smaller.

"Screw this," I said, and burst from the bubble and immediately formed another as I flew toward Spaz.

A lot happened in the next few seconds.

I never knew, and don't know to this day, where the capsule came from: whether it somehow escaped our gravity box, was somehow summoned from another part of the galaxy, or was in the vanguard of another swarm. But come it did, straight at me.

I saw the capsule in time to hit it with a beam, with the inevitable results: a disintegrated capsule, a silent explosion, and a shock wave that drove me toward the wall. For a moment, I was confused, unable to think of a command for my ring, and I was traveling fast. Maybe I would have saved myself, maybe not. I *did* survive, though, because Spaz ringed a flat cushion between me and the wall that slowed and stopped my movement, like the big mattress I'd put under that small plane about four million years ago. Where had Spaz learned to do *that*? He wasn't supposed to know how to do tricks with the ring. Had he learned from watching *me*?

I thought of all that later. At the moment, I just realized that I'd stopped without knowing exactly why. Then I saw the cushion and the green beam that seemed to be attached to it, and followed the beam to Spaz. Like something out of an old cowboy movie, right? One hombre savin' the bacon of another. Jimmy Stewart as me, John Wayne as Spaz.

I wanted to return the favor. But I couldn't. Spaz

was only yards from the wall. I couldn't possibly reach him before . . . whatever was going to happen, happened.

I'd forgotten about Gandy until I saw him hovering next to my bubble. Could he do anything? Then I remembered: He didn't want to.

Okay, it was up to me. I warped the hell out of space and sped toward Spaz, but I wasn't fast enough. He touched the wall and he just . . . *wasn't*. I was expecting—maybe I was *hoping* for—some kind of pyrotechnics. But there were no sparks, no electrical displays, no explosions, not even a shimmering as he vanished. He simply stopped being. As all sentient creatures would soon stop being.

The wall was unchanged. Spaz had died in vain, had failed.

And if he'd failed, so had I. The Oans were the winners.

Then the wall also stopped being. And I was rushing toward the emptiness where it had been, aware that Gandy was beside me, passing the place where I'd last seen Spaz, looking for Big Momma. . . .

We should have been inside her. We'd traveled far enough, certainly. But I could see nothing, not even Gandy.

Once, in high school, I'd crawled to the bottom of a cave with a spelunker friend, and when we turned off our flashlights, I'd experienced utter darkness. Compared to where I was now, the bottom of the cave was the sunniest day in July at noon on the beach. Oh, I knew the dream I'd had of a giant PC morphing into a big iMac and then into a mainframe was silly, but I'd expected to see *something*—vast tangles of exotic circuitry, transistors as big as moons, chips as big as Jupiter, a motherboard the size of the Milky Way. I'd expected to be impressed.

Suddenly, I was. Not because anything changed, but because I realized that I had never before experienced such *nothing*. Even in the void between galaxies, I'd seen stars. Even going to Pluto there had been a sense of existence around me—the void was somehow tangible. Here, now, there was an absolute *absence*, and though I'd been here only a short while, I was as lonely as a man stranded on a desert island for twenty years. How long could I stay sane? Was I already crazy?

"Gandy," I said, knowing that the sound of my voice could go no farther than the surface of the bubble, about an inch from my face, but needing to say it regardless, needing to acknowledge to myself that at least once, in the past, I had not been so terribly alone.

Then I felt as though my body had dissolved and my spirit had expanded to fill the entire universe and, for a nanosecond, I was happy. But only for a nanosecond. Almost immediately my spirit shrunk until it was smaller than an electron, and again I was insignificant, and this time I shrieked, *"Gandy!"*

Gandy. Ganthet the Oan. My mentor and my friend. The best friend I'd ever had—strange but absolutely true. The *second* best—that'd be Spaz, the warrior, the gentleman, the boon companion. . . .

I realized that my mind was unraveling. I had to think, while I still could.

Okay. Begin with where I was. Inside Big Momma, as planned? Sure, why not? Consider: The Oans could cram into a ring—a bauble about an inch in circumference, with a stone maybe an inch square and a half-inch high—technology that could access trillions of languages, the science of a million civilizations, that could generate energy beams, bend space-time, and allow Gandy to slip into and live comfortably inside the ring's confines. All that in a ring. Obviously, they didn't need to mess around with screws and wires. Big Momma was almost certainly not an aggregation of hardware, but some kind of pure energy, or something even stranger. Way beyond my comprehension, and probably beyond the comprehension of anyone from the Earth I'd left.

I'd imagined I could take Big Momma down with a little raw, old-fashioned ring power. Like Clint Eastwood ridin' in to face a low-down, mangy-ass owlhoot, I figured to wait till Big Momma had filled her fist and then throw down on her. Or something like that. But it's hard to hit a target when there's nothing to shoot at.

I had a sudden, chilling thought: What if I'd already failed? What if the Oans had already completed their project? I could have somehow been spared, maybe because I was inside Big Momma, and if that were so, I was more alone than anyone had ever been. There was no one else, anywhere. Or any*when*. By one line of reasoning, the Oans' time-twisting meant that nobody had *ever* existed, except me.

If I left Big Momma, would I go the way of the rest of my kind? Was that desirable?

No! I still had humankind's most reliable ally—survival instinct—and anyway, I hadn't exhausted my options. For openers, I could try to explore.

I willed the ring to form a huge flashlight, and apparently I understood enough about how a flashlight works because when I mentally commanded *On*, a wide beam cut through the blackness. A green beam, of course.

I saw nothing *but* the beam. But that was, oddly, encouraging. At least *light* could exist here. And the ring still responded to my commands. That was encouraging too.

I moved the flashlight around its axis: up, down, left, right, round and round in circles. Nothing. I warped a little space and moved the light and myself some distance—fifty miles, I'd guess—and repeated the flashlight fandango.

This time, as I swept the beam upward, I saw something other than the blackness. I wasn't sure what it was, but it was *something*.

I edged toward it and, allowing myself to express what I was feeling, I could honestly say my heart was filled with joy. I wasn't alone! That is, I wasn't the only object left in the universe. There was hope. . . .

What I saw wasn't a little blue guy in a red nightshirt. Whatever oddity in my brain made the Oans appear, like the funny dudes in garish nightwear, wasn't operating anymore, or I'd learned not to believe my senses.

Anyway, what I was seeing was Gandy—not the Gandy of the alley behind Omfrey's, but the Gandy who rode with me in a big car that smelled of leather and grandfather. . . .

Ganthet. A cold, unfriendly Oan who, a few minutes ago, I missed more than I'd ever missed anyone in my life.

I enlarged my bubble to encompass him, and when we could talk I asked, "Where are we? Did we make another jump through space and time?"

"No."

"Then we're inside Big Momma? I mean, the Oan computer?"

"Yes."

"Then where is it?"

"We are surrounded by it."

"It's invisible?"

"It is not invisible to me."

"But to me?"

"That is apparently the truth."

"So we're in the middle of a bunch of circuits and transistors and electrical stuff? Only I can't see them? I could ring up . . . I don't know . . . a big hammer and start breaking things?"

"No."

"I know you're not being deliberately difficult, Gandy, but . . . work with me, huh? Let's try very hard to communicate. Don't say anything, just answer my next question as completely as you can. Okay?

Here we go: What's Big Mom—*the computer*, made of?"

"It is comprised of relationships among subatomic particles."

Relationships? Well, I'd ended a few of those in my time by being inconsiderate or egotistical or forgetful or just a jerk, but I didn't think any of those methods would work with Momma.

What would?

"Is the computer sentient?" I asked Gandy. "If I talk to it, can it hear me?"

"It can hear you if you want it to hear you."

If I want . . .

"Works something like the ring?"

"The computer operates by a four-trillion-generation permutation of the technology that operates the rings."

Four trillion. I wondered if the Oans *ever* dealt with numbers like *one* or *two*. . . .

I was getting an idea that scared the hell out of me.

"Okay," I said, "for openers, let's cozy up the scene. Yo, computer, I want you to hear me. Answer in the voice of . . ."

I couldn't finish the sentence. Whose voice did I want the computer to speak in, and why did I *care* which voice it assumed?

"My mother's voice," I whispered.

"*All right,*" someone I knew to be Big Momma replied in a voice I knew to be my biological mother's— though, presumably, I hadn't heard her since I'd been born.

"Let's get some light here," I said, and immediately

everything was suffused in a soft ocher glow—everything being Gandy and me, since we were the only things around apart from a few relationships.

"BarcaLounger!" I ordered, and there one was. I reclined and, realizing that I was on a roll, said, "Let me see Gandy as he was—short blue dude in a red nightshirt."

The amorphous *whatever* that had been Gandy congealed into my old buddy, Red Nightshirt.

"This is *way* more like it," I said, and enjoyed the BarcaLounger for a few moments.

When I was damn good and ready to continue, I said, "Computer, from now on you'll answer to the name 'Big Momma.' Got that?"

"Yes, I have." The voice sent a chill down my spine. Excuse the cliché, but a chill really *did* go down my spine. For a moment, I considered going one step further and telling the computer to manifest itself in my mother's body, let me see what she looked like. But I decided not to muddle myself more than I already had.

"Okay, Momma, listen. Are there any sentient beings left in the universe, present company excepted? Did you finish the Oans' project?"

"Which question do you want me to answer, honey?"

"Both."

"Well, there are loads of sentient beings left and no, the project ain't finished yet."

My mother said "ain't"?

"Okay, brace yourself, 'cause here comes the biggie. Can I get inside you? Wait, let me rephrase. . . .

Can you integrate my consciousness into your own?"

"Shouldn't be a prob, sweets."

"Final question, Momma. Have you ever told anyone a story?"

"I don't understand stories, hon."

Of course you don't! You're the poisoned fruit from the poisoned tree. The Oans created you, and since they don't understand stories, neither do you.

I didn't say any of that aloud.

What I *did* say aloud was, "Okay, here's the program. I want to integrate my consciousness with yours, but I want to retain my own identity and thoughts. And when I say . . . when I *think* 'the end,' the integration ends, and we're separate beings again. We clear?"

"Clear as crystal."

"What do you hope to accomplish." This from Gandy.

"My mission."

"You could fail."

"You think? Look, Gandy, if you have a good idea—hell, even a *bad* idea—let's hear it. Otherwise, let me take the only shot I've got."

Guess what? Silence.

"Okay," I said, "wish me luck."

"Luck does not exist."

I had nothing to come back with, so I addressed the computer. "One more thing, Momma. I have to stay sane, as I normally define the word. No matter what happens, I don't go crazy. You cool with that?"

"Like an ice cube, hon."

"Okay, when I count to three, we integrate. One . . . two . . ."

One more syllable and the cosmic die would be cast and tumble across all of time and space and decide the fate, past and present, of the universe. I knew I might not survive—in fact, I'd have been surprised if I did—but that was the most minor of considerations.

". . . three . . ."

It shouldn't surprise anyone, this consciousness-integrating stunt. When Gandy had been hiding in my ring, he'd done it, though to a limited extent, and he'd done it again when I was in the Oan boot camp. And anytime I used the ring, whatever was inside it was reading my mind—which is to say, integrating its consciousness with mine. Some form of consciousness integration was a part of the Oans' repertoire.

Consciousness-integrating? Oh, *that* old parlor trick!

Nothing much happened on the outside. I continued to float in the ocher glow—at least I think I did. I was too busy to notice.

I have to admit, it was a great ride. If you could sell tickets to the trip I found myself taking, people would hock their family heirlooms and take out second mortgages to buy them.

Momma was receiving signals—input—from all over, and I mean, *all* over, from everywhere and from every*when*, too. Countless sights and smells and tastes and feelings—and not only the kind of sensations I'd always known, because Momma could see well into the infrared and ultraviolet and smell like a bloodhound and hear like a wolf. . . . I was over-whelmed, big time. *Big* time, because I was experiencing past as well as present. The smartest single thing I've ever done was to insist on my remaining sane because if I hadn't, I'm sure my mind would have been instantly nuked. As it was, well . . . it was a great ride.

It took some time for me to adjust—to get my mental bearings; exactly how *much* time, I couldn't say. Forty seconds? Two million years? A nanosecond?

As I'd realized when I was traveling with Spaz and Gandy, time had become almost meaningless. And so all I can say with any kind of certainty is that I didn't immediately get control of my faculties, whatever "immediately" means. When I did, I experienced flashes. I couldn't understand most of what I saw-heardsmelledtasted, either because the sensation passed too quickly or because it was from some-where/somewhen unimaginably alien. I'm pretty sure that I did glimpse the Justice League satellite circling a globe that was neither as blue nor as cloudy as the Earth I'd left and a star suddenly quintuple in size and comets crashing into other comets and something small and slimy crawling from a pool onto sand and a magnificent silver city crumbling and that I smelled something that filled me with desire and revulsion and I tasted something that made my belly feel like a chasm needing to be filled . . . that there were continual explosions of sightsoundsmelltaste that I was unable to fathom or control.

But I *was* able to communicate with Big Momma. It was like having a dialogue with myself, but I'd done that before, and so it was a lot more normal than whatever else was happening. Whatever "normal" means.

Anyway, my conversation with Momma went something like:

"Can we do a search?"

"What'cha wanna find, hon?"

"People named Hal and Di."

" 'Fraid not. We can't control what we're receiving. Sorry."

"Me too."

Okay, I had to try. Now it was time—there's that meaningless word again—to start the finish.

I remembered Gandy's reaction when I'd sarcastically asked him for information in the form of a haiku. He'd given it to me. He didn't understand anything that was not literal truth. Did the computer?

"Momma, I want to tell you a story. Actually, tell *us* a story, because you and I share the same consciousness, right?"

"I don't know, hon. . . . I don't like those stories. . . ."

"That's because you don't understand them. But you'll understand this one. You could even be the heroine."

"Oh-kayyy . . ."

I was taking the biggest gamble of all time (can't we get rid of that word?), and at the same time (damn!) the smallest, since all I was wagering was words (including the word "time"). And the words weren't even constructed of modulated air because they were being formed in the mind Momma and I shared.

I told her the story I just told you. Then I had to conclude it. "Momma, you can understand how it has to end, can't you? Really, only one ending is possible. I feel you twitch; you're resisting me. Let me explain: I'm the hero. The story has been about me. I'm the hero, but you made me the hero because you provided me with a heroic task to accomplish. In a way, we're the same being, you and I. You've been the cause of every heroic act I've performed.

"Oh, I'm grateful to you, Momma, because without you I'd be a slacker living in a basement, not the costumed adventurer who's roved the universe, battling monsters and loving a fair maiden and coming to value himself. That last—that's a great gift, and I am infinitely grateful to you for it.

"But the story has to end. I have to win.

"Don't worry about being defeated, Momma. Your defeat will be a victory because it will allow a magnificent deed to be done—and make no mistake, Momma, saving the universe is a magnificent deed.

"I salute you, Momma. You are far greater than me. You are the greatest being in the universe, and you're about to experience your greatest moment.

"We're ending the story, Momma. Right now, we're ending it. Soon, I'll use the ring to create an image of you, and then I'll use the ring to destroy it. Because I have to perform some act, something decisive. It would be unworthy of you to end the story with an ellipsis. . . . No, we must be emphatic!

"Of course, Momma, your destruction will only be symbolic. We both know that. You can't die. You're immortal. And when this story is told, back on Earth, you'll be twice immortal. That's part of why we humans tell stories—to make people and places immortal.

"Here's what will happen when your image vanishes. All the energy you're transmitting throughout the universe will dissipate, and the process of alteration will stop. If the damage already done can be reversed, good. If not, well, that's how it will have to be. But what I'm telling you—listen, Momma—what I'm telling you is that the universe will continue to change and grow, just as it always has.

"Are you ready? I'm creating your image and . . . Oh, Mother. You are beautiful. You're as I've always pictured you. Beautiful and kind, and your arms are outstretched with love.

"I extend the ring even as I turn my head away and I blast you with a bolt of green energy. And when I again look you are gone and my universe expands and contracts and shatters and re-forms and I weep. . . ."

And then I wept. Which was stupid.

PART THREE

1

This is what happened next:

The ocher glow was gone, which I hoped meant that Momma was gone too, or at least inoperative. I quickly formed a bubble, ringed up the flashlight, swung it around, and located Gandy. He hadn't moved. I extended the bubble around him and asked, "Do you know what I just did?"

"No."

"I destroyed Big Momma—I think." Suddenly my throat constricted and I wanted to cry again, but I didn't. I was a hero. Heroes don't cry. At least, in the movies they don't.

Then I was looking at Gandy's brothers, the rest of the Oans, more like the shimmering entity of Grandpa's car than the red-nightshirted midgets. I didn't know then, and don't know now, if they'd been lurking nearby or had sensed Momma's absence and came from wherever they'd been.

I liked them better in the nightshirts and so, experimentally, I mentally commanded the ring to let me see them that way. Funny little blue guys ready for bed weren't scary.

There was no air outside my bubble to allow for normal speech, and I'm not sure the Oans would have spoken normally if there had been. But Gandy communicated with them—somehow. I'm not sure how, any more than I'm sure how I knew it was happening. But I did, and it was.

I enlarged the bubble to encompass everyone—the several dozen Oans, Gandy, and me.

"Let's talk," I suggested.

"You destroyed our computer," an Oan said in the usual flat, uninflected voice, which left me wondering whether he was asking or telling.

"I did," I replied, and realized that I was about to try a bluff. A bluff is a kind of lie, and since the Oans couldn't grasp fiction of any sort, including lies, I thought I could probably fool them.

And if I couldn't? I might be able to kill them. That had been a possibility all along, but it hadn't occurred to me before. Zap 'em with the ring. Toast their silly little blue asses. Serve 'em right. Because, if I left matters as they were, they might just build another Momma and we'd be back where we started.

But I didn't want them to die. They weren't vicious nasties, villains in the grand manner, just old, old men made arrogant and unfeeling by having lived too long, and not well. It wasn't their fault that the universe had coughed up the circumstances that shaped them.

So I'd bluff.

"We waited until now to see how stupid you are," I said. "We could have stopped this ridiculous project at the beginning, but we wanted to know how far you'd take it." I looked toward my boots and shook my head. "At what point in your evolution did you lose intelligence? Don't bother answering—I'm not really interested. Here's something else you don't have to answer: Do you have any idea what we'll do if you ever try anything like this again?" As I was speaking, I ringed up a green version of Michelangelo's *David*. "We'll let you build your grand artwork, your frozen universe, and then?" I ringed up a hammer and with it smashed the David to atoms.

"Then, when we're done with your art, we'll deal with you," I concluded.

"We will all be nonexistent," an Oan said.

"What's goofy is, you believe that."

I stared at them, smiling.

They didn't move. I knew they could outwait me. Oans are good at waiting. I'm not.

"There's another possibility," I said after a while. "Ganthet told me about a hole into a pocket universe a guy named Kronus created once. A little universe, too young to have evolved life. You could create another hole, and once you're through it, you could . . ." I hesitated; I was really pulling this stuff out of my ear as I went along. I coughed, to explain why I'd stopped talking, and then I said, ". . . could create another mini-universe and make that as complex as this one, only in different, smaller ways. Then do your art.

I mean"—and I recalled something Gandy had said—"size is largely subjective."

What I'd just suggested was not the result of brilliant thinking. But it *had* required a mind not so utterly focused on one objective that it could conceive of no other—a trick the Oans had lost long ago.

"Yes," an Oan said.

"Meaning what?"

"We will do as you propose," Gandy said.

"One condition," I said. "You guys don't return to this universe. Agreed?"

"Yes," an Oan said.

"And in case something ever *forces* you to return, you don't remake things, for the sake of art or anything else."

"We agree to your terms," the Oan said.

They don't lie. They would have if they could, but they couldn't. So I believed him.

"Get busy," I ordered, hoping I sounded like Jack Webb in *D.I.* . . .

To tell the truth, I'm getting tired of writing about time contractions and other sci-fi mumbo jumbo. Let's leave it at this: The Oans, without the late Big Momma's help, efficiently and more quickly than I would have thought possible constructed some kind of portal into an elsewhere/when. Might have taken days, might have taken months, or longer. Again, for all practical purposes, time had stopped existing for me.

I constructed a cozy little mansion for myself, and watched the Oan activity from a green BarcaLounger next to a green swimming pool under a miniature green sun. I ringed up food when I needed to eat, and ringed up my favorite movies to amuse myself. And when I tired of watching them, I changed the endings. I mean, I'd always thought Bogie should have died at the end of *Casablanca*, and I hated Welles rubbing our noses in Freudian Meaning with the dumb sled bit at the end of *Citizen Kane*. My versions were better.

Eventually—whatever "eventually" meant—Gandy wafted down from my mini-sun and told me that the Oan portal was completed.

I sent a command to the ring, and the mansion, BarcaLounger, sun, and pool vanished, and we were floating in space, inside a bubble. I ringed up a flashlight and shone the beam on the Oans. I wanted to wish them a nice trip, but I was afraid any niceness on my part might soften the bluff, so I just nodded to them.

"You'll be coming back to Earth with me?" I asked Gandy.

"No. I shall accompany my brothers."

He was going *with* them?

"Why?"

Gandy was floating toward the Oans. I extended the bubble so I could continue talking with him as he moved.

"I am them," he said, now ten feet away.

"You're *not*. You stopped them. You're different!"

Twenty feet away. "If I am not them, what am I?"

I couldn't answer.

"How the hell am I going to get home without you?" I shouted.

"Trust the ring."

Gandy merged with the other Oans, becoming an indistinguishable part of a crowd, and then they compressed and diminished and went somewhere else. I was alone.

"*Trust the ring*," Gandy had said. Okay, I would. But first I allowed myself to savor where I was: at the very forefront of all that was being carried forward, into a time and space that existed simply because *I* was being carried forward into it.

I had what I guess was a flash of insight then: The same would be true if I were back in Mr. Gloinger's basement—each new second would exist because *I* was experiencing it.

I can't help feeling that there's something profound there. I just don't have any idea what it might be.

I'd trust the ring.

But to do what? Take me to Earth? I wasn't quite ready to return to Earth yet—I'm not sure why. I could search for Di and Hal, but if they were still alive, they could be anywhere and/or any*when*, and the chances of my stumbling onto them were infinitesimally tiny.

I could go anywhere in the universe, but there was no particular place I wanted to be.

In the end, I decided to return home.

"*Trust the ring*."

I ordered it to take me to Pluto.

I left the blackness, and was again in a universe with stars. I wished Gandy were with me so I could ask him if the ring had a kind of memory that computed the best way to get wherever it had been, or if it was programmed for any and every command I could give it. If that was true, why hadn't I been able to go anywhere I wanted earlier? Because I had to somehow "master" the ring?

I may never know.

I've described journeys through wormholes and travel at near–light speed already: no point in repeating myself. Suffice it to say that pretty soon I emerged from the last of the tunnels through time and space, and I recognized the patterns of stars, not because they were the familiar constellations I'd looked up at from Earth, but because I had nonetheless seen them before. I was somewhere near Pluto.

Only then did I realize how successful I'd been. In destroying Momma, I'd undone the various harms the Oans had caused. The wormhole back to my solar system existed; space-time was back to normal. Whatever "normal" means.

I sped up and landed on the planet. Again, I'm not sure why. I guess I just wasn't quite ready to breathe terrestrial air yet.

I gave myself a little tour. Everywhere was pretty much like everywhere else: dismal, dark, silent, cold. Real cold.

I remembered a sunny October day when I was about fourteen, walking around a block, and around, and around, passing the residence of a girl I desperately wanted to take to the movies, afraid she'd say no. That was how I was feeling about going home.

Eventually, I'd knocked on the girl's door and popped my big question. She'd said no.

Maybe I'd be luckier with Earth.

I up, up, and awayed, warped a little space, accelerated to about 95 percent of light speed, and commanded the ring: *Earth.* I'd never taken the Pluto-to-Earth route, but, what the hell, I trusted the ring.

I decelerated about three thousand miles from Earth's surface and began the final part of the trip at a much slower speed.

After I'd dropped maybe five hundred miles, I began to scan the various bits of flotsam orbiting the planet. I'd begun my grand adventure as a quest for a missing satellite, and I still wasn't certain if I'd found it.

And then . . . I had. The Justice League headquarters was exactly where it'd been, in geostationary orbit above the Earth's equator.

I approached, remembered how to open the airlock, and entered the satellite.

They were waiting in the inner chamber: Superman, Plastic Man, the Atom, the Flash—and Wonder Woman, who was smiling.

The Atom spoke first: "Well?"

For a moment, I couldn't remember why I had come to the satellite just before it vanished. Oh, yeah, to tell the Leaguers that I was ready to be a hero, that I wanted in.

But after all I'd experienced, that seemed superfluous.

"How was it?" I asked them.

"How was what?" Wonder Woman asked back, and for a second I flashed on a lovely, clumsy girl climbing from a swimming pool.

"Precambrian Earth. Traveling millions of years in time. You know."

"We don't," Superman said.

"Perhaps you'd better explain," Wonder Woman said.

I did. I told them the story I'd told to Big Momma, and of the few events that had happened since. Wonder Woman, Superman, the Flash, and Plastic Man listened attentively—Plastic Man even did me the honor of looking like an ordinary person.

At first the Atom was skeptical, but as I was speaking, he consulted the satellite's various instruments. And when I finished, he said, "It all makes sense. The earlier anomalies . . . caused by a disruption of the temporal field . . . all theoretical, of course."

"But the theory does support my story," I interrupted.

"Yeah, it does."

I placed myself in front of them and said, "But you remember *nothing*?"

"I *think* I had a momentary blackout," the Flash said.

The Atom: "Me too."

Plastic Man and Wonder Woman: "And me."

Superman: "So did I."

"Green Lantern is telling the truth." This from a speaker on the wall next to a video monitor: Batman, who'd been listening without my being aware he was present, if only as a bunch of electrons dancing on a screen. He *has* to teach me that trick someday.

"No disrespect, Bats, but how do *you* know?" Plastic Man asked.

"I do." Okay, case closed.

"I don't like it," Batman said.

I spoke to the monitor: "*What* don't you like?"

"The business of superbeings being no more than accidental by-products of the Oans' experiments."

"Why not?"

"It demeans us."

Interesting: He said "us." He considered himself the equal of Superman and the rest. Well, who was I to argue?

"You could look at it like that," Wonder Woman said. "Or you could merely be glad we exist at all."

"We're pretty handy to have around," Plastic Man said.

"Without us, the world wouldn't have a chance against the likes of Major Disaster, Doomsday, and Doctor Polaris," the Atom said.

"If *we* didn't exist," Batman said slowly, as though explaining the obvious to a bunch of dull first-graders, "*they* wouldn't exist either."

I wondered if the rest of them resented Batman as much as I did at that particular moment. But when he's right, he's right.

"Nothing we can do about it but be who we are," I said.

The monitor suddenly went black. Batman isn't big on dialogue and discussion.

"Anyway, ring-slinger, welcome back," Plastic Man said, slapping me on the shoulder from twelve feet away.

"Have you made your decision yet?" Superman asked.

"Yeah," I said. "I was on my way to tell you when you guys vanished. I'm in, if you still want me. I didn't think I could handle the super-hero business before, but now . . ."

"You've changed your mind," Wonder Woman said.

"Or had it changed for me."

"You'll answer your signal from now on?" the Atom asked.

"I promise."

"Okay, then," the Atom said, and actually shook my hand. Superman shook it next, and after him, the Flash and Plastic Man. Wonder Woman gave me a kiss on the cheek. If Batman had been present, he probably would have ignored me, but not because he didn't like me.

"I'll see you all soon," I said, and went into and out of the airlock, formed a bubble, and hung in space, gazing down at the blue-green world below. I'd seen a planet or two in my time, but none prettier than the Earth. Of course, I'm biased.

I warped a little space and went down, into the atmosphere, through some clouds and on over a vast, dark landmass dotted with tiny specks of light. Night in the United States of America from thirty thousand feet.

When I spotted my landmark river gleaming in the darkness, I dropped farther, to about five thousand feet, and dissolved my bubble.

The air stung me. Cold, it was: A few scattered snowflakes swirled around me, and flecks of ice were in the wind. I followed the river for a while and eventually landed in the park. I could have landed on Mr. Gloinger's rooftop—at this hour, in this weather, the chances of my being seen would have been slim. But I wanted to walk. The eastern sky was just beginning to lighten, and in the first crimson glow of dawn, I looked at the street I'd left only hours ago, or millions of years ago. Dirty pavement, crumbling buildings, overturned garbage cans, burned-out cars . . . so different from the clean void between the stars.

A cat crossed my path, but it was calico, not black, so I didn't worry.

I turned a corner that was once familiar but now seemed impossibly alien, and walked to Mr. Gloinger's house in the middle of the block. I stopped at the gate and stared. Something was changed, but for a couple of minutes I couldn't decide what. Then I realized that I was looking at a tree in the center of the yard, its outermost branches extending beyond the edge of the sidewalk, its top near the roof of the house. Its leaves were a reddish yellow, and there were clusters of tiny red berries all over it. Where the hell had *that* come from? There was no tree on the Gloinger property.

Then I remembered: the scrawny little stick that shivered in the wind. The dogwood. But it had been less than a foot high when I'd last seen it . . . how long ago? Twenty-four hours or a million years or *what*?

A man in a tan trench coat and black hat was passing the fence, hurrying, his head bowed to the wind. On his way to work, probably.

"Hey, mister," I called to him. "This is gonna sound stupid, but . . . can you tell me what day it is? And what date?"

He could tell me, and did. Just as I'd thought: In Earth time, I'd been gone only about thirty hours. Could a dogwood tree grow that big that quickly? Obviously not. So what had happened? I've never figured it out, but I do have a couple of possibilities: One, my memory was playing tricks on me and the dogwood had been big for years. That's the most likely scenario; and later, when I asked Mr. Gloinger about it, he said he'd planted the tree a decade back.

Which brings me to the second possibility: All the fooling around with the universe by the Oans had actually nipped and tucked the space-time continuum and reality *had* changed, if just a little.

I'll probably never know.

I moved past the dogwood and around the corner of the house, used my key, and entered my apartment. I'd reproduced this room—in green—while I was floating in space, mourning my failure to save Hal and Di. That copy, mostly an illusion created by the weird matter-energy synthesis of the Oans, seemed real, while this box I was standing in seemed as indistinct as my mother's photo.

I got rid of my costume and flopped down on the futon. The room was cold. I lay shivering beneath my thin blanket, trying to sleep, until the dirt-glazed window became as bright as it ever gets. Then I got up,

dressed in ordinary clothing—jeans, sweater, sneak-
ers—and went outside.

The city had awakened: Citizens were hurrying
along the sidewalks, bundled in coats and jackets,
heads down, going to places they had to be. I couldn't
see them as people. To me, they seemed to be only loose
accumulations of energy, ephemeral and meaningless. Objects—cars, buildings, pavement, fire hydrants,
everything that clutters urban avenues—seemed even
more meaningless.

I felt that way for several months.

2

Gradually, the world around me began to seem more substantial. I still saw it as fleeting and pretty pointless, but I could at least accept it for what it was without feeling monstrously disillusioned.

I sold a few drawings. Surprise, surprise. Now that I didn't care whether or not I was a commercial artist, I was.

I did a few super-hero acts, both with and without the Justice League.

One that I did on my own took me to Santa Prisca. You remember Santa Prisca? The island where the Justice League, minus me, put down a rebellion?

I did a little reading—well, a lot of reading—during my first weeks back, trying to acclimate myself to a world that seemed incredibly alien, despite its being *my* world.

Buried in the back of publications like the *New York Times* and *Foreign Affairs Quarterly* were stories about

how the Santa Priscan rebels were not hostile mili-
tants determined to impose military rule but, mostly,
simple fishermen whose families had lived on the
beaches for generations and whose fishing grounds
were being destroyed by the building of a luxury resort, now three-quarters completed.

I decided to fly east and warped a little space. On
the way to where I was going, I flew over a Navy con-
voy: a big ship—an aircraft carrier—and four smaller
ships that, I guess, were destroyers.

I arrived at the coast of Santa Prisca at an oppor-
tune moment. From a thousand feet up I saw a speedboat painted military green, with a machine gun
mounted on the bow, roaring around a rowboat that
was bobbing and tossing in the wake of the boat with
the machine gun. Two men wearing straw hats were
in the smaller craft, clutching the gunwales, trying not
to fall into the ocean.

I paused, hanging in midair, to consider the situation. Quite possibly, the straw hats were bad guys and
the four uniforms in the speedboat were lawmen just
doing their righteous duty. But I wouldn't have
wanted to bet a nickel on that. So I ring-formed two
sets of pincers and lifted both boats out of the water
and flew them back to the carrier, depositing them on
the big deck with all the airplanes. A lot of sailors
gaped, and two marines came running, pulling hand-
guns from holsters.

I told them who I was and what I wanted, and they
escorted the Santa Priscans and me to an inner cabin.
There, an officer in a khaki suit spoke Spanish to the

Santa Priscans and then, after maybe five minutes, turned to me and said that, in his opinion, the straw hats were innocents and the uniforms were bullies who had used their boat to have some nasty fun. I thanked the officer, and let the marines escort us back to the big deck.

I ring-formed a pair of large green hands and put the Santa Priscans back in their boats, bowed to the sailors and marines, who were applauding, and took off with the boats in tow.

Then I flew back to the coast of Santa Prisca and deposited the boats back in the ocean—that is, I put the rowboat back in the water. The gunboat I flew up high, very high, and tipped slightly so the men inside may have thought I was about to dump them—perish forbid!—and spoke two of the few Spanish words I know: *"No mas."*

I'm pretty sure they got the idea. They were looking distinctly pale when I finally put them, gently, back into the Caribbean.

Next, I went to the construction site, where a highrise hotel was complete except for the top floor and landscaping, and found someone who spoke English. This nice person took me inside the almost-finished building to another English-speaking fellow whose suit, I'm thinking, cost enough to pay the rent on my apartment for the next five years.

I asked him if there was any heavy labor left to be done. The man hemmed and hawed and finally admitted that the fourth of the resort's five swimming pools still needed to be dug. I asked him to show me where the pool was to be, and we went outside, into a blazing Caribbean midday, and he pointed to a barren stretch of ground.

I ring-formed a backhoe and about ninety seconds later, he had his pool excavation.

I then put a friendly hand on his shoulder. "Now, *mi amigo*," I said, using the part of my Spanish vocabulary I hadn't used on the gunboat crew, "I am going to suggest that it would be generous and gracious if you and your fine company gave jobs to the fishermen whose livelihood was lost. Jobs guaranteed for five years, maybe? With American-sized salaries? Purely as a gesture of goodwill. You don't have to. But I may return, and there are many, many things I can do with a green backhoe."

I smiled and went up.

Last week, the *Times* ran an article in the business section praising a certain developer of luxury resorts for using local labor.

Call what I did high-handed and I won't disagree. But I stipulate that it was no worse than what the other Leaguers had done when *they'd* visited Santa Prisca. I remembered a rule I'd learned in Green Lantern boot camp: "*One is never to use the ring to promote one's unique point of view.*" That's kind of what the League had done by interfering in what was none of its business. It was what the Oans themselves had apparently been doing for centuries with the Corps. I'm sure the Oans hadn't forgotten the rule itself, but they *had* forgotten the *meaning* of the rule.

Maybe there was a better way to handle the situation with the gunboat and the fishermen. If so, I wish I knew what it was. I wear a uniform of sorts, but unlike most uniform-wearers, I have no code of conduct, no set of rules to govern my actions. Sometimes, I envy people who do.

So I grope ahead, doing the best I can. The only rules I'll ever have are the ones I learn as I go along.

A couple of years have now passed. I learned that Hal Jordan survived the destruction of Oa because he returned to Earth and caused a lot of trouble before he finally disappeared forever. Another story for another time.

I never got a chance to see him again, much less ask him about Di.

I haven't spoken with any of the Oans, either. Phenomena that the Atom detected with Justice League equipment leads him to believe they're back in this universe, and who am I to disagree with the Atom?

I have an idea I'd like to share with Gandy and his brothers, about Kronus and all the disasters he caused by seeking the origin of everything. The Oans think the chaos occurred because he was trying to learn something he shouldn't have known. Maybe. But I wonder if the *machine* Kronus used might not be the culprit. It must have altered space and time, and if so, couldn't such meddling have affected what was being meddled with?

I haven't discussed any of this with the rest of the Justice League. I don't plan to. We don't exactly speak the same language, the Leaguers and I. But I'm a member in good standing nonetheless, and never, ever, do I ignore the Justice League signaler—though once, when it buzzed while I was kissing Jenny, I had to feign illness to get away without seeming like the rudest jerk in three counties.

Oh, yeah, Jenny. Forgot to mention Jenny, didn't I?

Jennifer Tulone, who'd helped me with what she called "computer questions." That Jenny. I'd spotted her a half-block ahead of me one bright May afternoon, thought *what the hell*, and ran, caught up to her, chatted, and, finally, offered coffee. This time, she didn't refuse.

We see each other every day. At first, she appeared to be the usual loose accumulation of energy and, if I think about it, she still does. But mostly she's this sturdy, curvy bundle of cuteness with pale blonde hair worn in a ponytail and amber eyes behind her glasses.

But you know that, don't you, Jen? And now that I've come to the end of my story, you know everything else, too, except maybe why I'm reluctant to give you the commitment you deserve and that I want you to have.

Here's why: Sometimes, early in the morning, as I sense the Earth turning beneath me, moving me into the sun, I rise into the emptiness and stare at the stars and again I want to be out there, as far as I can go, flinging myself across the void, searching for what I can probably never find. . . .

Acknowledgments

If I have seen further it is by standing on the shoulders of giants.

—Isaac Newton

Nobody writes a story like the one in this book by himself. Green Lantern, as a character, has been around for sixty-four years now, as has the fictional universe he inhabits.

I'll probably never know everyone who, by contributing to that universe, participated in the writing of this novel. However, I can and do happily acknowledge a few of them:

Green Lantern's earliest incarnation first appeared in *All-American Comics* #16, published in July 1940. The story was written by Bill Finger, the art created by Mart Nodell, and the cover illustrated by Sheldon Moldoff. Without them, there would have been no *later* incarnations to inspire me and many other writers.

In 1959, Julius Schwartz, one of the truly great editors, writer John Broome, and artist Gil Kane, reinvented the character, changing his raison d'être from magic to science. They have my admiration and gratitude.

Green Lantern's second reinvention happened one spring night in 1993 when Archie Goodwin, Mike Carlin, Kevin Dooley, Eddie Berganza, and I—DC Comics editors all—had dinner at a Manhattan restaurant to talk about a super hero whose popularity, sales indicated, was waning. For a couple of hours we discussed what we would like to see, and what we would *not* like to see, in a revamped Green Lantern. Then we returned to the office and offered the scripting job to Ron Marz. Later, Ron, Kevin, Eddie, and artist Daryl Banks expanded, amplified, and supplemented the ideas hatched over Italian food, and gave the world its newest Green Lantern, Kyle Rayner.

Kevin deserves special mention. He did yeoman editorial chores on Kyle's first appearances, and he contributed very directly to the book you hold. I sought his advice, information, and guidance at least twice during its writing, making both me and the phone company happy. He is valued, both as a colleague and friend.

I should thank a couple of other people:

The science herein is not real; it is, at best, *suggested* or maybe *inspired* by real science. But the ex-journalist in me wanted to get at least some facts right and in that, Dr. Jack Beuckman of St. Louis was helpful and deserves my appreciation. A man just never knows when an ex-roommate will come in handy.

When I'd drafted about three-quarters of the novel, I discovered I'd written myself into the proverbial corner. As we were driving away from a visit to Mark Twain's house in Hartford, Marifran McFarland

O'Neil made a suggestion and my problem was on its way to being solved. I—again!—have reason to be grateful to Mari, and I am totally delighted that she provided her help after we'd visited *Mark Twain*'s house!

Charlie Kochman has once more proven that he is, in the absolute best sense of the term, an old-fashioned editor.

Scott Peterson: Thanks for the reading and the encouragement.

Finally: On September 10, 2002, while lunching with Mia Wolff and her son Virgil, I experienced cardiac arrest and, for a while, lay clinically dead on the floor of the Sidewalk Cafe in Piermont, New York. I was revived by John Ingallinera, Lizzie Fagan, Michael O'Shea, and Bryan Holihan. If Mia had chosen another restaurant, or if John, Lizzie, Michael, and Bryan had been less resourceful, I wouldn't be here. I am grateful beyond expression to them all.

Dennis O'Neil
November 2003

About the Author

For over thirty years, editor and writer Dennis O'Neil put the "dark" in the Dark Knight and was the guiding force behind the Batman mythos at DC Comics. He has been called "a living legend," "a master of the comics form," and "the dean of American comics writers." He prefers to think of himself as, simply, "a working professional storyteller."

O'Neil began his career in the mid-sixties as Stan Lee's editorial assistant at Marvel Comics, and went on to become one of the industry's most successful and respected creators.

As a freelance writer and journalist, he has produced several novels and works of nonfiction—the national best-seller *Batman: Knightfall* (Bantam Books, 1994) and *The DC Comics Guide to Writing Comics* (Watson-Guptill, 2001)—as well as hundreds of comic books, reviews, teleplays, and short stories. During his forty-year career in comics, O'Neil has written for almost all of DC and Marvel's major titles, including *Green Lantern*, *Green Arrow*, *Shazam!*, *Spider-Man*, *Superman*, *Wonder Woman*, *Hawkman*, *The Atom*, *Iron Man*, *Daredevil*, *Justice League of America*, *The Question*, and *Azrael*.

An expert on comics, pop culture, and folklore/mythology, O'Neil is a popular guest at conventions and on radio and television. He has taught writing and lectured at numerous colleges and universities throughout the country, including the School of Visual Arts, UCLA, MIT, and the Learning Annex. He currently lives and works in New York with his wife, Marifran.

Not sure what to read next?

Visit Pocket Books online at
www.SimonSays.com

Reading suggestions for
you and your reading group

New release news

Author appearances

Online chats with your favorite writers

Special offers

And much, much more!

10421